CW00530847

Surviv:

Susan McRae

Susan McRae was born in Vancouver, Canada and is of mixed Ukrainian-British heritage. She came to the UK to study at Oxford, got her degree, married a Welshman and stayed. She spent the next twenty years undertaking sociological research into women's professional and family lives, and in academic management. She is the author of *Cross-class Families, Cohabiting Mothers, Women at the Top,* and editor of *Changing Britain: Families and Households in the 1990s. Surviving Ukraine* is her first novel.

A Note on the Text

Words and names can be political. This novel was conceived many months before the tragic events in Ukraine that began in February 2022. The place names used in the text are those current at the time of the events depicted, rather than those of the present day: Kiev, not Kyiv; Odessa, not Odesa; Lvov, not Lviv; Babi Yar, not Babyn Yar (and some others). I hope this was the right choice and that it offends no one.

1

The Beginning

It's hard to be happy standing on a corpse. Not for the first time, I try to shake the memory of my treachery from my mind. But I fail. I always do.

My life story began on the sixth of January, 1920 – Orthodox Christmas Eve – in a small, beautiful Ukrainian village nestled below hills topped by mile after mile of wheat fields; when and where I was born. I was a happy baby, a giggling toddler, and grew to be an inquisitive, cheerful child; adored by my sister – who had always wanted a brother – adoring my mother and in awe of my father. And when on Christmas Eve 1930 – my tenth birthday – I received the best birthday present *ever*: a tiny puppy I named Arkadiy, which means *bold*, I decided my life was perfect, at that moment and forever …

Mykhailo Oleksandrovich Salenko – Misha to his family and friends – woke in the half-light on the morning of his tenth birthday, wiggled his toes for a bit, and grinned. He was full of excitement and anticipation. Not just because it was his birthday, although that was important. He could smell cooking. That was good, too. He sniffed the air: fish balls, he reckoned; his favourite. Even better, because it was Christmas Eve, his Uncle Orest was coming to stay. Papa's brother was always funny. He made everyone laugh, even Mama. That was *very* good. And his cousin Kola would be with Uncle: that was *the* best. He never knew Kola's mother – his Aunt Lena – she died when Kola was born. But he was sure she would have loved his cousin just as much as he did.

Fully awake now, he shimmied down under his quilt, hiding his head beneath its warmth as the chill of his room caught him. They didn't have to go to Church to celebrate Christmas: another good thing. He knew about God and loved the Baby Jesus, of course. He wasn't too keen on incense, though, and was glad he didn't have to sit listening for hours on end like they did in the old days. He giggled. Mama wouldn't like to hear him say that.

And there would be mountains of food to eat because it was *Svyata Vechera* – Holy Supper. The only black spot was kutia. He surfaced from beneath his quilt, grimacing. Why would God want to spoil Christmas by inventing kutia? Either God didn't know about it or had never tasted it. No one, in his view, should have to eat that mush of cold cooked wheat kernels mixed with ground poppy seeds and water, gritty and sour, even if sweetened with honey.

The boy lay in bed waiting for his mother to bring him some tea. On balance, he reckoned Mama was the best, even if sometimes she had a scary temper. A cup of tea in bed was her birthday treat and he bet none of his classmates got one. He was also thinking about his chances of getting a puppy for a present. He'd been hoping for one for an entire year and didn't much mind what kind. He'd also prayed for one, secretly, although he wasn't quite sure prayers worked that way.

He disappeared back under his quilt. The bedroom was tiny and far too cold that morning. His father was the village schoolmaster – in Misha's eyes, an excellent job for a father to have – and the family home backed onto the schoolhouse. To the boy, the house was just the right size in just the right place: bigger than the farmers' white-washed cottages along the main street, smaller than the doctor's house which overlooked the square. It had two doors, one to the garden and the other through the schoolhouse to the street. Inside, two bedrooms opened off a long middle room, one for his parents and one shared by his sister, Nataliya, and his grandmother. His room was in the corridor to the schoolhouse, had a small window facing the garden, and used to be a storage cupboard. He moved in last summer and he loved it! Although that morning he wished it was a bit warmer. He was sure it was big enough for a puppy.

At last his mother arrived, carrying hot, sweet tea. 'Happy Birthday, Misha,' she said, bending to kiss him. 'And how are you this morning, my little one?'

'Ten isn't so little, you know,' he replied, but smiling so his mother would know he was glad to see her.

'I know, but you'll always be my little one, even when you're old and grey.' She ruffled his hair. 'Enjoy your tea but get up soon. There's lots for you to do.'

'Yes, Mama,' he said, thinking more about his hoped-for puppy than the holiness of the night to come.

'Where's Papa?'

Up and dressed, Misha had joined his mother and *baba* – his grandmother – in the kitchen where they had already started cooking that night's special supper. His father was nowhere to be seen, but if the boy had bothered to listen he'd have heard his sister singing softly to herself in her room.

'Happy birthday, Mykhailo Oleksandrovich.'

'Thank you, *Babtsia*,' he said and kissed his grandmother.

'I hope you had a good sleep because we've lots for you to do.'

'Yes, yes,' he replied, looking around: 'Mama, where's Papa?'

'Gone to meet your uncle and Kola. What do you want him for? Go tell Nataliya to hurry up. I need her here.'

Just then, the door opened and his father came in with his brother Orest.

'But where's Kola?' Misha asked, startled by his cousin's absence. 'Didn't he come with you?'

'He's on his way back to Kiev for misbehaving on the train, making far too much noise and not obeying his father.'

'Oleksandr, stop teasing your son, it's his birthday.'

Misha's eyes darted from father to uncle, back again to his father, deeply puzzled. Christmas without his cousin? He couldn't believe Uncle Orest would let Papa send Kola away.

His father shrugged. 'Well, maybe he's outside – have a look.'

The boy turned away slowly and went out the garden door, uncertain. His heart jumped with joy when he saw his cousin outside, a puppy in his arms. He darted over instantly.

'Happy birthday, Misha,' Kola said, handing over the tiny creature.

Beaming, Misha turned around to see his mother and father, *baba*, Nataliya, and Uncle Orest all laughing at him. He didn't mind one bit.

'Go on,' his mother said, 'you and Kola take the puppy to your room. I'll call you when I want you.'

An hour or so later, with the puppy sound asleep, the women of the household preparing that evening's meal, and the men catching up on several weeks of news and happenings, the two cousins headed outside and climbed the path leading upwards to the steppe. Kola was everything Misha thought a boy should be: brave and funny and smart and full of good ideas. People who saw them together often thought they were twins. Six months older, Kola was taller, by an inch or two. He was also stockier, looked more like a fighter, Misha thought. But with their thick dark hair, long thin faces, and bright blue eyes – well, it was the same story told twice.

There were some differences, of course: Misha was a bit too cautious, perhaps, although he loved to laugh and to see other people laugh. Kola was clever, sometimes impetuous, a risk-taker. But they liked being together, even if from time to time they seemed to not quite live in the same world.

'Misha, have you ever caught a lemming?' Kola asked after they'd been walking for a time.

'Have I ever caught a *what*?'

'A lemming, you know, a vole, a lemming; they live in burrows on the steppe.'

'I know what they are. How would I do that, even supposing I wanted to?'

'Well, you could put a rope, with a noose, over the entrance to its burrow and then, when the lemming put his head out, to go get some food maybe, you could pull the rope really fast and you'd catch it. Then you could have it for a pet.'

Misha groaned and looked sideways at his cousin. 'You've lived in a city too long. First of all, lemmings always have more than one entrance to their homes, so if one of them saw you sitting there, they'd probably just go out another way. Second, they only ever come out at night. And, third, if one ever did come out in the daytime, you'd probably get sunstroke waiting for it.'

'Oh'

They walked on in silence for a minute or two.

'I saw a football game in October.'

Misha stopped dead in his tracks. He looked at his cousin with something approaching awe: 'A real one?'

'Of course,' Kola replied, keeping his voice casual, as if such outings happened every day. 'Dynamo Kiev. My Pioneer brigade went. They were playing Odessa.'

'Oh.'

Walking again, Misha contemplated his cousin's good fortune without speaking for a short while. Then asked: 'Did they win?'

'Not likely!' Kola burst out, laughing. 'And it rained the whole time.'

Peace restored, the cousins linked arms and headed back down the path to the schoolhouse and Misha's birthday puppy.

It was almost dark before Yulia summoned the family back to the kitchen. An educated woman, she was part of the generation who expected equality and love in marriage; who were quick to divorce when one or both were absent, having too often watched their mothers live without either. But after sixteen years married, she remained content. Her husband was a kind man, a successful teacher, lacking the violence that stained many village homes, loving towards her and their children. They trusted each other and shared many things, above all, their hopes and fears for Nataliya and Misha. And if their equality was manifest more in thought than deed, she was untroubled: the household was her domain; the classroom, his. A matriarch indoors, she knew when a day depended upon her for success and today was one of those days.

'We're almost ready,' she said, 'but not quite. Nataliya, dear, you set the table. Misha and Kola, you bring some hay for Nataliya and watch for the first evening star, so we know when to begin. Oleksandr, you and Orest are to make sure the fire is built up and that there's plenty of wood in the house – and you will *not* talk politics and you will *not* drink too much vodka before supper, and don't forget the *didukh*.'

Uncle Orest groaned – in jest, Misha thought – and turned to Oleksandr: 'You remember the old saying, I'm sure: *God created the world and rested; God created the man and rested; God created the woman, and ever since no one has ever rested.'* His mother didn't laugh as much as Misha but he thought he saw her smile at *Baba*.

At length, Kola spotted the first star of the night and it was time to eat. Everyday clothes were changed for best. Places at table were taken. Misha's father lit the top-most candle in the tower of braided bread – the *kolach* – that Nataliya had earlier, carefully, placed on the family's best white cloth, then encircled with evergreen sprigs. Standing at the head of the table, Oleksandr raised a spoonful of kutia to his lips and spoke the words echoed down the centuries and across nations to welcome the holy festival of Christmas, even in a country that had abandoned religion:

'*Khrystos Rodyvsya!*' – Christ is Born!

The family answered him in a single voice:

'*Slavim Yoho!*' Let us glorify Him!

Then, to symbolize the bonds between themselves, and with those no longer living, each one took up a spoonful of kutia, Misha rather more reluctantly than the others, which his father obviously noticed.

'Eat your kutia, Mykhailo,' he said, but not too sternly. 'All of it.'

The boy gulped hard and did as he was told. Beside him, Kola laughed and asked for more.

Misha loved the night before Christmas. After fasting all day, by dinner time he was more than hungry. The evening meal was meatless but there were twelve dishes, which took a long, happy time to eat. After about an hour or maybe more, nothing much remained. The *kolach* tower was destroyed. Plates were scattered with remains of dried fruit compote. The room was warm and Misha was full. He giggled and poked Kola in the ribs when Uncle Orest stood up yet again, promising only one last toast: 'Well then, *Dobrym liudiam na zdorovja*' – 'To good people for good health' – then turned to his sister-in-law, grinning, with just one more: '*With borsch and cabbage, the house will not be deserted* – famous Ukrainian proverb,' he said, sitting down and laughing much harder than anyone else.

The ample food and the late hour began to take their toll. They decided to have one last song, their favourite, Carol of the Bells – and go to bed. Nataliya started, her voice was the best, and the rest soon joined in:

Hark! How the bells, sweet silver bells

All seem to say, throw cares away.

Christmas is here, bringing good cheer

To young and old, meek and bold.

Ding, dong, ding, dong …

Kola was half asleep and Misha felt his eyelids droop. He ruffled the fur of his new puppy, sleeping happily in the boy's lap. His life, he decided, was perfect, at that moment and forever.

He was wrong.

2

Part One

Holodomor

Between 1932 and 1933, the Soviet republic of Ukraine was all but destroyed by a man-made famine which estimates suggest killed between four and ten million Ukrainians, with the population in some rural villages obliterated. Behind this tragic event was retaliation for Ukrainian resistance against drive to collectivize agriculture, the undermining of Ukrainian nationalism, and forced expropriation of food and livestock for export in exchange for machinery to support the Stalinist regime. In recognition of its scale, the famine of 1932–33 is often called Holodomor, Ukrainian for "to kill by means of starvation".

Hovkova Village, Ukraine,1933

Misha was alone in a house that once rang with laughter. He'd lost track of time and wasn't sure how long he'd been on his own. His mother had been alive in January. He knew that, because one day she said it was his thirteenth birthday. But he didn't know when January was. After she was gone,

15

he'd turned the mirror to face the wall. He didn't want to see himself. His eyes were still blue, his hair still black but the contrast with his pale, gaunt skin was too frightening. Without the mirror, he could remember the chubby but fit boy he used to be.

Winter felt endless. The autumn harvest had been poor and too many people had too little food. The summer before, the village had looked and felt almost normal. Farmers and farmers' wives worked on the rich black soil surrounding the village, harvesting and planting. Fruit and vegetables grew in garden plots, giving hungry people precious food. Children tramped in the woods, singing out to their friends, their brothers and sisters. Old men and old women sat side-by-side in the square. Sunshine soothed them and gave them hope.

But even Misha had known it was a cruel illusion. The old were silent, haunted by the thought that this could be their last day or their last week. Not-quite-feral children searched for food, calling out when they found something, anything, living or dead. Soldiers guarded the men and women who harvested the fields and planted next year's crops; guarded the full-to-bursting church-cum-storehouse that held enough grain for every man, woman and child in the village; grain that would instead be sold to give Stalin money for guns. The warm summer sunshine turned into the cold grey days of autumn, and everywhere there was hunger – endless, relentless hunger – and death.

He remembered his birthday. It had been very cold. The village was always cold in January. Because he was stronger than his mother, he had made their soup and she had promised to eat some. They had soup every day, before it got dark, in front of the stove, trying to keep warm. They were luckier than most and had lots of wood to burn: desks and chairs from the schoolhouse. He had loved being the schoolmaster's son – at least until the children began to die. As the numbers too ill to attend school mounted, as the numbers dying from lack of food grew, it became evident the school would close, ending both Papa's job and his food rations. And so, as spring gradually turned into summer, his father left home, telling the family he would be gone no more than two weeks. He had to find food somehow, he'd said, or they would starve like the others. He would go to the Dnieper and catch fish, some to eat now and some to salt for winter. Fish to keep the family alive, he said. But he never came back. Mama had always believed he would return – or pretended to believe – until her last days.

When, January, she said it was his birthday, the boy had added extra mushrooms to their soup – mushrooms his sister, Natalya, picked and dried the autumn before. They would be good for his mother and they could pretend it was a party.

But then she refused to eat.

Tears slipped down the boy's cheeks as he remembered. He brushed them away: *It's pointless to cry in a dead house in a dead village*. Mama had cried when he tried to make her eat. You, not me, she said. Not hungry –

He hadn't believed her.

There were no mushrooms left now. No potatoes either. As soon as it was light, he'd get up, go outside, and hunt for acorns. Perhaps he'd spot a marmot. He was so hungry and so tired. He slept for a while, the smell of mushrooms dancing in his head. He could almost taste them: silky white mushrooms… silky… white –

After a time, Misha opened his eyes and saw his sister Nataliya come into the room. Four years older, she was a paler, more delicate version of her brother; her hair more brown than black; her skin translucent, without the ruddy healthiness of the boy; her body lithe where his was sturdy. He smiled, happy she was there. He talked to her most nights, too hungry to sleep, not quite dreaming. She lay beside him and held his hand and comforted him. He told her he was frightened, afraid he might die, that he missed her and Mama and Papa, that Papa would be home soon with lots of fish. For a while, they argued about what Mama should cook with the fish Papa brought home. She wanted baked fish stuffed with mushrooms and breadcrumbs but he preferred fried fish balls; they were tastier. She stopped their argument with a laugh, telling her little brother that Zvi was waiting for him outside. Zvi! The boy's heart soared. He always knew that one day he would see his best friend again, after his father, Dr Rosen, was falsely denounced and the police took him away. He shook his head, still angry. Papa had said the doctor had done nothing wrong and that the family would come back to the village; that Zvi would come back. But they didn't. Then Papa left.

He woke with a start. The house was cold. While he had dozed, lost in the past, the fire in the stove had gone out. He went to the schoolroom to fetch another chair to break up for firewood. He paused outside his father's classroom and placed his hand on the closed door, the door that kept his sister safe. He knew she lived only in his mind, in his dreams; knew he wouldn't see her again, she wouldn't talk to him or hold his hand or tell him a friend had come to call. She was gone and he wept with loneliness, remembering her. Remembering, and blaming himself, even though months had passed since the awful day she'd been caught outside while looking for food.

He had almost finished the jigsaw puzzle he'd been working on for several days when his mother brought him a woven shopping basket, telling him to go looking for acorns, to make their flour last longer; and mushrooms. He'd moaned, saying he'd gone last time. He wanted to finish his puzzle. Couldn't Nataliya go? His sister had laughed and taken the basket. Ignoring their mother who told her to wear a shawl because it was cold and might rain, she had disappeared through the schoolroom door, saying she'd be back before any rain arrived.

But when the rain started, she hadn't returned. He could still see the cold, slashing rain turning the street beyond the schoolhouse to mud. The temperature had dropped dangerously low. Wind rocked the tallest trees, flinging brown, broken leaves swirling to the ground. He'd heard his mother pacing back and forth, talking to herself. She came to his room, bringing a heavy coat and an old hat, telling him he must go and find Nataliya, admonishing him to hurry. Once outside, he turned around to smile and wave to his mother standing in the open doorway. He was frightened for his sister, but didn't want Mama to know.

He had found Nataliya almost immediately, lying barely conscious on the path beside the river. Her basket was missing and the muddy path badly churned up. He didn't waste time looking for the people who'd hurt her. They'd be long gone after other prey. He lifted her to her feet and started for home as soon as she was able to walk. His father should have been there with him.

Mama was watching for them at the schoolhouse window and ran out into the rain to help half-carry her daughter the rest of the way. The girl was soaking wet and filthy; her clothes foul. Mama had gently washed the mud from her body and put her to bed. Exhausted by her misadventure, she slept until the afternoon of the following day. When at last she told them what had happened, she cried as she talked. She'd found about two dozen acorns and almost half-a-basket of mushrooms. She'd started home, excited by her good fortune but worried Mama had been right about the weather. Suddenly, without having seen or heard anything, she was surrounded by four or five or six children – she couldn't say how many or if they were boys or girls or both –

filthy children who hit her and pushed her, shouting at her to give them the basket. One of them must have knocked her out because she remembered nothing else except Misha helping her to her feet and bringing her home.

She shuddered as she finished her story. 'I don't like remembering, Mama,' she said. 'They were horrible creatures, not like real children at all.'

Her mother hushed her. Told her they probably hadn't eaten for a long time. That their parents were most likely dead. 'Sleep now,' she said, 'you can get up tomorrow.'

But Nataliya never got up again. Only days later, her mother, brother and grandmother were standing together in the schoolhouse saying farewell. Misha had carried his sister's featherlight body – washed and anointed with scented oil, wrapped in the red and black *rushnyk* their grandmother had embroidered for her wedding day – into the classroom that had been his father's and rested her on his desk, boughs of winter-flowering viburnum at her head, cut by him that morning. She would spend the winter there, where Oleksandr had been, among his things, and then, in the spring, they would bury her.

Yulia lit the candles she'd brought to the classroom. 'Nataliya, my beloved daughter, *I say to you, the hour is coming, and now is, when the dead will hear the voice of the Son of God; and those who hear will live.*' She fell silent. When she spoke again, the pain in her voice was palpable. 'God bless you, my daughter, I will cherish you forever.'

'We should have *kolach*,' *Baba* said, 'bread, braided with fruit. Jesus said, *I am the bread of life.*' Her voice was bitter.

'Yes, I know, Sofiya, but we haven't any.'

'I hoped to live long enough to see her married, my only granddaughter.' Tears flowed from *Baba*'s eyes as she stroked the embroidered cloth enclosing the tiny body. 'She chose the pattern herself, all those beautiful birds and flowers. I never dreamt it would be her shroud.'

'Don't cry, *Baba*.' Misha put his arms around his grandmother. 'She wouldn't want you to cry.' He turned to his mother, seeking solace in his grief: 'I'm glad we decided to keep her here, Mama. I wouldn't want her in the barn with all the other people.'

'I'm glad too,' Yulia said. 'But come now, Misha, Sofiya, it's time. Kiss Nataliya – you first, Misha, then Sofiya, and then me. One last kiss from each of us and then she will rest.'

Misha shivered at the memory. *I should have gone instead. Papa should have been there.*

He woke late the next day. A hazy mid-day sun was trying to warm the village. He left home to forage for nettles, burdock leaves, anything to add to his meagre soups. He knew he needed more than pickings from the wild to survive, but he couldn't steal from the already-dead. He shuddered as he thought of it, knowing others did, knowing the day might yet come.

Outside, horrors surrounded him: children with the look of dying old men, bellies bloated, eyes hollow, lifeless; walking skeletons who had once been healthy men and women, his neighbours perhaps. And dead bodies, so many dead bodies, lying half-covered by filthy frozen snow where the once-living had fallen and died, or piled deep in alleyways, or heaped in carts: all waiting for the ground to thaw; shrivelled, unshriven. He looked at the dead and the not-yet-dead and knew that had it not been for his mother, he too would lie among them.

He spotted a cluster of men and boys gathered outside the abandoned village store and was surprised to recognise one of the older boys from school among them: Ivan Ivanovich. He'd thought he was dead. The shop was dark. He wondered why they were there. Could there be food? Real food? Or only rumours? A scuffle broke out between two men standing a few feet away. He craned his neck to see if they were fighting over food. At the same time, an old crone in filthy rags came from behind and pushed her way past, leering at him. She pinched his arm and cackled: 'You'd be good to eat, my pretty one. There's still meat on you.' She dropped his arm and scuttled away through the crowd. He was glad he wasn't alone and drew closer to the others, trying to listen.

He'd guessed right. They had heard there would be bread, but there was none, only stories of bread; and of dreadful, inhuman things, of disappeared children, stolen in the full light of day; of missing fingers, hands, limbs from the daily harvest of the dead. They'd have died anyway, an old man had been heard to say when taken away, his children dead and dismembered.

The wind turned icy. He smelled snow in the air and hoped the clouds overhead kept hold until he was home. An old man lunged towards him. Fearing the worst, he swerved to escape him. The man stumbled to the ground at his feet. His mouth fell open. His lips were black. No words came from them. His eyes clung to the boy, imploring him to do something. He watched, frozen, unable to move, knowing he was helpless. He shivered uncontrollably as the old man died.

Emotionally and physically drained, Misha gave up his search for food and headed home. Once there, he locked himself inside and fell into the chair by the stove, hoping its warmth would ease the chill enveloping him. He was dizzy. The room seemed to spin around his head. He closed his eyes and held tight to the arms of the chair, afraid he would pass out or faint or stop breathing. After a minute, perhaps less, he heard a noise outside the house. He half-rose from the chair, ready to run if necessary. The house was dark. He hoped that whoever was outside would think it empty, would think there was nothing inside to eat. The nearest window rattled. He fell back, relief flooding through him. *It's the wind. Only the wind*

–

Chapter 3

Winter finally began to lose its grip. Clumps of dirty grey snow clung on outside doorways but the linden trees around the square were turning green. In the fields surrounding the village, winter wheat slowly edged its way up through the fast melting snow. If Misha could have seen twenty miles, he'd have caught sight of the Dnieper finally free of ice and the willows along its banks getting ready for spring. It was still cold but there was hope in the air. Spring meant food. Dormice. Mushrooms. Spring meant summer not too far off. Berries. Apples. He let himself dream. Perhaps he'd live. 'But I must get to Kiev.' He spoke aloud, to no one. 'There'd be food in Kiev. I must. I must.'

He looked out the window. It was growing dark. Icy. He looked down at his swollen belly, his stick-like legs. In his heart, he knew he was not strong enough to leave the village, even if they took the roadblocks away. Kiev was too far. 'Maybe Uncle will come,' he said, talking to his reflection.

'Mama wrote to him before she died, begging him to rescue me. He didn't come: maybe he's dead. But my cousin, Kola, will be there. He'll come. Kola will come. Or Papa … aahhhhhhh –'

He pushed away from the window. There was a cracked face looking in; a face with only one eye, with blood dripping. His head swam, the room whirled around him and he tumbled to the floor. After some minutes, he came to, shivering violently. He crawled closer to the stove and struggled into his chair, wrapping a rug around himself. He was frightened by his dreams – visions, hallucinations – by whatever they were. He feared his mind was shrivelling along with his body. He told himself he must eat a second bowl of soup. He couldn't spare the food but was afraid he'd die in his sleep without it.

He knew who the face in the window belonged to: his father's assistant, Misha's teacher, Petro Dmytrovich. Misha's teacher who without reason had denounced the village doctor, Zvi's father, and had him taken away. Who'd forced Papa to help expel the village shopkeeper and all the best farmers, the supposed *kulaks*; forced him to take part in food raids against villagers who had little or no food. Petro Dmytrovich, the man who Papa murdered.

He had seen them that day, walking through the village, arguing so ferociously they didn't see him. He'd darted into the shadows. He thought it was strange, the two of them being together at that hour. School was long over for the day and he'd never seen them together away from the schoolhouse like that, arguing. All he could hear was something about hidden grain and seeds: Papa saying that one of the students had told him where it was hidden but would he – Papa – please not tell her father as he'd skin her alive if he found out, she'd said.

He decided to follow them, despite his mother's injunction against staying out alone. They walked through the village, Misha trailing behind in the growing dusk. It was very quiet and very cold. Everyone who could be inside was inside. He thought it might snow. He watched the two men stop at a shed where his father took out a small spade. Then they headed down the path leading to the river. Once over the

31

footbridge, his father turned downstream. With Petro Dmytrovich following behind, he walked to a grove of tall bushes and scrub-trees several yards inland. Here, the pair separated. The boy followed his father, using the scrubby bushes to keep hidden. Not long afterward, Petro Dmytrovich called out to bring the spade, that he'd found a patch of ground that looked like it had recently been dug over.

Misha crept as close as he dared, practically holding his breath. He watched his father watching Petro Dmytrovich clear the rough ground. His teacher uncovered a wooden box, handed the spade over, and kneeled down to pull the box to the surface. He was puzzled to see his father raise the spade high over his head, holding it on the slant, exposing the sharpest edge. Then, without a word, his father slashed the spade into the back of Petro Dmytrovich's head. The young teacher fell face down into the dirt, gasping, clawing the ground, trying to crawl forward, struggling to escape. Once more, his father raised the spade high over his head and brought it down, and again. Petro Dmytrovich's skull split open and his brains spilled out.

Misha staggered backwards, terrified. He rustled some bushes and froze instantly, eyes closed, afraid his father had heard. When he looked again, his father was opening the wooden box. Taking out a handful of the grain inside, he scattered it around the surface of the hole and trod upon it, making it look as if it had been accidentally spilled. He left the upturned box with its lid open beside the hole, picked up the spade and threw it as far as he could into the surrounding woods. Taking some old gloves from his trouser pocket, he put them on and slowly turned Petro Dmytrovich over. With one last look at the dead man, he left the way he'd come.

The boy was too frightened to move, too frightened to breathe. He was freezing cold and shaking. He shuddered. He felt ready to puke. Minutes passed before he came out of hiding. He went to the dead teacher. Blood was everywhere. One eye was gone. His stomach heaved. He walked around the blood, keeping his shoes clear. There was so much blood. So much blood. He didn't like Petro Dmytrovich – Mama didn't either, not after what he had tried to do to his sister, Nataliya – but he wasn't sure he deserved to die like that.

Nobody did, to his mind. Even after all the evil things he'd made Papa do. The dead eye stared at him and he lost his fight against nausea. Coming to himself, he shivered hard, from fear, not cold. After what felt like forever, snow began to drift down. He watched snowflakes settle on the body. Then fled.

Misha ran through the dying light and settling snow. He knew the way well and was soon outside the darkened schoolhouse. He crept silently through its unlocked door, along the empty, dark corridor to his room. Arkadiy bounded at him as he entered, eager to welcome him home. He acted quickly to stifle his barks. He didn't want his parents to know he was home. He didn't want his father to know. Changing rapidly, he'd climbed into bed, barely noticing the ice-cold sheets. He couldn't face his father. Or his mother. He couldn't stop seeing the blood.

He slept very little that night. Each time he drifted away, pictures of his father lifting the spade higher and higher, and of his teacher's broken head, had flooded his mind. Each time, he'd woken with tears wetting his cheeks, and when morning finally came, he was too ill to leave his bed. His sister sat with him, told him silly stories and brought him bread and soup; his mother did as well. But not his father. For a day and a night, he didn't see his father and wondered if Papa knew he'd been there, knew he'd seen. He told himself he would never ask why; never say he knew. But neither would he ever forget.

On the third day, by which time his teacher's body had been found, his mama let him rest until late afternoon but then insisted he dressed and join the family for supper. He entered the room where the others were gathered, quietly, without attracting attention. Papa and *Baba* – his Grandmama – were sitting side-by-side; Papa talking, *Baba* nodding and smiling at his words. Mama and Nataliya were conferring about something in the oven, plainly pleased with the progress of that day's meal. Their happy tranquillity overwhelmed him. Against his will, tears filled his eyes. He turned away so his mother wouldn't see, but not quickly enough. She caught his arm and pulled him around to face her, demanding to know why he was crying. When the boy refused to speak, she questioned her husband, asking why their son was upset:

'What's going on?' she said. 'First he's too ill to get up. Now he's in tears. What don't I know?'

'What do you mean? He's unhappy because his teacher is dead. Nothing more.'

'That's nonsense,' she snapped.

A dreadful silence had followed. Misha was weeping openly now, as his pent-up misery cascaded out. He wanted his father to speak, to say what he'd done. But Oleksandr said nothing, rubbing his face as if he was very, very tired. His mother tried to console him, enveloping her son in her arms, telling him he'd done nothing wrong, asking him why he cried. Confronted with his continuing silence, she turned back to face her husband, not speaking as the seconds ticked by, just looking from him to her son.

When at last she spoke, her voice was past sadness. 'Was it you, my dear husband? Did you kill Petro

Dmytrovich? I never quite believed he had left for Moscow, however much he wanted to be there, at the centre of things; not with the snow falling so heavily and the village closed and guarded. But I didn't think for one moment you had killed him. But you did – didn't you? And somehow, your son saw you and made himself sick as a result.' She sighed deeply. 'What have you done to us?'

Oleksandr was defiant. 'Nothing – I swear. No one will ever think it was me, not the way I planned it. They'll think it was someone hiding food and seeds. It was the only way to protect Nataliya, to protect all of you. You know that.'

'I don't know that. And they will come looking for you – you, the only person Petro Dmytrovich told he was leaving for Moscow. How is that going to keep our children safe? You've brought us all into danger. I thought you had more sense.'

Oleksandr responded angrily: 'I had no choice.' He started towards his wife.

Misha flinched at his father's words: something in his voice frightened him. Although worried his father might harm him, he put himself between his parents, pushing his father back, telling him to leave his mother alone.

His father's anger had evaporated instantly. He moved to the far end of the room and sat down, hiding his face in his hands. Within minutes, he was on his feet again, begging his wife's forgiveness. 'I'll leave,' he said. 'You'll be safe that way.'

'The village is closed. You'll be arrested if you try.'

'There are ways –

'You'd leave us to face the winter alone? Leave us without rations? No. You stay.'

Within days, Petro Dmytrovich was declared a victim of roving bandits by the local militia, who buried him and promptly forgot him. After the family had learned of his role in the teacher's death, Misha's father had grown quieter, more distant. There was precious little laughter and no joy between father and mother, between father and children. The boy still loved his father. All his life – until that night in the woods – he had admired him, had been proud to be his son. Now he was conflicted: glad Papa was still at home and sorry that he had not left; thinking they'd survive without him, not wanting him to go.

But Oleksandr went nonetheless, when the weather warmed, when fish could be caught. And one night, many months later, when Misha was alone with his mother in the room she had once shared with her husband, he had finally asked the question that never left him, no matter how hard he tried to banish it: *Is my papa dead?* His mother had answered no. Papa had gone to catch fish in the Dnieper, so they wouldn't starve. He hadn't come back because he'd been arrested. Leaving the village was forbidden. Fishing in the Dnieper was forbidden. He must have been arrested.

Her son had not believed his mother then, and still did not. He thought his father was dead for the simple reason that, if alive, he would have come back or let them know somehow or told Uncle Orest in Kiev or done something – anything, but not simply disappear. Not that.

The boy was asleep in his chair, dreaming of food – the wonderful food of Holy Supper – and the day when his best birthday present *ever*, Arkadiy, came into his life, the day he turned ten. Poor Arkadiy. He'd been almost the last dog alive in the village. Then one day, the boy had left the garden door open. The dog went out when no one was watching and disappeared. Mama said some poor man or woman would perhaps live a bit longer in finding him. He wished this had made him less sad but it didn't. He had pretended for a while that his pet was visiting a lady dog somewhere but, in his heart, he knew the truth. He missed him still and tears slipped down his cheeks even as he slept.

Waking from his dreams and hungry as usual, he slipped on a coat and went outside, intent on finding something to eat. As he passed the old church-now-storehouse, he kept his head down and eyes averted from the soldiers who guarded its doors, awaiting the transfer of the village's confiscated seed and grain to Moscow where it would be traded for money and goods to build Stalin's new industrial world. He turned up the path alongside, looking for fresh pickings. A woman was gathering something from the ground behind the church. She waved as he went by and called his name. Misha recognised her and waved back. Suddenly, two of the soldiers were beside him, running towards the woman. They shouted at her to stop or they'd shoot. Either she didn't hear them or didn't believe them. She continued to pick up what the boy realised must be fallen grain, lost when supplies were taken away.

He was stunned. They wouldn't shoot someone just for picking up a tiny handful of fallen grain, would they? When the soldiers first came to the village, he had thought it exciting. He'd been out with Papa when they arrived. They watched in the dusk as the trucks drove by, bumper to bumper, a seemingly-magical chain of light created by filthy exhaust spewing from each truck glowing in the headlights of another coming up behind They reminded him of the toy train he'd had when he was a baby, that he used to pull across the floor with a string. But Papa hadn't liked them.

He watched as the soldiers raised their rifles. One yelled *stand up*. The other shot. He gasped as the woman fell to the ground, suddenly frightened. There was no one else in sight and he feared the soldiers would not want a witness to their foul cruelty. But as they brushed past him, to retrieve the body he supposed, the one who had fired simply smirked at him, saying *Stealing state property, she was.*

His eyes filled with tears. Why shoot people picking up a few forgotten grains, grains that are no good to anyone, people who are only hoping to live a little longer? It wasn't right. He wiped his face and headed home. Whatever he had there to eat would have to do.

Finally, the miracle happened and the siege of the countryside was lifted. Moscow needed Ukraine alive. Forced grain and seed collections stopped. Roadblocks were taken away. Not long afterwards, thousands of tons of seed were made available for the next year's harvest. Life could begin again.

But the miracle had come too late for Misha's mother. No longer strong enough to leave her bed, she had slipped in and out of consciousness for a week and more. One cold, bright morning he could not wake her. He lay down beside her, devastated, weeping and remembering, until evening. When night fell, he kissed her cold lips and left her, closing the door behind him. His heart was broken.

The boy was alone in a house that once rang with laughter but was now filled with the dead. His dead. In time, they would demand to be buried but until then, they were his and he kept them close: Mama in the room she had shared with Papa. Nataliya alone in her father's classroom. *Baba* in the room that had been hers and Nataliya's. But no Papa. Alive or dead. Mama had believed he was still alive, until she herself died. Did the schoolmaster's son hope his father still lived? Sometimes. Always. He rocked back and forth in his chair as he sat talking to himself. 'There's food somewhere … lots and lots of food… there must be. Why can't I find some? Or just leave? Papa left … Mama wouldn't have died if he'd stayed.' He fell quiet for a time. 'I don't want to die. I don't want to die.'

'Mykhailo! Misha! Are you there?'

A voice boomed from outside, a fist banged on the locked door.

'Misha, open up. It's Orest, your Uncle Orest, and Kola. Open the door.'

Misha flung the door open and rushed into his uncle's arms. 'Oh, *Dyad'ko*,' he cried, 'I'm so hungry.'

4

Part Two

Terror

In fear of an approaching war with Germany and Japan, Joseph Stalin took steps to rid the Soviet Union of all "enemies of the people" and all "spies and hidden infiltrators". Throughout 1937 and 1938, thousands of random arrests, deportations, and executions took place. In February 1938 alone, 30,000 Ukrainians were arrested and 2,000 shot. By the Autumn of that year, virtually every family in Ukraine had either lost a relative or knew someone whose relation had disappeared or was imprisoned.

Kiev, September 1937

High on a hill above the Dnieper Misha was sitting under a tree waiting for his cousin Kola who was late. He didn't mind waiting, not on St. Volodymyr's Hill, his escape from the unnatural quiet of the crowded, cowed streets below. Years later, he'd learn to call these times *The Great Terror* but while he was living through them, it was the silence he noticed most. His childhood village had been silent only at the end, when the birds and animals and children were dead. Here in Kiev, silence – and fear – held sway.

As he waited, he kept the ruins of St Michael's Cathedral behind him – destroyed by the Bolsheviks the previous year – and watched the river and the birds, the trees swaying in the wind. Sometimes he would call to mind the narrow river that flowed through the woods behind Hovkova village and think about Mama and Papa, about his sister and grandmother and his life there: his life before. Mostly, though, he simply sat and listened – to the birdsong, the wind, and the distant river traffic. He'd tell himself it was best not to remember too much. That was the past. This was now.

It wasn't always easy, though, not to remember. He was seventeen, almost a man. When his uncle rescued him from the famine four years ago, he'd been a child, an all-but-dead child. A week or two longer, maybe only a few days, and he would have died; alone and unremarked.

Kiev also suffered during those years. Long, cold queues for bread had been widespread, and the streets had filled with thousands of men, women and children seeking refuge from the countryside; with hundreds who died each day. Then at last it ended and there was food. Food, and for him, a new family. Food alone would not have saved him, he knew that. To live, he needed a family: Kola who thought that, like him, Misha could do anything, survive anything; and Uncle Orest, especially Uncle Orest, who healed his body, held him when he cried, and woke him from dreams gone bad. And if, from time to time, his eyes blurred, if the pictures in his mind came too near – too vivid – he told himself there were others who had suffered more, who were suffering still. *I just have to get along somehow, like Papa used to say – Papa … I'm still not sure he did right.* He hadn't told his uncle about the murder. He hadn't told Kola. He often thought about doing so but felt it would be disloyal, somehow.

'Damn,' Misha muttered aloud, jumping to his feet, irritated He was tired of waiting, but not just that. His cousin wasn't only late, he was bringing someone to meet him, some so-called friend. He headed down the road linking the Upper Town to Podil. It bloody well wasn't the right time to be making new friends. It was hard enough to know if old ones could be trusted. After Kirov was assassinated three years before and the purges began, it was the Party bosses and their acolytes who'd been arrested. But as the months passed, the terror had spread downwards and outwards, a miasma covering the city as widely and suddenly as the Dnieper covered the flood plain. Arrests became random. The next one to be caught could be you or your brother or your wife. Only fools and drunkards talked in the street or made new friends. But that was his cousin Kola: smart, definitely, but also reckless. His first year as a student at the Aviation Institute had only just begun. He couldn't have known this person for more than a week or two at best. Far too soon to call him a friend.

After a few minutes walking downhill, he spotted the two men coming around a bend. 'Hey, Kola!' he called out. 'You're late.' He looked around for somewhere open to sit, somewhere they could see both the river and anyone approaching, where they wouldn't be overlooked or overheard.

'Hi, sorry we're late.' Kola gave him a hug. 'This is Borys Andrusiv, Misha. Bobby, my cousin Mykhailo Salenko.'

Misha looked at the tall, well-built man standing in front of him, who wasn't the stranger he had expected: 'Oh, shit.'

Astounded, Kola watched his friend Bobby shove his cousin hard. Misha stumbled backwards only just staying upright.

'She's barely fifteen. What the hell do you think you're up to?' Bobby shouted.

'You're who – her brother? I haven't done anything. I just like her, that's all.'

'Guys, guys, calm down.' Kola stepped between them. 'Bobby, leave him alone. Misha, what's this all about? How do you two know each other?'

Confronted by his cousin, Misha looked abashed. He stuttered: 'There … there's this girl, Mariya. We met accidentally, in the market. We had coffee. That's all. I like her. I think she likes me.'

'She's only fifteen.'

Kola grinned at his friend. 'Well, Bobby, that's old enough to have a boyfriend. You know that. I know that. So get over it. Let's sit down. Okay? Let you two get to know each other a bit better.' He tugged his cousin's sleeve, then tempted him with food: 'I brought some almond rolls. Come on, Bobby, you too.'

The trio settled on a patch of open grassland overlooking the river. Kola and Misha sat side-by-side, leaning slightly against each other for support. They still looked like brothers, with their matching narrow faces, dark curly hair, and blue eyes, but they'd lost the twin-like looks of childhood, perhaps because of the famine, perhaps because they were just getting older. Kola used to be taller but now ceded an inch or so to Misha, although he still carried more weight, still looked more a fighter than his younger cousin. Misha's years in a village under siege had left him lean and wiry.

Lounging on the grass, his face turned to catch the afternoon sun, Bobby couldn't have presented a greater contrast. With light-coloured hair, hazel eyes, and a round, vigorous-looking face, he didn't look Slavic although, like his sister, he might have been mistaken for someone from the north, around Chernihiv perhaps, where the centuries-old Nordic invasion still showed in people's faces. He spoke Ukrainian like a native, though, and dressed like one as well.

Outwardly calm, Misha was rattled inside. He'd let Bobby think he and Mariya had only met once, which wasn't precisely true. They'd met in the market three times now, for coffee and donuts, although last time – only a few days ago – their time together had ended abruptly, oddly. They'd been sitting quietly amidst the bustle and confusion of shoppers coming and going; of sellers hawking their wares. Not talking much, just enjoying each other's company. He had wondered what it would be like to kiss her, hoped he'd get the chance one day soon. She was so pretty. Then, without warning, she'd leapt to her feet, said she was sorry but she had to go, and hurried away towards the nearest exit. Astonished by her sudden departure, Misha was equally surprised to see her accosted by a good-looking young man who proceeded to berate her for something and hustle her out the doorway. Tossing enough money on the table for their food and drink, he hastened after her but to no avail. There was no sight of either Mariya or the young man who, Misha guessed – hoped – was her brother or at least a friend and not someone wishing to do her harm. Which proved to be the case, as the encounter with Bobby had so aptly demonstrated.

Coming back to the present day and deciding Bobby and Kola had talked airplanes long enough, Misha questioned Mariya's brother about his name. 'Bobby sounds American – is that right?'

'Absolutely right, Mykhailo. It is American, because I'm an A-MER-I-CAN,' Bobby drawled the word in English. 'Or at least I was born there, just like my sister,' he added with a smirk.

In truth, Mariya had told Misha she'd come with her family from the United States, and why. But he wanted to hear Bobby's version of events, to see if he'd tell the same story. If he did, and Misha believed Mariya, then he'd have to believe Bobby as well. It only made sense.

'So, what's an American doing living in Kiev?'

Bobby replied amiably. 'I'd have thought Mariya would have told you. We were born in Detroit. Our dad was a car worker: a senior engineer at Ford's River Rouge Plant. You know Ford?'

'*You can have any colour you like as long as it's black*,' the cousins chimed together.

'That's the man. Well, about six or seven years ago he sold the Soviet Union the whole shebang – blueprints, machinery, spare parts – everything needed to make 75,000 Model A Fords, plus five years' technical assistance; all for forty million dollars in gold. My dad was part of the deal and we came over in March '31. About a thousand Americans arrived every week that year: qualified engineers, like my dad, and factory workers, plumbers, electricians, artists, doctors, professors. You name it, we were coming.'

'Coming for what?'

Bobby laughed. 'This was the Promised Land! The workers' paradise, where the working man was king, or at least well-paid, housed and fed.' He paused to finish his almond roll. Then picked up his story again. 'My father's own job was pretty secure. And it probably would've been secure for a while longer. But millions didn't have jobs. You know about the Depression, I guess. Well, there we were in the great USA with people sleeping rough in public parks, soup kitchens everywhere, and millions of men and women, and kids too, riding the trains back and forth across the country looking for work. And meanwhile, there were the newspapers extolling the wonders of the USSR, all the new factories and new industries, and jobs – lots of jobs. Big advertisements. *Americans – we want you*!' Taking a pack of cigarettes from his jacket pocket, he shook one out for himself and passed the rest around. He exhaled a cloud of cheap smoke. 'Dad knew his factory would close sooner or later, so he signed on the dotted line and off we went – mom and pop and two little kiddies, chasing the Russian dream. We ended up at the automobile plant in Kharkiv, and Dad became a foreman on the assembly line.'

Misha jumped to his feet. He wanted a moment to think. He shook his left leg. 'Sorry. Bloody thing's gone to sleep.' He tramped back and forth for a minute or two. Bobby was elaborating Mariya's story. Unless they were conspiring together to hoodwink Kola and him … but why would they? He and his cousin were just students: no money, no important relatives. He decided to accept Bobby for what he clearly seemed to be: a friendly, interesting, used-to-be American. Unless, and until, he had reasons to do otherwise. He rejoined the others, curious to hear the rest.

'Sorry about that. How did you get the name Borys Andrusiv?'

Bobby looked at him, puzzled. 'You don't know? There were thousands of Americans here, and it happened to most of them. With my family, it was at the factory. There was an office there for foreigners to hand in their passports for registration. My father was told they'd be returned whenever we wanted them and given registration documents to sign. He signed and – hey, presto! We were Soviet citizens. Later, he got papers for us so we could travel to other parts of the country if we wanted, and Bobby Andrews became Borys Andrusiv.'

'And your passports?' Misha asked. Kola shot him a warning look. Bobby just shrugged, watching the smoke from his cigarette drift upwards. 'It didn't seem to matter much in the beginning, being without them, the passports. But later... well, it mattered later.' He shivered as he spoke. 'Look, I'm getting cold and it's getting late. I'd better go home. My sister Mary – Mariya – will be waiting for me.'

The sun, which was high when they met, had slipped behind the tall trees lining the western edge of the park, casting long shadows across the open grassland. But it wasn't cold and Misha wondered if there were other reasons why Borys – Bobby – suddenly wanted to leave. He said nothing, though, letting his doubts pass for the moment at least. He got to his feet.

'Sure, let's go. You live in Podil, right? We'll walk you down and take the funicular back up. Okay with you, Kola?'

'Why not, there aren't many people around. Let's walk.'

The road down was steep and cobble-stoned and traversed the hill as it dropped towards the river. As they turned a corner, two men came into view, heading towards them. Each one thinking the men might be police, they fell silent until they passed by and then spoke only of inconsequential things until they parted at the funicular in Podil. After Bobby left, Kola asked Misha what he thought of him.

'I liked him.' Misha grinned. 'I like his sister, too.'

'Do I get to meet her?'

'Maybe.'

'We could invite them for a meal? See what Papa thinks of them.

'Good idea. Uncle could cook *Chicken Sichenyky*, with creamed mushrooms. Makes me hungry just thinking of it.'

Kola laughed and took his arm. 'You're always hungry. Let's go home.'

I was running across snow-covered fields, alone and happy, surprisingly warm under the winter sun, finally free to explore the tumbled-down remains of tumuli scattered across the field hidden under the snow. I knew if I was allowed to look, I'd find buried treasure. Old coins, rings maybe; left behind by the Romans or the Scythians. They always buried money and jewels with bodies hundreds of years ago and I knew I'd find some. I didn't know why Papa hadn't stopped me this time. He always stopped me. Said it's disrespectful. There were so many mounds. Not big ones like the Black Grave but dozens and dozens of small ones. Which one? Which one? I ran from one to another. Which had the treasure – this one? That one? I swept the snow from the nearest mound –

'Ahhh – w-what?' Misha woke gasping, frightened and confused. He fell back onto his pillow. He'd been dreaming about tumuli, but when he swept the snow away it wasn't buried treasure he'd found but Papa. He twisted onto his stomach and sunk his head into the pillow, trying to stop his tears. He couldn't shake the image of his father's blackened, broken face from his mind. He lay still, exhausted.

After a few moments, the bedroom door clicked open. He turned over. Of course it was his uncle, asking if he was alright. He nodded. His uncle waited, giving him time to recover. After a bit, he managed a smile. 'I'm okay,' he said.

'Good. We all have them, bad dreams. Scoot over.' Orest sat on the bed beside his nephew. 'Your papa?'

He nodded.

'I know sometimes you think your father was wrong to have left you and Nataliya, to have left your mother. But you mustn't ever forget he was trying to save your lives. To get food. He loved you all very much and would never have abandoned you. He acted from love, my boy, remember that, from love.' He ruffled Misha's hair, smiling. 'Losing people is hard, it hurts, but you mustn't let the pain win. You'll survive better if you don't.' He got to his feet. 'It's late now, almost nine, so you need to get going. Don't you have a special lecture this morning? Kola's gone and I'm off as well. Have some breakfast and remember, it was only a dream.'

Not quite an hour later, Misha slipped into an empty space on a bench in the Great Hall of the Agriculture Institute of Kiev. He was a first year agronomy student. As a young boy, he'd often thought of becoming a farmer, mostly – childishly – because he loved the sight of wheat, top-heavy, golden, swaying in the wind, ready for harvest. It wasn't the beauty of wheat fields that drove him now, though, but a craving for knowledge: how to secure food supplies, to overcome hunger and banish famine; to stop people dying like his family. His parents had believed the famine was the result of political malevolence; his uncle still did. Misha was not sure he agreed, or at least not entirely. In his view, there must have been more to it than malice. Political ill will alone was not enough, or too evil, to explain the deaths of so many millions. He simply could not accept that people were wilfully starved. Not the right science – that was his opinion – the science hadn't got it right.

It was the first time he'd been in the Great Hall. 'Have I missed anything?' he asked his neighbour, whom he recognised from a lecture the previous week, and received a friendly *Not yet* in return. He watched the room fill up, wondering how many it held – a few hundred at least – and admired the oak-covered, windowless walls. *Great Cave* might be a better name: an immense, three-sided cave with tiered rows of oak benches that rose up and up and up; the pride of the Institute. The room around him was humming with whispered conversations as the gathering of students, research assistants, and professors waited for the day's celebrated speaker, Trofim Lysenko, one of Stalin's famous *barefoot scientists* – uneducated, untrained – whose new biology was going to make the Soviet Union a world leader in food production.

Soon the side doors opened and the Rector entered with Comrade Lysenko. Yegor Tomenko, one of the Institute's most respected professors and a particular hero of Misha's, followed a few steps behind. He would reply to Lysenko's lecture.

Misha was astonished by Lysenko. This insignificant, sullen-looking man was the future of Soviet agriculture? He had a dejected look, with pale skin, concave cheeks and pronounced cheekbones. He looked dull, bored with himself and the world. But then, wasting no time on preliminaries, he began to speak, and revealed himself not dull, not boring, but a charlatan! Darwin was wrong. Mendel was wrong. The chromosome theory of heredity was wrong. The whole of Western science was wrong and only Lysenko was right. He rubbished Professor Tomenko. *The saviour of Soviet agriculture? Not bloody likely.*

When Lysenko was finished, Professor Tomenko stepped forward. His opening remarks praised Darwin – fulsomely. From the benches behind, beside, and in front of Misha, there rose an uproar of catcalls, hissing, and hoots. After a noticeably extended, seemingly unconcerned pause, the Rector moved forward to restore order. Professor Tomenko began again, but when he suggested that the evidence for a new Soviet biology was weak, and that Comrade Lysenko was very good, an expert perhaps, at producing findings from experiments before they were finished, be they of potatoes, peas, or trees in Siberia, he was shouted down as a traitor and forced to leave the podium. The Rector thanked Academician Lysenko at length for his brilliant lecture and contribution to Soviet science, invited applause, and escorted his honoured guest from the Hall. Professor Tomenko was left to find his own way out.

Shaken, Misha made his way down the stairs amidst a crowd of chattering, laughing, wide-eyed students and researchers. He found himself walking alongside his seatmate, who introduced himself as Fedir Wendelko, one of the research staff. Forgetting in the excitement of the moment the ever-present need for vigilance, Misha said he thought the boo-ing and catcalls were unfair on Professor Tomenko.

'Komsomol thugs, probably, and not entirely unexpected,' Fedir replied. 'You're new, aren't you? Follow me.' Fedir steered Misha to a quiet corner of a courtyard momentarily empty. 'You should have been here last May. The Rector was accused of *Lack of Vigilance* and to meet the criticism, he convened a purge meeting.'

To Misha's surprise, Fedir laughed out loud.

'Teachers and students denouncing each other. Everyone calling for true Soviet self-criticism. The Komsomol taking turns praising Lysenko and condemning Tomenko. They went after the Professor pretty viciously, but he's internationally respected for his work and eventually they backed off. But now that Lysenko's the rising star, Tomenko looks like fair game. I don't fancy his chances. Say, how about a coffee?'

By this time, Misha had remembered where they were and when they lived. His sense of caution around strangers had revived and he was thinking that this man not only talked too much but also too freely to someone he had just met. He was attracted by Fedir's friendliness and reminded of his childhood friend, Zvi Rosen – the same dark, clever eyes, the same pale skin – but drew back nonetheless. 'Well, perhaps another day,' he said. 'I'm a bit short of time today.'

'Sure, any time. I'm here most days. I'll look out for you. *Bu vayl* – bye!'

Misha left the Institute with his head spinning from the morning's events. The wind was cool but the sun warm. He walked along Shevchenko Boulevard looking for somewhere cheap to eat. After a time, too hungry to walk any further, he jumped on a trolley bus heading towards the University where his uncle worked. He'd go to the covered market on Bessarabka Square and combine lunch with shopping for some sausage and fruit from Odessa for that night's meal. If he had enough money, he'd get some cheap cigarettes as well.

As usual for that time on a weekday, the bus was filled to capacity, with much jostling for seats. Still distracted, he took no notice of the various comings and goings. Perhaps if he had, he'd have seen the startled expression on the face of a passenger who pushed past him heading towards the rear of the trolley. But he didn't, and in another ten minutes or so, he jumped off and crossed over the square into the market

Misha loved the sounds and sights and smells of Bessarabka Market. He especially loved to sit, nurse a small coffee and some sweet bread, and watch the fruit sellers –

their plums and apples and oranges geometrically arranged in perfect pyramids – as they haggled with their buyers, mostly women but a few men also, over the price of a bit of fruit. It was something his mother would have loved. From their faces, he could tell it was a game, a serious one perhaps, but a game nonetheless, with buyers and sellers randomly changing places as winners or losers. That day it looked like the sellers were winning, perhaps because of the shortage of fruit from the South.

Unable to make his coffee last any longer, he tossed a few coins on the table, got up and headed for the nearest exit. The aisles were crowded and he stood back between two stalls to allow an elderly couple to pass. Suddenly, no more than ten feet away, coming toward him, was Zvi Rosen. It couldn't be – but it was. He waited until his long-lost friend was about to pass and stepped forward into his path.

'Zvi,' he said, hearing his voice catch, 'Zvi, it's me, Misha.'

'Excuse me?'

'It's Misha. Don't you recognise me? Oh, Zvi, I always knew I'd see you again. But here, in Kiev –'

'I'm sorry, you have made a mistake,' the young man interrupted. His dark eyes held no sign of recognition; he simply looked politely baffled. 'My name is Binyamin. I know no one by that other name. Would you let me pass, please?'

'But Zvi…?'

'Let me pass,' he said again, this time with a hard edge to his voice. Startled by it, Misha stood aside to let the stranger disappear into the crowded market. Only this was no stranger. Even that cold, clipped voice, the 'I've had enough now' voice, belonged to Zvi, his easy-going village friend, who could so swiftly mimic the authority of his doctor-father.

It was Zvi. I know it was. Whatever he said.

He couldn't wait to get home, to tell Kola. Ever since they were boys, the cousins had talked about seeing Zvi again one day, sooner or later. Bubbling over with excitement, he burst into the apartment and told his cousin about the lecture and the catcalls and how afterwards he'd gone to the market for lunch and there, in the market, in the flesh, was Zvi. He told him all this and Kola didn't believe him.

'But it *was* him,' Misha insisted. 'I know it was.'

'You must be mistaken,' Kola retorted. 'Even if Zvi is still alive – which would be a bit of a miracle – and calling himself Binyamin maybe to stay safe, how likely is it you'd just bump into him in the market?'

'I don't know, but it was him,' Misha replied, equally adamant. How could anyone – leastways Kola – think he wouldn't know his childhood friend?

'Was who?' Unheard, Orest had come into the apartment, taken off his coat and hat, and joined the pair in the kitchen. 'What don't you know, Misha?'

'I saw Zvi Rosen today, but he said he wasn't Zvi.' Misha repeated his story, hoping his uncle would believe him, would believe that Zvi was still alive and somewhere here in Kiev. In this, he was disappointed.

'Remember this morning? You dreamt about your childhood. Then you went to this lecture where you say you met one of the researchers who reminded you of Zvi. Well, I think when you saw this other young man, the one in the market, with dark hair and dark eyes like Zvi, you saw what you wanted to see. I'm sorry, Misha, but I think it was another dream; a wide-awake one, perhaps, but still only a dream.' Orest put his arm around his nephew's shoulders. 'You're having a rough day, aren't you? Come and sit down.'

A knock at the apartment door stopped them. Orest told Misha to sit down and Kola to make coffee, that he would go to the door. A moment later, he opened it to find a young man with dark hair, pale skin, and dark eyes standing on the threshold.

'Professor Salenko, my name is Zvi Rosen. May I come in?'

For one glorious moment, in a small apartment off Pan'kivs'ka street, just minutes from the University, there was silence, amazement, incredulity. The clocks stopped, the world held its breath. Then, an explosion of sound: shouts of joy, hoots of laughter, everyone speaking, no one listening, until, at length, Orest convinced three excited young men to sit down and be quiet.

'Well, Zvi,' he said when calm prevailed. 'I'd say the first thing you need to do is to explain how you got here, to this apartment.' He peered closely at the long-lost friend. 'Haven't I seen you somewhere?'

Zvi was sitting on the couch beside Misha who had yet to stop smiling. 'Yes sir, you have. I'm a student in the History Faculty.'

'Binyamin…'

'Chovnik. Yes sir. I got here today because I followed you from the University. We didn't meet more than once or twice when I was a child but I recognised your name and thought you must be Misha's uncle. I thought Misha was dead.'

'I thought you were in Siberia.'

'But when I saw him on the trolley bus today –'

Misha reeled forward, eyes wide with surprise. 'You saw me on the bus?'

'Yes,' Zvi said, pulling him back onto the couch. 'So I followed you because I thought I must be mistaken or crazy or something. But then it was you –'

'But you… you said …why didn't you admit you were you? I mean, obviously you knew I recognised you.'

'I'm sorry about that, Misha, truly, but there were too many people around. I didn't want to be noticed.' He laughed. 'I knew you'd get excited and shout.'

'Well, you could've winked or something. Kola here thought I was crazy when I told him I'd seen you. And Uncle thought I was dreaming.'

'Misha, quit picking on him. He's here now, isn't he?' Orest got to his feet and headed to the kitchen. 'This calls for a celebration. Kola, you get the glasses, I'll get the vodka.'

Zvi looked around the apartment, plainly curious to see how a university professor lived. 'It's nice to see all the books. I can't afford to buy many.'

'They're mostly Uncle's but also a few of Papa's I brought with me. There's more in Uncle's bedroom – ask him, I'm sure he'd let you borrow some.' Misha followed his friend's gaze around the room. 'I've been living here since April 1933. There's this room and two bedrooms, Uncle's and one I share with Kola. But see that door at the end, on the right? A room through there used to be part of this apartment. Apparently, the neighbours either knew someone important or did something important and the room was given to them. The door was just sealed up this side and papered over on the other side. Can you believe it?' Misha shook his head at the absurdity.

'Believe what?' Orest returned, carrying vodka, sugared almonds, and caraway pretzels.

'I was telling Zvi about the room that used to be yours.'

'Patronage: the first principle of communism. I keep the door unpapered to remind me. But come, stand up, let's toast our long-lost Zvi, returned to us at last.'

Kola handed his father and cousin small crystal glasses, which Orest filled with vodka. They spoke as one: 'To Zvi. Long life, happiness, and good health!'

'Thank you, thank you so much. I can't tell you how happy I am to be here with you, with Misha. I – I – ' Zvi's voice faltered as he tried to go on.

Kola handed him a glass of vodka. 'Drink up, Zvi, and have a pretzel!'

'To the prodigal, returned!' Orest raised his glass again.

'To my old best friend!' Misha added, raising his. 'But how did you get to Kiev? I thought you followed your father north. Is your mother here too?'

Misha's questions reminded them that Zvi had not left Hovkova village by choice. In official eyes he was a *Son of an Enemy of the People*; a dangerous label to wear during times of denunciation and terror. Thoughts of Dr Yakov Rosen's arrest and banishment quickly replaced the light-hearted gaiety that had marked Zvi's reappearance. Misha took his friend's arm and guided him back to the couch. Kola and Orest put aside their vodka and sat facing them.

'Both my parents are dead,' Zvi began, his normally pale complexion flushed with emotion. 'After Papa's trial, after he was found guilty, Mama and I thought he'd be sent to the Solovetsky Islands right away. That's what your papa thought too, Misha, do you remember?'

Misha nodded. 'I was so angry with him. Before he went to Kharkiv for the trial, he told me it was all a big mistake – that your father had done nothing wrong – that everything would be okay and that you all would be coming home soon. And then you didn't. It took me a long time to realise it wasn't his fault.'

'Poor Misha.' Zvi smiled wistfully at him as if seeing the ten-year-old boy who'd been a cherished part of his lost childhood. 'Papa was kept in Kharkiv prison month after month. When I got a bit older or when Mama wasn't well enough, I'd take parcels for him to the prison. I'd line up with dozens of other relatives, all waiting to hand theirs in. We never knew for sure if Papa got the parcels, but other people waiting said the guards wouldn't take them, the parcels, unless he was still in there' – the young man's voice faltered for a moment – 'May I have some water, please, or tea?'

Kola jumped to his feet. 'I'll get it. Tea for you too, Misha? Papa?'

Glass in hand, Zvi continued his story. 'Then one day about a year later, in the summer, I tried to hand in a parcel and the guard said Papa had been transferred to another place. Of course, I thought that meant he'd finally been sent to a camp, although the guard wouldn't say where he'd gone. But after I left, a woman who had been queuing nearby caught up with me in the street and said it meant Papa had died. That *another place* was their way of telling the relatives. I spent a long time walking around the city, trying to think how I could tell Mama. She wasn't very strong, not since the baby died and I was –'

'Baby?' Misha interrupted. 'I don't remember a baby.'

'Mama was expecting a baby when we went to Kharkiv for Papa's trial. I think that's why your father came with us, to make sure she was okay. She had a little boy after the trial, at the end of November. We called him Nathan. It used to make her so sad that Papa had never seen him. He died that same winter, not even three months old. Mama was never really the same afterwards. So I didn't know how I was going to tell her about Papa, but of course I had to. After that she gave up wanting to live.' Zvi's voice wavered. 'She used to apologise to me – to me! – for wanting to die. She'd say she wanted to join Papa and Nathan.'

'When did that happen?' Kola asked, his voice gentle.

'At the end of September, in that same year, 1931.' Zvi was quiet for a few moments. When he began again, his voice was stronger. 'That left me, age eleven, an orphan, living with strangers – well, friends, obviously, but not relatives. I had the address of cousins in Poland and in Kiev, and since Kiev is a lot closer than Lvov, I came here. On the train, which took endless days because I kept getting bumped off. At every station, there were hundreds of people trying to get on: people fleeing villages because they didn't want to be part of the collective farms; people who had been thrown out of villages because they were supposed kulaks. Men and women everywhere, dragging small wooden carts filled with odd bits of furniture, carrying roped cartons or old suitcases. Lots of children, too, so nobody took much notice of me.

'The worst were the locked livestock trains, heading north, full of people. Whenever one of them stopped in a station, you could hear the people inside, banging on the wagon sides, crying for water or food or air. They'd shout they couldn't breathe, that there were too many of them crammed inside. They'd beg someone to open the doors. But of course no one dared. The soldiers saw to that.'

Zvi stopped, shaking his head as if to clear the pictures from his mind. He laughed quietly, almost to himself. 'So finally I get here to Kiev, to the house of my cousin. Can you imagine those poor people? An eleven-year-old boy shows up out of the blue, hardly any money or clothes, father a convicted traitor, and says he's a cousin with nowhere else to go.'

'But they took you in?'

'They took me in. I was family. I could've been a traitor and they would've taken me in… *probably*.' He smiled. 'They hid me in an awful room in the cellar, cold and damp most of the time. I couldn't go to school or shopping or anywhere. Fortunately, the neighbours were members of the same synagogue, so we didn't have to worry too much if I was seen inside the house, just not outside. Then my cousin's son, Binyamin – he was only a year older than me but quite frail – fell ill with pneumonia and never recovered. I stayed hidden for a few more months after he died and in September used his papers to register at a school on the other side of Podil where he wasn't known. Ever since I've been Binyamin Chovnik, son of Leah and Isaac and brother of Rachel and Zoya.' He grinned. 'Sometimes I worry that someone from Hovkova village will recognise me, like you did, Misha. But as most people seem to think one Jew looks pretty much like another, I just get on with life as Binyamin. Including being a student in your faculty, Professor Salenko.'

'Please, Zvi – Binyamin – from today, you are my nephew. You must call me *Dyad'ko*,' Orest chuckled. 'Although maybe not at the University; that might not be wise.'

'Thank you, Professor … Uncle. I'm very grateful.' He turned to Misha, looking pleased. 'That makes us cousins, doesn't it? But what about you? How did you come to be living here?'

Misha had known his turn would come, that he would have to tell his own story. He didn't want to – he didn't like talking about the past – but it was Zvi asking, so he had no choice.

'After the roadblocks in the countryside were lifted,' he began only to fall silent at the eruption of insistent knocking at the door. For the briefest of moments, his silence hung between them, palpable, as if fear itself was waiting outside the apartment.

Kola spoke first, his voice bright: 'I'll go. I'm not expecting anyone, are you?' He looked at his father who shook his head.

Opening the door, Kola was surprised to find his fellow student outside. 'Bobby! What brings you here?'

'He did it! Vancouver – Chkalov – 63 hours non-stop! Can you believe it?' The newcomer pushed past Kola into the apartment, excitement pouring out of him. He came to an abrupt halt when he realised his friend wasn't alone. 'Oops, sorry. I shouldn't have just barged in.'

'It's okay.' Kola took his arm. 'Papa, this is the friend from the Institute I told you about, Borys Andrusiv – we call him Bobby. You know my cousin. And this is –'

'Binyamin Chovnik,' said Zvi, coming forward to shake hands. 'I'm one of Professor Salenko's students. I was just leaving.'

'Please, don't go because of me,' Bobby said, looking embarrassed.

'Borys – Bobby: you're very welcome. Kola, bring a chair for your friend.' Orest put a hand on Zvi's arm to stay his departure. 'Binyamin, don't go yet. Let's hear Bobby's news. You're a historian, so I doubt you know about this Chkalov character: Stalin's favourite pilot. All the flyboys, like these two,' – he waved in the direction of Kola and Bobby – 'want to be just like him and all the girls want to marry him. Knows more tricks than a circus-full of clowns.'

Misha brought fresh tea for everyone and they settled down to listen.

'It was on the loudspeakers and Radio Kossior, 5,288 miles from Moscow to Vancouver, Washington, USA – I've got an aunt there,' – Bobby interrupted himself – 'It seems the first twenty-four hours were okay, nothing much happened. But when they were going over the North Pole, the plane's compass stopped working and they had to fly by dead reckoning and a solar indicator. Then they started to burn fuel way too fast, because of headwinds and storms, and the plane kept icing up, and they nearly ran out of oxygen.'

'It sounds like a miracle they got there,' Kola interjected.

'We don't believe in miracles.' Misha grinned at his cousin.

'I forgot.'

'Be quiet, you two. Go on, Bobby.'

'Well, that's it, really. Except when they arrived, there were crowds of Americans cheering them and bigwigs waiting for them. Apparently – I don't know if I believe this – when Chkalov jumped out of the cockpit, he shouted back into the plane, "Look, there's General Marshall" and his two co-pilots couldn't figure out whether there was a general waiting to greet them or a marshal.' – Bobby laughed at his own story – 'Anyway, they're going to stay for a month, go all over the country and meet President Roosevelt.'

'Well, that has the look of an 'Order of the Red Banner' for them.' Orest sounded amused. 'Chkalov will probably end up elected something important and never go flying again.'

'That would be a pity, wouldn't it?' said Zvi, standing up. 'I enjoyed your story but I'm afraid I must go now. I have to catch the Twenty-one.'

'The tram to Podil?' asked Bobby. 'I live there too. I'll come with you.'

'Please, no, don't leave on my account.'

'I insist. I probably shouldn't have just dropped in anyway.'

Zvi and Bobby eventually left together, after Bobby promised to come back soon and Zvi agreed to meet Misha the following day. Kola and Orest disappeared into the kitchen to begin preparations for the evening meal but Misha couldn't settle. He paced back and forth in the living room, thinking about the odd coincidence. After a time, he joined the others in the kitchen.

'Kola, how did Bobby know where we live?'

'I don't know. I must have told him. Why?'

'Don't you think it strange he shows up, just when Zvi is here? Then wants to go to Podil with him – maybe find out where he lives?'

'No, I don't. You're paranoid. Bobby's just friendly. I thought you liked him, wanted Papa to make dinner for him and his sister. He was excited about Chkalov, that's all. Papa, you tell him.'

'Tell him what, exactly?'

'That he's too suspicious. That Bobby's not spying on Zvi or whatever it is he thinks he's doing.'

'Since I only met him for the first time half an hour ago, I don't think I can do that. He seems genuine but these days suspicions have a nasty habit of coming true.'

'I know, but –'

'But nothing – you're old enough to know that. You have to be careful. We all have to be careful.' Orest smiled at his son, whose face was flushed. 'Tell you what, you invite him for coffee later this week. I'll see what I think of him. He says he has an aunt in the United States. Does that make him some sort of American? Is that where the Bobby comes from? Not the best background for an informer.'

'He was born there. But it's a long story and you should hear it from him.'

'Okay, you invite him and I'll listen.' Orest turned to his nephew. 'Happy?'

'Yes, *Dyad'ko*, thanks.' Misha opened the oven to see what smelled so good. 'I'm hungry. Let's eat.'

It was the next day. Zvi and Misha were tramping through woodland high on Volodymyr's Hill. Misha kept pinching himself. Despite his boyhood bravado that he and Zvi would meet again someday – *for sure* – he didn't quite believe his friend was really beside him. He felt he'd got a part of his family back. As they walked, Misha told him about Hovkova village in the years after he left. Zvi knew about the push to collectivise the farms, of course, and about the famine that came in its wake. What he wanted to hear was about *their* village, *their* school friends, *Misha's* family, *Misha*.

'Do you remember Andriy Stepanovich?'

'Short, with squinty eyes? His family had the land near the old oak?'

'That's him. He was the first of our classmates to die, along with his mother. Andriy died from fever from the boggy land they were given after they left the village, and his mother from a broken heart, according to Mama.'

They walked on, following a narrow trail winding upwards through linden and oak and birch, soft underfoot and canopied overhead. After a time, Misha picked up the story again:

'Stalin said that rapid, compulsory collectivization was never his idea in the first place – all the fault of over-zealous officials, apparently – and if farmers wanted to leave the collective farms, they could. Simple. Then, the farmers were told that if they did leave, they wouldn't get their *own* land back, or their own cow or horse. Instead, they'd be given land somewhere outside the village. After all, the collective farm wasn't going anywhere: they were, not the land. When Andriy's father heard this, he leapt to his feet, swearing and yelling *it's all a bloody joke*. He wanted to know how he could be sure the government wouldn't change its mind again. If we leave, he asked, how do we know we won't just have to come back later? Which he did, both leave and come back, but without Andriy and his mother. It was very sad. I was very sad. But it was nowhere near as awful as watching all the others die one by one after the famine took hold, including lots of our friends – Ivan Pavlovich, Mykola Ruslanovich, Stepan Ivanovich, and their sisters and most of their brothers.'

Zvi took Misha's arm and they continued along the path in silence. Misha knew it was time to speak about his own lost family. They propped themselves in front of the monument to Volodyhmyr the Great, high above the river, and watched the small boats far below cut glinting trails through the Dnieper. Zvi waited for his friend to begin.

'It took more than a year, maybe two years for collectivization to end up in famine. Papa left the year I was twelve. His access to rations had pretty much dried up by then. He said fruit and vegetables wouldn't be enough to stave off starvation when the weather turned, and what we needed was fish from the Dnieper. Mama didn't want him to go – but he did – and never came back.' Misha paused to catch his breath, holding up his hand to keep Zvi silent. He wanted to get it out.

'It was bad enough without Papa but then it got worse. Summer turned into a wet, miserable autumn and then into a vicious winter. Nataliya was caught and beaten while she looked for acorns and died of pneumonia in December. Mama had asked me to go instead of her but I was busy with something stupid, nothing really, and Nataliya went in my place and died instead of me –'

'No, Misha. Not that. It wasn't your fault.'

'But if *I'd* gone –'

'It wasn't your fault. You can't blame yourself for what others did.'

Misha shrugged. 'Then Baba stopped eating, told Mama to give her food to me. She died a few weeks after Nataliya. We couldn't bury them. The ground was frozen. There were corpses everywhere: on the lanes, in barns, in the woods. So they stayed in the house with us. Then Mama… she died… and I was alone.' A picture of his mother, shrunken and cold, rocking in her chair, admonishing him not to go outside, crept into his mind. He took a deep breath and shook himself back to the present. 'But not for long. At least I don't think it was very long. I was only half-conscious most of the time. Then one day, Uncle Orest and Kola banged on the door until I heard them. They took me back to Kiev and back to life, and here I am still – and fit as a fiddle, as you can see.'

Misha couldn't hide the tears welling in his eyes. Zvi held him tight. They didn't speak. They didn't need words. They knew each other's pain. Soon, Misha shook free and found his battered pack of cigarettes. Zvi didn't want one – he never did – and lit one for himself.

'Your mama and mine were great friends, weren't they?' Zvi said. 'Sometimes I think I loved yours almost as much as my own – you could always talk to her. And our fathers: they were such good friends. Yours was a wonderful teacher. Thought I was pretty smart, didn't he?' He punched his friend gently on the shoulder.

Misha half-smiled. 'Smarter than me at least.'

'Did you ever find out what happened to him?'

'No, Uncle Orest tried, but nothing.'

'I've never forgotten him, Misha. He was so good to my mother and me.' He laughed, lightly. 'On the train to Papa's trial, he told me this ridiculous story about a nose that turns into a major. I thought it was just a funny story, but when I got older and had dealings with *apparatchiks* and sundry petty officials, it took on quite a different meaning. I found out later it was made into an opera. You must miss him very much.'

That is truer than you can imagine, my friend: seeing Papa's image in my uncle every day, loving him, Papa's brother – so like him but not him – 'I do miss him,' he said, and then fell silent for a few moments.

'There's something else – something I wasn't sure I'd ever get the chance to tell you. Prepare to be surprised,' he paused briefly, for effect if he was honest. 'It was our teacher, Petro Dmytrovich, who denounced your father.'

Zvi looked astounded and signed for him carry on. Misha told him about a quarrel he overheard between his mother and their teacher, when Petro Dmytrovich had said Papa shouldn't be so friendly with Dr Rosen, that it might be dangerous, and about a discussion his parents had about the trial when they thought he wasn't within hearing distance.

Zvi listened with closed eyes, silent, absorbing his words. 'Because we're Jews, I suppose,' he said quietly, as if speaking to himself.

'Yes, maybe, but I think mostly because of your house. He took your house and made it into offices for him and his Party cronies, and put in a jail – a jail – in Hovkova of all places.' – Misha was still incredulous almost ten years later – 'I couldn't believe my eyes the first time I was there, when Papa made me go to a meeting with him. The wall separating your father's office from the family rooms was gone. Instead, there was a large single room filled with benches and chairs, with a raised platform at one end. In the centre of the platform was a long table covered with a red cloth and four chairs. Behind these, curtained walls were covered with huge pictures of Lenin and Stalin and banners proclaiming the glories of collectivization and the penalties of opposition: *Comrade, come and join our kolkhoz! The heroic period of our socialist construction has arrived! Those who do not join the kolkhoz are enemies of Soviet power!* When I read the banners, I laughed – inside – and thought that your mother would not have liked them decorating her house.

'Then he started expelling so-called *kulaks* – including the Dudyks, who ran the village shop, remember? so the shop shut down. After that, he began carrying out food raids, forcing my papa to take part in all of it. Which wasn't so good for me. An old woman died during one raid: she wouldn't tell them where she'd hidden their seed cache. It turned out she was the grandmother of one of the older students and from then on, I was given a lot of trouble at school. I think if I hadn't been the teacher's son, they would have beaten me up. But worse than my problems, he attacked Nataliya. I don't think he – you know – but whatever he did, it was enough to make her terrified and miserable.'

Misha paused briefly. He could still picture his sister rushing through the open front door of Zvi's old house. He had been sitting on a bench across the road, wishing he had a gun so that he could shoot Petro Dmytrovich for making his father do such evil things. Suddenly, there was Nataliya, obviously miserable and frightened. He'd leapt to his feet, demanding to know why she'd been in the house. When they both had calmed down, she told him she'd been passing by the house when Petro Dmytrovich called from the front door, asking her to wait, saying that he had a parcel for Father, and would she please take it home with her. Misha had asked her why she didn't simply wait outside.

'Because he never came back,' she'd said, 'and I felt foolish just standing there in the doorway, and I thought it'd be rude to leave.' – She blushed then, and stumbled over her words – 'I… I suppose was curious about what they'd done to the doctor's house. I wondered what the jail looked like. I told myself it was the middle of the day: what harm could there be stepping inside for just a moment? But when I got inside, Petro Dmytrovich was nowhere to be seen. I walked to the back of the long room and looked through a door at the end.' She shuddered and stopped speaking.

Misha, worried she'd cry again, said she didn't have to say anymore. They could go home or walk along the river for a while. She said she was okay, that she'd rather tell him. She went on to say that the teacher had suddenly appeared while she was looking through the door, grinning at her, saying he knew she wanted to see the jail. She told him she didn't, that she simply wanted the package. He grabbed her arm and pulled her through the doorway, promising not to lock her in. He kept laughing, but once they were next to the jail, he stopped. His voice went hard and cold. He pushed her though its open doorway, following her inside. She tried to get out of the small room but couldn't get past him. She struggled to keep her voice calm, asking him to please let her pass.

She was crying as told her brother. 'Oh, Misha he's vile … he pulled me down beside him onto one of the benches, saying he was sure I'd like him to kiss me. I told him I just wanted to go home. Then he touched me… where he shouldn't… and tried to pull my skirt up. He kept saying he was sure I'd like him to kiss me. Then suddenly he just let me go, laughing, telling me to be off.'

With his sister's tears still vivid in his mind, Misha resumed his sorry tale: 'Our teacher threatened Nataliya to keep quiet, said it would be Papa who paid the price if she said anything. But I'm pretty sure she told my mother who told my father. Petro Dmytrovich was a bastard, that's certain, but he paid the price in the end' – he paused – 'Papa murdered him, Zvi, in the woods, with a spade.'

Zvi gaped at him, stunned.

'I've never told anyone, not Kola, not Uncle, but I was there. I saw them together, arguing. So I followed them secretly. They went over the bridge into the woods. Papa hit him over the head with a spade, not just once but two or three times. Blood was everywhere. It was disgusting. I was terrified and stayed hidden until Papa left so he didn't know I'd seen. It snowed that night and they didn't find the body for about three days. They never found out who killed him. I don't think they tried very hard.'

Misha paused, caught his breath. 'To this day, I'm still not sure if what Papa did was right – or evil.'

Zvi looked dazed. 'I'm glad you told me,' he said, but then stopped. After a short time, he astounded Misha. 'Your father did the right thing – absolutely. What I would have done if I'd had the chance. That first day, at his trial, Papa pleaded not guilty. I'll never forget his words: *I am not a traitor. I have never conspired against the Soviet State, never worked to overthrow the State through an armed uprising, never worked to build an independent Ukraine. I am a doctor. That is my work. I am not guilty.* So, they took him away and tortured him, in the prison, overnight, tortured him until he became old and stooped and frightened. And when they brought him back the next day, he said he had been mistaken – mistaken! – when he'd said he was not guilty. He said he'd been afraid to admit the truth but now he fully and completely confessed that he was guilty of all the charges against him. Then they took him away and Mama and I never saw him again.'

Bile churned inside Misha, creeping upwards. Cold sweat drenched him. He took Zvi's hand. He wanted to weep – with him, for him, for Zvi's father and for his own.

'Oh Zvi, I didn't know. Your poor papa – '

'Hush – don't – it was a long time ago. And I'm glad your father did what he did, Misha, very glad.'

Misha felt a knot of anger dissolve inside him. What had been unforgiveable was now forgiven. He smiled at his long-lost friend, and knew from that day forward his life would be easier.

Chapter 8

A few days after Bobby had turned up at the apartment uninvited, excited by Chkalov's flight, he came back for coffee and cake, and inspection by Orest. Misha watched as his uncle fell victim to the American's infectious good humour.

'Well, you see, sir, we came over on the S.S. Leviathan.' Bobby laughed. 'I was only a kid at the time, of course, and none of us knew what was coming, but looking back, I don't think life gets more absurd than that, do you?'

'Hobbes' Prince of Hell brought you here?' Orest's laughter joined Bobby's. 'That's rich.'

Bemused, Misha looked at Kola, who shrugged. 'Perhaps one of you could tell us what's so funny?'

In an instant, the father/uncle disappeared and Orest Salenko, Professor of History and University Lecturer, surfaced. 'The *Leviathan* is a book by Thomas Hobbes, written during the English Civil War, in which he argues that the only way to avoid total chaos – a war of all against all – is through the submission of the people to a strong central government; to an absolute ruler, to whom they would give up their right of self-government. So, you see –'

'Yes, we see.' Kola interrupted the lecture, smiling.

Bobby went on to tell them about his time in Kharkiv during the famine, saying it was one of the reasons he had wanted to meet Misha, after Kola told him his cousin had lived through the catastrophe in a village. He said that his family had been luckier than most. His father was well paid, with access to special food stores for foreigners. Although this kept them alive, it also had a nasty side. Thousands of people in Kharkiv were starving and everyone knew Americans had food. Strangers would knock on their door, asking for food, scraps, anything they could spare. Sometimes people fought over their garbage. Legally, they weren't allowed to give anyone anything, so they had to be careful. But his mother and father had become good friends with a Ukrainian engineer and his family who lived close by, and helped them whenever they could with food, and with medicine when their little girl got sick.

'Both my parents were arrested eventually,' he said. 'probably because of the help they gave them. But of course I don't know for sure.'

Misha glanced at his cousin, eyebrows raised. Kola shook his head slightly. He hadn't known about the arrests.

'Before that, after we'd been in Kharkiv for about three years, my mom wanted to go back to the States. The famine years had been awful. Things in the factory weren't as good as they said they would be. She didn't like the way my sister was being educated: too anti-American. But when my dad asked for our passports, they refused to give them back. Told him he was too valuable, a specialist, that he was needed in the factory, and so on. That was September 1934. Later we learned thousands of other Americans were also trying to get their papers back, without any luck. Then they started to disappear.'

'Disappear?'

'That's right: Americans, our friends, other Americans from Dad's factory. In spring 1935. At least, that's when Mom and Dad first noticed people were missing. Two men they knew had gone to the American Embassy after it opened in Moscow, trying to get new passports. They never came back. Their wives never returned either, after they went to Moscow looking for them. Then my father was arrested and three days later they came back and took Mom, which is why Mariya and I came to Kiev. We think my mother's in the Lukyanivska, at least they keep accepting our parcels for her. Dad, we think, got sent North ….'

As the afternoon wore on, Bobby told them about the teacher who recommended him to the Aviation Institute, his journey to Kiev with his sister, and how they'd struggled to find somewhere to live. By the time he consumed several cups of coffee, two or possibly three sweet rolls, finished his story and made his farewells, Uncle Orest had long been won over.

'I tell you what, boys, we'll invite him and his sister for dinner, along with Zvi and his cousin Rachel. It's been far too long since we've had any female company in this apartment. It'll be a *zastillya* – a celebration of friendship – what do you say to that?'

A day or two later, Misha invited Zvi to the dinner. After some friendly debate, he agreed, with one condition – he was Binyamin Chovnik, not Zvi Rosen.

'I'm sure your uncle – our uncle – is right about Bobby. He's probably perfectly *kosher*.' Zvi smirked at his joke. 'But I'd rather be careful than sorry. I'm Binyamin, okay?'

Misha didn't say no.

Chapter 9

The night of the dinner was moonless, windy and wet. Zvi and his cousin Rachel arrived first, both covered in dark, drab raincoats; protection against the foul weather. With coats, hats, and umbrellas set aside, the quick-witted Jewish intellectual stood transformed into an 18th-century Cossack marauder, in deep red *sharovary* – pantaloons – tucked into soft black boots and paired with a hip-length white tunic and an embroidered, sleeveless waistcoat. At his side, a classical Semitic beauty with sparkling eyes, dark curling hair piled high on her head, and pale, unblemished skin. In traditional dress like her cousin, the narrowness of her waist was accented by the brilliant red and black woven *poias* – belt – encircling her heavily embroidered blouse. Orest, himself resplendent in a dull gold Ottoman kaftan and brown pantaloons, ushered them into the kitchen where Kola and Misha were preparing *zakuska* plates – little bites of food to tempt the appetite – each dressed like the other in green pantaloons and highly elaborate belts over plain white collarless shirts, once again looking more like twins than cousins.

But it was Bobby who stole the show. Arriving with his sister, Mariya, not many minutes later, he shunned Orest's outstretched hand and kept his coat on and buttoned as if still cold from the wind and rain. Misha greeted Mariya and introduced her to the others, who all admired the distinctive black and red cross-stitch of her traditional costume. His sister feted, Bobby removed his coat, to reveal to great laughter, an American baseball shirt, with 'Kharkiv Auto Works' blazoned across the front and a large number 10 on the back.

'Wait,' he said, 'I'm not finished.' With a flourish, he removed a small, ragged baseball cap from the pocket of his trousers and placed it on his head. 'There,' he said, pirouetting for all to admire, '*American traditional.*'

They waited for dinner to cook standing around a small table covered with *zakuska* plates, drinks in hand, listening to Bobby's stories about baseball in the Soviet Union.

'The funniest thing was the Russian teams objecting to players stealing bases. They thought it was some sort of capitalist deviation that shouldn't be allowed.' He took a sip of his vodka. 'That made me laugh – that, and hearing them yell, *niet* out – *niet* out. But that was later on. At first, it was Americans playing Americans: Gorky auto workers against Moscow auto workers, that kind of thing, with maybe two bats and a ball, and one old glove between them. Then the government got involved and decided baseball should be a national sport. Then it got serious, at least for a while. Rulebooks translated into Russian, new equipment ordered, Americans asked to coach.'

'Do I remember a game on the radio?' Orest asked. 'Around three or four years ago?'

'July 1934. It was the first live broadcast over Soviet radio. It was great. I can't remember who won, probably Gorky, they always seemed to. Do you remember, Mariya?'

His sister shook her head, and he continued. 'I guess that was the heyday – 1934, 1935 – Soviet and American teams played against each other. There was an inter-city league. Kharkiv Auto Works even managed to win a couple of games, with our Dad as pitcher.'

'I remember that,' said Mariya.

'I thought you might.' Bobby smiled at his sister. 'Then it all started to go wrong. Baseball and show trials don't mix. The American players began to think it might be a good idea to keep their heads down. Then they disappeared, almost one at a time. It was very strange. By summer, there was little or no baseball left in the country, and Mariya and I had gone from Kharkiv. Months later, we heard US embassy staff in Moscow had listened to the World Series on the radio, while eating hot dogs. I'd have enjoyed that, but I guess our little radio would have been too feeble to have picked it up anyway.'

'The feebleness of your little radio would probably have saved your lives. Listening to programmes in English is highly suspect. It would have been almost be mandatory for someone, a neighbour perhaps, or a visitor to the building, to denounce you.' Orest tipped the last of his vodka into his mouth. 'Drink up,' he said. 'Time to eat.'

Misha was watching Kola squirm, enjoying his cousin's obvious discomfort, wondering if Uncle had noticed. Kola had glowered at him when they'd sat down to dinner and Misha grabbed the seat between Mariya and Rachel; presumably the spot Kola wanted. He was now trying to think of interesting things to say to Rachel from across the table, with little sign of succeeding. Misha grinned inside. Rachel was two years older than Kola. Why would she be interested in him?

'Rachel, Binyamin tells me you're a teacher.'

'Yes, that's right.' Rachel smiled and continued eating.

'Where's your school?' Kola tried again. 'Is it close to where you live?'

'Not far.' She smiled again.

'Oh, that's good.' Kola took a bite of food and appeared to ruminate. After a few moments he came back with: 'So, do have you any trouble with the Komsomol? Trying to get rid of students, I mean, you know, children of kulaks who've come back or people who've been arrested. Any purges in the staff room?'

'Kola!' His father laughed. 'I hardly think Rachel wants to discuss purges at the dinner table. Can't you think of anything better to ask?'

'I was just –'

'It's okay –'

Kola and Rachel spoke simultaneously, then both stopped. After a moment, she took pity on him.

'My school is a middle school, in a good area of Podil, with an excellent head teacher. We have about 400 students. I teach them Mathematics. And yes, we have had trouble with Komsomol: there are two on the staff. They wanted to expel a boy whose parents were arrested, for failing to denounce them. The Head wouldn't hear of it. She quoted Stalin to them: *a son does not answer for his father* and they backed off. She said to us: "There are no enemies of the people studying in this school". She's very brave and I admire her immensely.' She paused briefly. 'And no, we haven't had any purges in the staff room.' She lowered her eyes and smiled to herself, before taking another bite of the meal in front of her.

'That's lucky,' Kola said; a bit lamely, Misha thought.

'Bobby,' Orest called from the opposite end of the table, perhaps a little more loudly than necessary, 'Do you like Kiev?'

Bobby grinned. 'I think it's got the craziest buildings in the world.'

'Crazy? What do you mean, crazy?' Orest turned to Mariya. 'What about you, child, do you think Kiev is crazy?'

Mariya shook her head but before she was able to speak, her brother started up again. 'Not the city, Prof, the buildings. I mean, there's one building with stucco owls all over the front, one that has a concrete lion on the roof, another with stone dogs, one with cats, and one with the face of a woman who weeps when it rains. Those are crazy buildings.'

'You forgot the haunted house, Bobby.'

'And there's a haunted house,' Bobby said, triumphant.

Misha ignored Bobby and looked at Mariya. 'I didn't know that. Whereabouts?'

Mariya blushed. Misha thought she looked even prettier than usual.

'On St. Andrew's descent. It looks like a fairy tale castle but it makes horrible noises when the wind blows. A neighbour told me that the man who had it built cheated his workers somehow, and they got back at him by putting empty pots and bottles inside the walls, and they wail when it's windy.' She blushed again. 'I could show you sometime, if you'd like.'

Misha said he would like that very much. He sipped his wine. Could think of nothing else to say to her, not with his uncle and the others listening. Drank some more wine.

For a few minutes, contentment reigned. The last bits of dinner disappeared from plates. Wine glasses emptied. Orest asked Mariya and Rachel to clear the dirty dishes while he retrieved the apple cake – his speciality – that he'd made for dessert. Kola and Bobby entertained Misha with tales of heroic pilots and brilliant aircraft designers.

'Areoflot's flying passenger planes to Prague now,' said Bobby. 'Four hundred roubles one-way.'

'I doubt many people would want to spend half a month's wages to get to Prague.'

'You just wait a few years,' Bobby replied. 'It'll get cheaper. We'll all be doing it before too long.'

'Doing what?' Orest was back in the room, carrying a cake and large jug of hot custard.

'Flying, Papa. Flying all over the world.'

'Stalin's latest heroes. Pilots. Pilots and planes: the new opiate of the people.' He divided the cake into seven more or less equal pieces while he talked. 'I hear he's started arresting them, and Tupolev. Imagine, the country's best aircraft designer charged with espionage, and Alknis, who we all thought was Commander of the Red Army Air Force, turns out he's actually head of a Latvian fascist organisation. Madness!' He handed Mariya the laden plate. 'Mariya, take a slice for yourself, there's custard too, and pass the plate to the others. I think I'll have more wine.'

While Orest refilled his glass, Rachel asked Bobby why he'd decided to study aviation.

'Chance, really. When I was fifteen, the same age as Sis here, I happened to meet an American named Victor Herman who'd come to Kharkiv with his dad for a baseball game. Sometime before, he'd driven a truck from Gorky to Moscow on a propaganda trip: one of the first Ford trucks to be delivered. As a result, he got invited to a reception where he met Marshal Tukhachevsky who helped him get into aviation school. Just before I met him, he'd set a new world freefall record, jumping out of a plane at 24,000 feet and waiting 142 seconds before opening his parachute. Well, I thought this was fantastic. I mean, flying a plane is amazing, but jumping out of one – wow! So I reckoned I'd train as a pilot and see what came next. That's how Kola and I met. I was telling some students about the jump, and he told us about seeing parachutists in the park when he – '

'Tukhachevsky. Now his problem was being too popular. Like Kirov. The trouble with being too popular is that you end up dead.'

'Papa – we're talking about flying.'

'Yes, and I'm talking about dead heroes. We've got far too many of them in this country.'

Kola jumped in, before his father could continue: 'I'm sure you're right, Papa, but it's a celebration tonight, remember? It's the first time we've all been together. You could tell us stories about Great-grandpa Stepan or we could listen to some music. Perhaps we could sing.' He smiled across the table. 'How about you, Rachel? Do you sing?'

A few days later, Misha was in the lab at the Institute peering through a large microscope, trying to understand why Triticum, a hybrid of wheat and rye, was better than either grain grown by itself – if in fact it was. He'd been delighted to find the lab empty when he arrived and wondered vaguely about the absence of the usual crowd of noisy students competing for space. Hearing the door behind him pushed open, he supposed the peace and quiet had been too good to last for long.

'Hey, you!'

Surprised by the harsh shout, Misha turned to see two men he didn't recognise advancing towards him. Before he had a chance to ask what they wanted or who they were, one of them grabbed his arm and yanked him off the stool.

'Khrushchev's here in ten minutes. Why aren't you in the Hall waiting? Think you know it all already, do you?

Jerk.' The man shoved Misha towards the door. 'Get there, now!'

Misha was both frightened of the men and annoyed with himself. He'd bloody well forgotten that the new First Secretary was speaking today. It doesn't pay to forget that kind of thing, not if you want to stay healthy. He started to excuse himself when the door opened again and Fedir Wendelko came in.

'Tomas, Ivan, don't often see you guys here. What's up?'

'This jerk thinks he's too smart to listen to Khrushchev. We were changing his mind.'

'Misha? Him too smart? Don't think so. He was just waiting for me. You about ready to go, Misha?'

Fedir headed back to the door, with a highly relieved Misha in tow. Once outside the lab, he thanked Fedir for rescuing him and they set off together for the Great Hall. While they walked, Misha puzzled over Fedir's fortuitous arrival. They'd had no plans to meet. At least not that day, when all who could were expected to attend Khrushchev's talk. They had met once or twice for coffee since Lysenko's lecture. Both of them thought Professor Tomenko was right about the charlatan's so-called New Soviet biology: that it would likely do more harm than good. Fedir certainly had been right about Tomenko's fate. Barely a week passed after the lecture before he disappeared, along with three researchers who had worked with him. It would be a long time before anyone at Kiev's Institute of Agriculture said anything good about Charles Darwin again.

Misha liked Fedir and thought he was clever. Indeed, he had asked for his help after a difficult lecture more than once. But he was not sure he trusted him, not yet.

Fedir had graduated two years ago and now worked as a researcher in plant biology. He was from the north and his family still lived there. He seemed to have a ready supply of money which, Misha had to admit, was very welcome as he paid for their coffee and cakes. He was good-looking but didn't pay much attention to girls. Misha wasn't sure why he had reminded him of Zvi that first day when they'd met at Lysenko's lecture. They were very different: one tall, the other not; Zvi's hair straight and short, Fedir's a bit long and curly. Maybe it was his dark eyes.

He was very ambitious. He worked hard, asked toadyish questions at lectures and in the lab. He told Misha he should do the same. It wasn't hypocritical, he said, or morally bankrupt to do so. It was a matter of not calling attention to yourself for the wrong reasons. You want to be noticed for the right reasons: you live longer that way. That was his formula; that, and trying not to join the bastards.

But as they walked to the Great Hall, Misha couldn't help thinking that his timely rescue from the two thugs was odd. It felt staged. But why? He, Misha, seemed an unlikely target for an informer, if that's what Fedir was. But then –

'What's that?' Fedir had spoken but Misha had been too many miles away to hear.

Fedir gestured ahead to the open lecture room door: 'I said: listen to the cheering and clapping … I suspect our speaker has arrived. Quick, let's get inside.'

Khrushchev was on the podium, grinning broadly; his worker's cap giving him a boyish air. The pair scooted up the stairs to seats far in the back. Within minutes of their sitting down, the Rector called for silence. Then, without any introduction, Khrushchev took centre stage:

'Comrades!' he boomed, spreading his arms wide as if to hug his audience. 'You are the future of our great country. You will teach our peasants to forget their old ways: no more *lapty* – shoes made from trees – like the ones I wore as a child; no more wooden ploughs. Your education will lead the way to modernity. Your education is the most important thing … and here I am, disturbing it!'

While Khrushchev paused for the laughter he obviously expected, Fedir leaned towards Misha. 'I could work for him,' he whispered. 'I like what he's said so far.'

'Maybe.' Misha murmured, keeping his eyes on the stage. 'Let's hear the rest.'

But Khrushchev moved on from peasants and the countryside to the grave dangers facing Ukraine and the entire Soviet Union: Nazi Germany and its fascist allies, saboteurs and spies, internal enemies and provocateurs; urging his audience to greater and greater levels of vigilance.

'Nothing new there,' Misha muttered to Fedir.

'True enough, but – '

'But isn't he one of the bastards?'

Misha was sitting on a bench in the Botanical Garden waiting for Mariya to finish work, trying to remember what kind of tree was in front of him. He knew what it wasn't. It wasn't an olive tree, like the ones in Yalta, nor a walnut, nor a hazelnut. Perhaps it was a pistachio, although not one a thousand years old like in the Nikitsky. He tried to convince himself to get up and look at the label, after all there were about 8,000 trees in the garden and he couldn't be expected to recognise all of them. But he stayed sitting, not really caring one way or another. What he cared about was Mariya, who was going to show him the haunted house.

They'd made their plans at dinner last week, before she and Bobby had *hit the road*, American slang for "let's go now" according to Bobby, which added another phrase to his smattering of English. Since then, he'd been ticking off the days. Kola might be crazy about Rachel, but Misha thought

121

Mariya was the prettiest girl he'd ever seen. He especially liked her smile, and her eyes – they were a light brown with flecks of gold – her tiny hands, and her voice, soft with a lilt in it. She was about the right height and –

'Hello, Mykhailo.'

Startled, Misha jumped to his feet. He felt his face reddening, his heart thumping. There she was, in front of him, ready for their walk.

'Mariya, I'm sorry, I didn't see you. I was looking… looking … looking at a tree.'

'Well, it's a good place to do that, isn't it?' she said, smiling. 'What's that one there?' She pointed to the very one he had failed to identify.

'I'm not sure. A pistachio, I think. You sit here. I'll go look.' He hurried across the path, ducked under the low branches of the tree, read the small white label in the ground at the base of the trunk, hurried back and sat down beside her.

'I was right, it's a pistachio.'

'What's that?'

'A pistachio? It's a nut. Do you like them?'

'Yes, I know they're nuts, and I like them very much,' she said, laughing. 'What I meant was, what's that?' She pointed to the small silver spider dangling from its chain around Misha's neck.

Chagrined, he blushed for the second time in as many minutes. *This is not going according to plan.* 'It's – it was my mother's. I didn't realise it had fallen out. Of course, you know what a pistachio is.' He held up the small charm so that she could see it properly, before tucking it back inside his shirt. 'Do you know the story? Mama used to tell me and my sister when we were young: *The Spider's Gift.*'

'Of course, I do. About Christmas and how the people were too poor to have presents or decorate a tree, and how baby spiders spun webs of silver while they slept, covering the tree and turning paper ornaments into gold.' She laughed again. 'But tell me, how about you, do you like pistachios?'

'Yes, I do,' he said, at the same time asking himself why they kept going on about pistachios; who cares about a stupid nut tree? Suddenly, a harsh voice intervened.

'Good afternoon, Comrade Andrusiva.'

A middle-aged man wearing a dark raincoat and grey trilby set low on his forehead had stopped in front of the couple. To Misha's surprise, Mariya appeared to know him.

'Good afternoon, Comrade Yelenchuk.'

'Finished your work early, I see.' The man nodded in Misha's direction. 'This is your brother?'

Mariya stood, drawing Misha up as well. 'No, not my brother. He's a friend, Mykhailo Salenko. We are going for a walk.'

Yelenchuk looked at Misha: 'Salenko, you say? A relative of our learned Professor Salenko, perhaps?'

'My uncle.'

'I see. Yes. Your uncle … of course.' Yelenchuk's eyes narrowed but not quickly enough. He turned to Mariya. 'Goodbye, Comrade Andrusiva. I hope you enjoy your walk. Comrade Salenko.' He nodded briefly. 'A pleasure to meet you.'

Once Yelenchuk was safely out of hearing, Mariya told Misha that he was the University's NKVD officer. She'd been surprised he knew her name. He'd never actually spoken to her before, even though she often cleaned his room and she'd seen him many times, patrolling the corridors.

'Spying, more likely,' Misha replied.

'Well, maybe, but more like watching, making sure there's no trouble. That's his job, isn't it, to watch for troublemakers?'

'I guess so,' Misha said, not wanting to argue. 'But I didn't like him and I don't think he liked me. Why was he so interested in my uncle?'

'He's interested in everybody, isn't he? Not just your uncle.' She took his arm. 'Let's forget him and go for our walk. Otherwise it'll get too late.'

'You're right. Let's go.'

They left the garden, crossed the courtyard at the heart of the university and passed through the black and red pillars guarding its entrance. When they reached Volodymyr'ska Street Misha proposed a trolley bus ride to the top of St Andrew's Descent and a walk down to Podil from there, which would take them past the haunted house. He said they'd make the most of their day together that way and Mariya readily agreed. In truth, he wanted time to think, which the silence of the bus would give him.

As the trolley made its way across the Upper Town, Misha puzzled over Yelenchuk. *Why so interested in Uncle Orest? Why so hostile? That look in his eyes – brrr. I wonder if something is happening at the university we don't know about. I'll ask Zvi –*

'This is our stop, I think,' Mariya said, touching him lightly on the arm.

Misha flushed slightly, realising with his companion's gentle words just how absorbed he'd been in his own thoughts. He rose to his feet with an apology, taking her hand to help her down the trolley steps to the road. Enough of worrying, he told himself. Today is Mariya and me …

'Did you know there were over 400 churches in Kiev during the Middle Ages? And to celebrate the 900th anniversary of St Volodymyr's conversion to Christianity in 1888, they invited the Archbishop of Canterbury, England, to a huge gathering of priests?' Misha was showing off but couldn't stop himself. 'He wasn't able to come but sent a letter to the Metropolitan of Kiev, saying he'd be there *in spirit*.'

Mariya laughed gleefully. 'Of course I didn't know that – how could I? How do you know? It's not the kind of thing they teach us in school.'

'No, but my papa was a teacher and he knew everything.'

They were standing on the terrace of St Andrew's church overlooking Podil and the Dnieper, leaning against the balustrade that edged the terrace, admiring the river almost 700 feet below.

'Were you very young when he died?'

'He disappeared when I was twelve. He went to get fish during the famine and didn't come back. I suppose he's dead: it's been five years. But sometimes I like to think he's still alive, in a prison maybe, or a camp, and one day he'll come back. They say people do, sometimes.'

Mariya rested her hand over Misha's. 'I feel the same way about my father. It's very hard though, to keep hoping. And my mother. I still take parcels to the prison, but –' Tears filled her eyes. She took her hand away.

'Don't cry, Mariya, please don't cry. I'm sure your mama's okay. They wouldn't go on taking the parcels if she wasn't. That's how they do it.' He drew her away from the railing. 'There's a 500-year-old linden tree over here, come see it. They're sacred trees, you know. They make icons out of the wood. A monk planted this one on his mother's grave.'

Misha blanched as he heard his own words, cursing himself inwardly: you're a bloody idiot. You're trying to make her stop crying about her mother and you talk about some monk and his mother's grave. He glanced sideways at her as they walked towards the tree. She'd stopped crying. Maybe she hadn't noticed his stupidity. Ask her about herself, he told himself; Fedir said girls like to talk about themselves.

'Do you like your job at the University?'

'My job? No, not really. I like the other girls, but I don't like the work very much. It's just cleaning, people's offices mainly. I'm only doing it to help Bobby, until he finishes at the Institute, and then I'll go back to school myself. Is this the tree? It's very big.'

A gust of wind chased early dead leaves across the empty churchyard where the tree stood encircled by tombstones. Mariya shivered noticeably.

'I think that's enough trees for today, don't you?' Misha said, taking her arm again. 'Let's walk down the hill. It might not be so windy in Podil.'

They left St Andrew's and started down the long, cobble-stoned descent which carved a wide S around the Zamkova Hora hill. 'You'd like to go back to school, would you?'

'Oh, yes.' Her face lit up. 'I loved my school in Kharkiv. The teachers were so kind.'

'Better than in America?'

'I think so,' she said, hesitantly. 'I don't really remember school in Detroit. I was only ten when we left. Bobby says it was better there, but then,' she giggled, 'he always got into trouble in school here. He especially didn't like the marching. I don't think he'd ever be a good revolutionary.'

'But you liked marching?'

'Oh, yes.' Mariya appeared not to have noticed the trace of surprise in Misha's voice. 'We marched every public holiday, the whole school. I used to love wearing my red tie – I was a Young Pioneer – and the songs. I loved the songs. Bobby thought being a Pioneer was just a good way of going on outings, but I knew it was more important than that.'

She smiled proudly. 'When I was twelve, I was allowed to take care of the Lenin Corner: you know, put up pictures, find good parts of his speeches to copy out. It was because I always finished my work plans on time. I certainly never had my red tie taken away for making trouble, like Bobby did.'

They walked on without speaking for a few minutes; time Misha spent wondering what to say next. If truth be told, he'd been more like Bobby, once the initial thrill of becoming a Young Pioneer wore off. He smiled inwardly, remembering the day he'd come home sporting his Pioneer tie and badge, bursting through the door like a small whirlwind, spilling noise and excitement in all directions; hoping his father would bring him a Pioneer cap from Kharkiv. Kharkiv. At the time, Papa had been at the trial of Zvi Rosen's father. His teacher, Petro Dmytrovich, was the village's Young Pioneer Leader and had come home with Misha after the ceremony. He'd said something to Mama and Baba about the Rosens not coming back for a long, long time – if ever, which drove his mother into a rage, and got Misha and his sister kicked out into the garden.

Perhaps Mariya had a better Young Pioneer leader than Petro Dmytrovich. She was certainly very keen. Maybe it was different in the cities. Misha remembered how much Kola had liked his Pioneer trips. That must be it – he assured himself – it was better in the cities. She's so pretty. And sweet, she's so... His reverie evaporated when he noticed Mariya was pointing to an odd-looking building on the right just ahead.

'That's the haunted house, the one with the black spire.'

A few more paces brought them to the front of the currently silent five-storey mock-gothic building which apparently wailed when the wind blew.

'I think you have to be inside to hear the noises,' Mariya said.

'It's the first time I've seen a haunted house with a barber shop and a butcher's in the basement. Of course, it's also the first time I've seen a haunted house.' Misha smiled wickedly. 'Maybe the story about the workers leaving things in the walls and chimneys isn't true. Maybe the barber and the butcher got together and it really is haunted. You know, the barber's customers and the butcher's knives …'

'Oh stop. That's horrible.' She pulled away.

'I'm sorry. I was only joking. I didn't mean to upset you – forgive me… please?'

She smiled and he took her arm once more. Five minutes' brisk walking brought them to the bottom of the hill and into Kontractova Square. As they crossed the square, they passed the remains of an old fountain.

'Did you ever see this fountain before it was destroyed?' Misha asked.

She shook her head.

'That's a pity. My uncle brought me here to see it not long after I came to live with them, because my father had liked it. Uncle said it always made Papa laugh. It was a funny old thing. Supposed to be Samson and the Lion – do you know about Samson?'

Once again, the young girl shook her head.

'He's in the Bible. He was given superhuman strength by God and one of the things he did was wrestle a lion. Who knows why? The fountain was Samson tearing open the lion's mouth, except in this case the lion looked more like a pussy cat and Samson looked all skinny like he'd only just survived the famine.' He laughed. 'Anyway, it's gone now; which is a shame because I liked it.'

'Are you religious?'

'Because I liked an old fountain?' He looked at her, disconcerted.

'You seem to know a lot about churches and the Bible and things like that.'

'Well, we used to celebrate Christmas before the famine and I once prayed for a puppy. Does that make me religious?'

'Marx said – '

'I know what Marx said,' Misha interrupted, laughing gently. 'I hope you don't believe *everything* they told us in school?'

'No, of course not,' Mariya retorted, blushing; but fell quiet afterwards.

They passed out of the square into Konstiantynivs'ka Street, which they followed until the first road past the synagogue when they turned down towards the apartment block where Mariya and Bobby lived. The street was quiet. Few people and fewer vehicles. Mariya held his arm and they both knew their afternoon together was ending. In another minute, they were standing in front of her apartment building. He took her hand.

'I'm sorry I talked so much about myself and trees and things. I planned to spend the afternoon talking about you. Will you forgive me?'

'Of course, I forgive you, Misha, except I'm not sure why you think I'd like to talk about myself for a whole afternoon. You don't think I'm vain, do you?'

'Vain? No, of course I don't think that,' he stammered, blushing once more. 'I think you're –'

'I'm only teasing.' She smiled at him. 'I've had a lovely afternoon. Will I see you again?'

'Next week?'

'Next week.' She reached up and kissed him lightly on the cheek. 'Bye till then.'

Misha retraced his steps to Kontractova Square where he could catch a tram to Bessarabka Market. He'd walk home from there. That went alright, he thought, walking a bit taller, rubbing his cheek lightly. She must like me or she wouldn't have kissed me. He smiled broadly. She is wonderful – wonderful – wonderful! He skipped on the pavement squares like a child at play. Calm down, he told himself sternly, or they'll put you in there. He glanced towards the old lunatic asylum on the corner. They'll re-open it just for you! Bobby seems so American most of the time but she hardly does. Probably because she was just a little girl when she arrived here. She's definitely a much better *comrade citizen* than either me or her brother. Her school turned her into a good Soviet citizen. She's still young, though, she could change. He would help her change. He smiled broadly. She wouldn't have kissed me if she didn't like me.

Chapter 12

It was January sixth, 1938, Misha's eighteenth birthday. The friends were gathered as before in the apartment off Pan'kivs'ka street, for lunch this time, not dinner. The streets at night were too dark and too cold; suffused with scuttling shadows, speeding cars with headlamps dimmed and windows darkened; sounds too like screams for comfort. Lunch was better.

Misha let his mind drift backwards in time. He'd been born on Christmas Eve, and for as long as he could remember, the birthdays of his childhood meant Uncle Orest and Kola coming to stay, Uncle's ridiculous jokes and toasts, and the wonderful food of *Svyata Vechera* – Holy Supper – that his Mama and Baba would make: wonderful – except for the kutia, of course. As a boy, he'd never understood why God wanted to spoil Christmas by inventing kutia. He smiled inwardly: what a silly boy he'd been sometimes; after all, it was only cold cooked wheat kernels and poppy seeds soaked in honey. He could still see his father standing at the head of the table, reciting the words that welcomed the holy festival of Christmas: *Khrystos Rodyvsya! Slavim Yoho*! And raising his spoonful of kutia to his lips, glaring at Misha to do likewise. Still feel his reluctance to do so.

Sitting at the table that afternoon, however, he knew he'd be more than willing to obey his father and eat his kutia if it meant those times could come back with it. He watched Uncle Orest watching them – the young people at table with him – eating and laughing and flirting. He could almost read his uncle's mind as he looked at Rachel, a beauty sitting between two gallants. Kola so happy to be sitting beside her; Bobby a natural charmer: might she love one of them? Misha chuckled quietly. And if she did, which one? That was the question.

Orest turned to him next, sitting beside Mariya. Misha smiled at him, hoping he looked as nonchalant as he was pretending to be. As Orest looked away, a shadow crossed his face. Misha followed the direction of his uncle's eyes: the suitcase by the door. The one each household had waiting, just in case. A few basics inside: underwear, soap, a clean shirt. Misha knew his uncle was worried. The terror was very great. Arrests were coming thick and fast. Would one of them get caught?

'Papa?'

'Mmm… sorry, Kola, did you say something?'

'Yes, Papa.' Kola's tone was indulgent. 'I asked if it's time yet.'

'Time? Oh yes, time. Of course.' Orest glanced around the table: 'Definitely. Let's clear these plates,' he said, standing. 'No, no, Rachel, you stay there. Binyamin and Kola can help.'

The table was quickly cleared and Orest returned carrying a towering bread-cake, topped with a single, lit candle. '*Babka in Rum*, Misha, happy birthday!'

Misha leapt to his feet, whooping with delight, more like the ten-year-old boy he'd once been getting a long-wished-for puppy as a birthday present, than a man of eighteen. 'Rum Baba! Where did you get it? You didn't make it, that's certain. I'd have seen you.'

'I queued for two hours yesterday, then took it to your uncle's office,' Zvi interrupted, 'that's how he got it. It's from Djima's on the Kreschatyk. It was damned cold, too.' He glanced at Mariya as he spoke, an odd look crossed his face and was quickly gone.

Misha wondered what the look meant. Nothing probably. Maybe she'd queued with him. He gave his old friend a bear hug and planted a kiss on each cheek. 'The biggest piece shall be your reward! Someone give me a knife.'

'Balzac said that Ukrainians made the best cake and bread in the world, because they grow the world's best wheat.'

Misha goggled at his uncle. 'Who?'

Uncle Orest looked at Zvi: 'Binyamin?'

'Honoré de Balzac, French novelist and playwright. Born 1799, Paris; lived Verkhivnia, 1847 to 1850, 150 kilometres from where you are now sitting. Married a beautiful Ukrainian lady – there are no other kind, I am reliably informed – named Ewelina Hanska, also known as

Eva, in 1850, in Berdychiv, 200 kilometres from where etc. etc.. Sadly, he died five months later. Rumour has it Madame Balzac was asleep at the time of her husband's departure.'

The table dissolved into incredulous laughter, from which Bobby recovered first. 'How do you know all that?' he asked.

'Amazing intelligence, I'd say,' replied Zvi.

Rachel shook her head at her cousin, still laughing. 'Amazing conceit, I'd say.'

'I always told my Papa you were the smartest person I knew, after him, of course,' Misha said, still laughing. 'But this is ridiculous!' He reached out a hand to his friend. 'Give me your plate; you've earned a second piece.'

'Rachel, I've seen the others recently but not you. How is it at your school?'

'Not so good, Orest Ivanovich. We've lost a great many students. They simply stop coming, one by one. We rarely learn why. And our head teacher was arrested last week. She was sheltering a girl, a really sweet, clever little girl whose mother and father have been sent to camps, and someone denounced her. It must have been someone from the school. Who else would have known? It's so unbelievable, that someone could be arrested simply for helping a child.'

Misha noticed Mariya, whose eyes had not left Rachel, lean forward in her chair, as if to speak. Instead, she dropped her gaze back to the half-finished cake in front of her and said nothing; perhaps feeling too shy, as the youngest in the room; perhaps deterred by Orest who could be heard muttering, 'Only too bloody believable – too many bloody informers.'

Flushed with anger and wine, Orest suddenly banged his fist on the table, rattling the cutlery. 'People who think that denouncing others is the new religion, like that bloody Nikolayenko woman. *Twenty-nine people*. She denounced *twenty-nine people* last week, our Polia, our Heroic Denunciatrix. Says she can detect an enemy of the people just by looking at them, by the look in their eyes. And the bloody fool believes her.'

He shook his head in disgust. 'She wrote to him – to Stalin. After the local party threw her out for being a nuisance.' He mimicked an old lady's voice: '*Oh, it's not me, dear Leader, it's not me. It's the Party – they're all traitors, Trotskyites. Not me'*. And Stalin agreed with her! With a crazy fantasist! I don't think there's anyone left in the local Party now, and half the Ukrainian Central Committee's gone: arrested, dead, who knows? I don't know who's crazier – the old moustache or the old woman.'

'Papa – '

Orest brought his wine glass to his mouth, forgot to drink, and put it down again. 'Papa nothing,' he retorted. 'We're all friends here.' He waved his arm around to encircle the table, narrowly missing his glass of wine. 'Just think about it. Everyone knows we're headed for war. So what does he do? He wipes out the Red Army brass: three out of five field-marshals, most of the army commanders and commissars, almost all admirals, and bloody near the whole supreme military council. Pah! He's living with the birds, in *Nephelokokkugia*.' He looked across the table at Zvi, his arm stretched out, palm upwards, as if showcasing the young scholar.

Zvi complied with his unspoken request: 'Cloud cuckoo land. From 'The Birds', a comedy by Aristophanes. It means someone who lives in a fantasy world.'

'Right. And now we've got bloody Khrushchev.' Orest laughed loudly for several moments, both astonishing and alarming the young people surrounding him. 'They say he was appointed First Secretary because he's one of the few party members shorter than Stalin, him and Yezhov. Mind you, Yezhov's a dwarf. '

'Papa – it's Misha's birthday.'

In an instant, Orest changed both tone and direction: 'Quite right, my boy, quite right.' He clapped his hands and grinned: 'O-KAY KIDS – I got that from you, Bobby – this is a party and there's still some Rum Baba left. We can't let Misha eat it all, can we? How about you, Mariya? Haven't finished what you've got? Well, eat up. What about you, Rachel, you'd like more cake, wouldn't you? Bobby, hand Rachel's plate to Misha …'

The cake was soon gone and the celebration over. Bobby left first, claiming an appointment he couldn't break. He asked Misha if he would walk Mariya home, which naturally he was happy to do. Mariya teased her brother about having a secret girlfriend, telling the others how he often disappeared for hours on end without saying where he was going or when he was coming back. Bobby laughed and, keeping his secrets, if secrets he had, waved farewell.

Three months had passed since Misha and Mariya first had coffee and cakes together in the covered market. Misha was in love and he believed Mariya felt the same. They took the tram to Podil but alighted early in order to prolong their time together. It was dusk, and cold. The streets were covered by a thin slick of frost that was almost ice. They watched their breath float upwards in clouds as they walked, arm in arm. No one was near and the world felt as if it was theirs alone. After a time, Misha heard a rough grinding motor in the distance and soon a large, unmarked truck passed. He watched it go by.

'I was told you can hear the trucks at night on this street, carrying bodies to Bykivnya Forest.'

'What do you mean?' Mariya pulled away from him, as if stung. 'I don't understand.'

'Political prisoners, party members, intellectuals, poets. All the people they've tortured and shot. There are huge fences surrounding the forest and it's where they bury the bodies. Hundreds of them. The trucks bring them at night. You must have heard the trucks.'

'I've heard nothing.' The girl looked confused, frightened. 'I'm sure you must be mistaken. Bobby's never said anything.'

'You know people are being arrested, at night usually, and tried in secret. Well, then they're shot and brought here. The soldiers bring them.'

'You shouldn't talk about such things. Those people are guilty. They confessed.' She sounded angry.

'Mariya, Mariya,' He spoke her name softly, not wanting to frighten her. 'Your mama and papa – they weren't guilty, were they?'

'But that was a mistake. Bobby said so. An awful mistake.'

'It was certainly a mistake to be an American.'

Misha was quiet for a moment, realising he had spoken harshly. She was very young, not yet sixteen. He shouldn't expect her to understand what was happening; after all, he didn't, not fully, and he was almost three years older.

He looked at her troubled face. 'Let's keep walking,' he said, gently. 'It's getting dark.'

They walked on in silence. After a while, she put her arm through his once again. 'Why do they confess then, if they're not guilty?' Her voice seemed to hold a hint of defiance.

'I don't know. But they're killing thousands and they can't all be guilty. Uncle says one sure way of getting shot is to deny everything. Maybe they hope Stalin will forgive them if they confess, and let them go.'

'Stalin! He probably doesn't even know about it. It's that nasty dwarf who's doing everything, not Stalin. Everyone knows that.'

147

'Yezhov? Stalin's Commissar? I doubt even the Head of the NKVD can shoot a hundred thousand party members without Stalin hearing.'

'Well, I don't think we should be talking about such things anyway.'

'You're right, of course.' He smiled at her. 'Look, here's your apartment building.

Once inside, Misha stayed Mariya's hand as she reached for the light switch. Ribbons of gold and silver were streaming through the windows, transforming an everyday apartment into a magical inn filled with dancing shadows. They both knew it was the streetlamp below, not moonlight. Even so, it felt to them as if hundreds of candles had been lit in welcome. They were spellbound. They discarded their coats and winter shoes and sat side-by-side on the sofa. Mariya put her hand in Misha's and leaned against his chest. He stroked her hair gently, luxuriating in its smell. He could feel his excitement growing and drew her close, murmuring her name.

After a time, she pulled away, ever so slightly. 'Misha, what you said about the trucks… is it true?'

'Yes, my love, it's true.'

'Bobby never said.' Her voice was tiny, childlike in its hesitancy. She let several moments pass before asking: 'Do other people know? People at your Institute, people at the university – do they know?'

'Yes, my sweet. They know.'

'Oh, Misha, hold me tight, please, hold me tight.'

Chapter 13

The summons Misha's uncle Orest half-expected, half-feared came in April: He was to report immediately to the President of the University. He returned the book he'd been reading to its place on the shelf, straightened some papers lying on the desk, and put the top back on his pen. He looked around the room that had been his office for over 20 years. Almost an eyrie, he thought, in its corner niche at the far end of a corridor on the top floor of the building, overlooking the courtyard on one side and Kiev spreading out below the hill on the other. 'I wonder if I'll be back,' he said softly to himself as he closed the door behind him.

The hallway, the stairs, and the courtyard Orest crossed to reach the President's room were empty. In place of students, bits of paper tumbling in the wind across paving stones. In place of professors, crows cawing at invisible enemies or each other. There were still students, and teachers to teach them. But the buzz and bustle of normal university life had dried up, withered, in six short weeks from the death of Ukraine's Premier to the NKVD swamping the campus.

Denounced as a nationalist saboteur, expelled from the Party and about to be arrested, Premier Panas Lyubchenko had first shot his wife and then himself, in order to escape his anti-Soviet entanglements – or so the newspapers said. Undoubtedly mourned by many in private, it was not his death that stung but hers: the whirlwind of propinquity, of guilt by association, the foundation of terror as practiced by Moscow. When one man fell, all who had known him, helped him, worked for him, or loved him were sucked down inexorably to disaster. Nadia Krupenik, wife of Premier Lyubchenko, had been a Kiev University lecturer.

One dead wife, and inescapable waves of suspicion engulfed the university, threatening entire departments with extinction, bringing down the best and brightest professors, the keenest students. Where better to hide sabotage and espionage – apparently – than in a university? Who better to recruit saboteurs and spies – evidently – than university teachers? They had started with Law, and worked their way through Biology, Philosophy, Physics, and Mathematics. Now it was History's turn.

Orest knocked lightly on the President's door and entered when invited to do so.

'Professor Salenko, please come in, sit down.' The President indicated a chair facing his desk. 'You know Comrade Yelenchuk?'

Orest nodded at the University's resident NKVD officer sitting to the side of the desk, his back to the windows. Of course he knew Yelenchuk; who did not? He preyed on the campus like a wolf circling a herd of caribou. He knew Yelenchuk; everyone did.

A third man was sitting in a small alcove on the far side of the room, where the privileged took tea with the President. No effort was made to introduce him and he remained seated and silent. NKVD higher-up probably, Orest thought, sent to watch the watchers.

'You wished to see me?'

'Yes,' the President replied, 'there are some questions, to which there must be –'

'Answers – good answers,' Yelenchuk interrupted, his tone curt. 'Answers you will give me.'

Orest looked at the red-faced, unpleasant man sneering at him, his breath sour. He had thought that when this day came, when it was his turn, he would be frightened. Instead, he felt calm, almost relaxed, as if he'd be letting himself down to fear this bully.

'I'm happy to answer your questions.'

Yelenchuk stood up and leaned across the desk towards Orest. 'It was not accidental, I am sure, that Nadia Krupenik was employed at this university. Under such cover, one person may corrupt many. Tell me, for how long had you known her?'

'I did not know her. There are hundreds of professors and lecturers here. I know fifty perhaps, by sight at least, but I did not know Krupenik.'

'You are sure of that? Her husband – your father – both Social Revolutionaries. How could you not know her?'

'That was a long time ago. My father died when Lyubchenko was fourteen years old. I did not know her.'

'What about Kravchuk? Krimsky? Shteppa? For how long did you know them?'

'I did not know them.'

'You don't know many of your colleagues, it seems. Why is that, Professor Salenko?'

The President intervened: 'It is a very large campus, Comrade Yelenchuk. I myself do not know all of the staff, although I do know a great many, of course. And some students also. I'm sure Professor Salenko knows as many colleagues as is proper and correct. Is that not so?' He smiled at Orest, obviously pleased with his robust defence of the professor.

'That is as may be,' said Yelenchuk, moderating his tone and changing tack. 'Professor Salenko, in 1929 you travelled to Germany – that is correct?'

Orest nodded.

'You gave two lectures on Hegel, on his *Philosophy of Right* – that is also correct?'

154

'Yes, at the University of Heidelberg.'

'And later that same year, you invited Professor K. Schmidt here, to give a lecture, also on Hegel. Yes?'

'Yes, he is a world expert and I wanted our students to have the benefit of hearing him speak.'

'That was when you became a foreign agent – a fascist spy – was it not?' Yelenchuk's restrained tone belied the menace of his words. 'When you went to Germany. Or perhaps when your spy-master came here?'

Orest's astonishment at the accusation stunned him into momentary silence. He sputtered when he could speak again. 'A German spy – me? Ridiculous. And it's equally ridiculous to suggest that Karl Schmidt, who must be over 80 by now and is highly distinguished, that he's – what did you call him, a spy-master? The whole idea is farcical.' He sat back in his chair, crossing his legs. 'Herr Schmidt is a scholar. I am a scholar. Nothing more.'

'It is you who are ridiculous, to think we will believe your lies.' Yelenchuk's voice coarsened with anger. 'You give lectures on rightist philosophy, on the supremacy of family and society over the State. You consort with our enemies, inviting them into the heart of our city to corrupt our youth. Then you say you are a scholar, nothing more.' He banged his fist on the President's desk. 'We are not fools.'

'That is enough for today.' The man in the alcove spoke quietly, with the implacable chill of authority. He rose from his chair. 'Perhaps the professor would be so kind as to join us again another day. Shall we say Monday at the same time?'

Orest nodded. 'Yes, but I –'

'Fine, good. We'll talk again.' The unnamed man cut across Orest's words. 'Until Monday, then.'

The President's door closed behind Orest. Dazed by the suddenness of his reprieve, he stumbled towards the stairwell. Deep shadows marked his way as the last of the sun filtered through heavily draped windows. Dark, he thought, it's almost dark. What time is it? He shuddered violently. My god, I need a drink. The bell in the clock tower chimed – one, two, three, four – four; it's four o'clock. Fifteen minutes. I was in there for barely fifteen minutes. Christ. It felt like a lifetime. He shivered. I need a drink.

He left the university through the back entrance, skirted the Botanical Garden, and headed up Tarasivs'ka Street to a small bar he knew was always open. He drank two vodkas in quick succession and ordered a third. What do I tell the boys? Do I tell them? Kola knows things aren't good at the university. I had to tell him that much after getting drunk at Misha's birthday dinner. Well, almost drunk. He twirled the vodka in its small glass. Lit another cigarette. Misha – I can't tell Misha. He's had too much worry already in his life. I can't add more. There's no point in telling either one. Nothing might happen on Monday. And if it does, well, it'll be soon enough then. He drained his glass. It'll be soon enough on Monday.

Monday dawned cool and cloudless. Orest woke late, enveloped in a preternatural calm. Whatever happened today could not be worse than his fear of what might happen.

At the appointed time, he knocked on the President's door, waiting as before to be asked to enter. To his surprise, the unnamed man from the alcove opened the door and invited him in. A quick glance around the room revealed empty chairs surrounding the President's desk and Yelenchuk sitting in the alcove. Puzzled, he asked if the President had been delayed.

'The President will not be with us today. My name is Plushenko. Please, come this way.'

Orest followed Plushenko to the alcove, where the two men joined Yelenchuk. He sat down and waited.

'As is well known,' Plushenko began. 'Trotskyism has descended into a crazed band of wreckers, spies, and murderers, intent on destroying our great country while serving the interests of war-mongering foreign states…'

Half-listening to the familiar litany, Orest wondered about the President's absence.

'… Complacency has allowed this to happen; complacency and a lack of vigilance. Sadly, our finest University has not escaped the depredations of those who would help our enemies. In the highest office there has been self-satisfaction where there should have been vigilance; complacency where there should have been watchfulness…'

Orest was stunned. If he understood correctly, the President had been arrested.

Plushenko was still talking. 'We believe we have exposed all of the conspirators and wreckers, from the top downwards. But we must all be vigilant, must we not, Professor Salenko? Always vigilant.'

'Yes, of course we must.' Orest hastened to agree.

Plushenko nodded. 'I knew that I could count on you. Yelenchuk here –' He tapped his colleague lightly on the arm. 'He thought you would not help us to be vigilant. He thinks you should be arrested.' He laughed. 'Well, not today.' He stood, as did the other two, quickly following his lead. 'Yelenchuk will be in touch.'

As the President's door closed behind him for the second time, Orest again stood dazed in the darkening corridor. If I'm not very much mistaken, he thought, I've just agreed to become an informer. He shook his head in disbelief. That's not going to happen. I don't know what is – but not that. That much is certain.

Chapter 14

The great adventure was set to begin. Misha, Kola, and Bobby were waiting impatiently to be gone. A bag of food and beer was packed; not quite enough for three young men but plenty to get them through the night. Coats and hats were by the door. The weather outlook was good, thus nothing was needed by way of extras to ward off torrential spring rain. All that was missing was Orest, having disappeared from the apartment twenty minutes earlier, saying he'd be right back.

'We have to leave in ten minutes, whether or not he's back, or we'll miss our train.' Bobby looked at Kola and Misha for agreement.

'Yes – yes, we'll go,' Misha replied. 'Don't worry so much.'

'He said he'd be back, so he'll be back,' said Kola. 'Although I have no idea where he's gone.'

The trio were going to the May Day air show in Kharkiv; Kola and Bobby to see the new Polikarpov I-16 in action – most of the staff and students at the Aviation Institute were going – and Misha simply for fun. He had at first demurred, arguing he had too much to do. This carried little weight with the other two. Kola claimed it would do him good to look up at the skies for a day, rather than at the trees and plants and dirt which were his usual fare; while Bobby simply insisted he come along. Misha had been happy to capitulate. Like Kola, he'd never seen Kharkiv or an air show. But where was Uncle Orest?

Two minutes later he came through the door, bearing gifts: a fat, spicy *sardelky* and a heavy coil of *kobasa*.

'Uncle Orest!' Misha's grin belied the admonishment in his words. 'That's enough sausage for six people for a week. We're only away for two days.'

'Well,' Orest drawled: 'I know how much you and Kola eat and I'm sure Bobby's just as bad. Put it in your bag and quit complaining.'

'I thought you'd gone to your meeting,' Kola chipped in, while at the same time relieving his cousin of the sausage. 'What's it about, anyway?'

'Nothing important. Meeting the new President – I haven't yet – a quick hello and glass of vodka after lunch, that sort of thing.'

And so, after three quick hugs, they were off. The great adventure had begun.

The train slowly made its way through Kiev, heading towards the Dnieper. Misha gazed out the window, lost in thoughts of Mariya.

'What's that? Did you say something?' He turned away from the train window to Kola and Bobby sitting opposite.

'Poker.' Kola waved a deck of cards. 'Fancy losing some money?'

'Why not?' Misha pointed out the window to the Victoria-era suspension bridge close by the girdered railway bridge; one built by an Englishman, the other by a Russian. 'Fantastic, isn't it?'

When he'd lost most of his money, Misha decided he'd be better off dozing and dreaming. An hour or so later, he surfaced long enough to ask where they were. Told they'd just passed the old Rurik fortress at Lubny, which he appeared to have missed sight of entirely, to the unwarranted – in Misha's opinion – amusement of his companions, he leaned back into his seat and closed his eyes once more.

'Hey, Misha, wake up.' Kola kicked his cousin's foot.

Misha opened his half-closed eyes, his smile languid. 'I wasn't sleeping.'

'Look out the window. We're here! Poltava, the site of Peter the Great's great victory. What do you think would've happened if the Swedes and Ukrainians had defeated him?'

'We'd all be Cossacks.'

'I suppose.'

After a night on hard wooden benches in the railway station, the weary, but excited threesome left Poltava at dawn, bound for Kharkiv. They had seen next-to-nothing of the first city and expected to see about the same of the second, but an air show awaited them and that was enough.

Surprised but delighted their journey proved uneventful, and that the train arrived on time, they followed the crowd from the station across Pryvokzaina Square to the special coaches which would take them to the airport about ten kilometres away. The mood on the coach was festive: whole families breakfasting, parents smiling and laughing, children chattering. Misha couldn't remember when he'd seen people so unguarded. It was a magical mini-world, a mobile cocoon harbouring the travellers inside from the harsh realities outside. His uncle was right: planes and pilots truly were an opiate. He was pleased with his recall of the word: opiate, something that causes a false sense of contentment. Kola had to look it up after his father used it, but Misha had known both what it meant and that it was a reference to Marx and religion. Zvi's not the only clever one, he thought, chuckling to himself.

He watched a woman sitting a few rows ahead lean across the centre aisle and kiss a young girl, her daughter, presumably. It's just human nature, wanting to be happy, wanting not to be frightened or lonely. It's just normal. He glanced at Kola and Bobby sitting across the aisle. Uncle Orest was certain that Kola had fallen in love with Zvi's cousin Rachel. Misha wasn't so sure, but if it was true, then he hoped his cousin was as lucky as himself. Mariya was perfect and pretty and –

'What?' he exclaimed, startled, as Bobby clicked his fingers in front of his face.

'I said, stop dreaming about your lady-love and look out the window. You've never been here before.'

'I wasn't –'

'You were!' Bobby and Kola replied in unison, gleefully.

'More seriously,' said Bobby. 'When we get there, there could be some important people around, so you two leave everything to me.'

'Yes, boss,' Misha said.

'Boss-y, more like,' laughed Kola.

'Idiots – I'm travelling with idiots.'

A few minutes later, the coach arrived at the airfield and spilled its inhabitants onto the tarmac. The trio headed towards the terminal half a mile away, wending their way through hundreds of others with the same destination in mind. It was May Day and the buoyant mood of the coach carried over into the crowds. Up ahead, they saw bunting and flags and a marching band. The flying hadn't started yet but the festivities had, and as they drew closer, they heard snatches of martial music, as if blown to them personally by the wind.

Years later, Misha would remember the air show as an enchanted happy outing, a tale from the pages of a child's storybook rather than a day in the real life of a Soviet citizen in 1938. The sky was perfectly blue and filled with mountains of fleecy-white clouds. The sun was warm and the wind was gentle. The crowds were friendly. The music improved. Two Ukrainian air regiments were there testing their new fighter planes, getting ready for the war Stalin said was coming. They explored the aircraft on show on the ground; oohed and aahed with excitement as planes took to the air, spinning and rolling and diving. Best of all, Valery Chkalov, Polikarpov's favourite test pilot and the country's official daredevil, was there to fly the latest and very best monoplane, the I-16.

'It's got a thirty-foot wingspan, two machine guns, and carries 250 pounds of bombs,' Kola was instructing Misha.

'I still think the cockpit's too far back, whatever you say,' Bobby put in. 'If I'd designed it, I'd have brought it more forward.'

'Maybe.'

They were inspecting the plane on the ground, waiting for Chkalov to show what it could do in the air.

'He never carries a parachute, you know. He told Stalin that it's his job to fly and land the plane, not let it crash and burn.'

'Let's hope they never collide.'

All at once, Chkalov was there, over their heads, dipping and diving, racing across the sky at three hundred miles an hour, a bright red flash against the perfect blue. Another pass and another; a deep, deep dive and recovery; then barrel rolls, over and over, each one lasting a second and a half, the crowd cheering wildly as the tiny plane looped and rolled with its cockpit open. Finally, a wing dip in farewell and he was gone.

'I think I finally get it, why you two want to be pilots,' Misha said, grinning from ear to ear. 'That was amazing.'

'Glad you came after all?'

'You bet.'

The day ended too soon. They retraced their steps to the coach, caught the train, changed at Poltava and arrived back in Kiev early the next morning, exhausted, but exhilarated. Kola and Misha waved Bobby off to his tram home and not long after, climbed the steps to their apartment.

'Papa, we're back,' Kola called out, unmindful of the fact it was half past six in the morning and his father was most likely still sleeping. Not getting a reply, he looked into his bedroom. It was empty.

'He can't be at the University at this hour, can he?'

'It seems unlikely, but where else would he be? He hasn't got a girlfriend we don't know about, does he?'

'At his age?'

Misha wandered around the small apartment, as if the empty rooms could tell him where his uncle was.

'Misha –'

Misha spun around quickly, frightened by Kola's tone of voice.

'His keys – these are his keys, for the apartment and his office. He never goes anywhere without them.' Kola slumped against the wall, suddenly faint. 'The suitcase, what about the suitcase?' He darted back to the door. 'It's gone.

He's been arrested! I just know it.' There was panic in his voice. 'He's been arrested.'

'You don't know that.' Misha put an arm around his cousin. 'Come and sit down. We need to think.'

Misha settled Kola on the couch, sat across from him and started talking; thinking aloud: 'We can probably assume he's not at the University, if his keys are here, especially this early. So he *might* have been arrested, but only maybe. I don't remember the suitcase being by the door when we left, and there's no sign of any search for papers or anything out of place. But we can't just go to the NKVD and say, excuse me, do you happen to have arrested my uncle – my father? They'd simply arrest us as well.'

Kola was grim-faced, silent, fighting back tears. Misha kept talking, trying to allay his cousin's fears as well as his own.

'We don't know he's been arrested, Kola. He's likely just gone out without his keys. I do it all the time. So do you –
'

'Do you think your chum Fedir denounced him? I saw him the other day chatting up some obvious NKVD thugs.'

Misha was shaken by Kola's suggestion. Speaking rapidly, to hide from his cousin – from himself as well? – that this had been his own first thought, he said: 'Fedir? Why on earth would he denounce Uncle Orest? He's never even met him.'

'Oh, I don't know. Someone must have said something, someone must –'

'What about Bobby? He's always asking about Uncle, always very interested in what he's doing. We don't really know much about him.'

'We know more about him than your friend Fedir. The idea is ridiculous.'

'Let's not argue. I'm sure we're both right. Let's do this: you stay here in case Uncle comes home. If he finds the apartment empty, he'll start worrying about us. I'll go to Zvi's. If something's happened at the University, he might know about it or be able to find out. I'll go now, even though it's still pretty early. Try not to worry. He'll probably be back before me.'

Misha grabbed his jacket and left the apartment before Kola could disagree. He was badly shaken. Not simply by Kola's suggestion about Fedir, which echoed his doubts about his friend, but by his own accusation of Bobby. He liked Bobby. He was in love with his sister. He had been suspicious of him at first, but thought he'd got over his distrust. Could he have been wrong to do so? Could Bobby have denounced Uncle Orest? Could Fedir?

Chapter 15

Orest was still missing when Misha returned home. Kola, hearing footsteps, hurried to the door, his face crestfallen when his cousin came in. Misha knew that the look of grief and fear on Kola's face was mirrored by his own but tried to calm his cousin – and himself – with optimism. He had talked to Zvi, who reminded him that Orest gave an early morning lecture on Mondays, so perhaps he was at the University after all. Zvi had heard nothing of any trouble relating specifically to Orest. The NKVD had been prowling the campus for several weeks now, hunting so-called saboteurs and spies, but when he'd seen Orest three days ago, all appeared well. He'd go to the History Department mid-morning, make some cautious enquiries, and come to the apartment as soon as possible afterwards.

'I went to Bobby's as well, but no one was there. I pushed a message under the door, asking him to come over as soon as he can. I said it was urgent. We'll just have to wait. They'll both be here soon.'

'There must be something we can do.' Kola was pacing the living room, nervous and angry and frightened, unable to sit down or stand still. 'Someone we can call. We can't just do nothing.'

'Right now, all we can do is wait. Zvi will be here as soon as possible. He'll find out anything there is to know at the University. Maybe Uncle did just forget his keys. We don't know he's been arrested, not for certain.'

'I feel it, Misha. Inside. I'm sure – sure they've taken him.' Kola began pacing again. 'Oh God,' he howled. 'There must be something we can do.'

'There's the door; it's probably Zvi.'

Kola ran to the door and flung it open. 'Bobby – Mariya … I – we – we don't know where my father is. We think he's –'

'Kola,' Bobby interrupted him. 'Can we come in? We know what's happened.'

175

At one and the same time both puzzled and hopeful, Kola stood back to let them enter and followed them through to the sitting area. 'What do you mean, you know?'

'Tell them, Mary.' Bobby's voice was harsh.

Despite his fears for Orest, Misha was delighted to see Mariya arrive with her brother. He was crossing the room, smiling, to draw her to his side when Bobby's words stopped him. 'Tell us what?' he asked, suddenly frightened. She looked so pale.

'I can't,' Mariya cried. 'You, Bobby, you have to do it, please, for me.'

'No, Mary. This is your doing. You tell it.'

'I want to sit down.' She was flushed and her voice trembled.

Misha went to her at once. 'Here,' he said, taking her arm. 'Come and sit here by me.'

'No – I can't.' She pulled away, her eyes averted. 'There – I'll sit there,' she pointed to a single wooden chair behind the table.

Misha let her go, mystified.

'Mariya, what do you know?' Kola asked gently. 'Please don't be frightened. We just need to know… please.'

For the first time since entering the apartment, Mariya looked directly at Misha. 'Do you remember when Comrade Yelenchuk saw us together in the Botanical Garden? When he found out you were Professor Salenko's nephew? Well, that's when it started. Not then exactly, a few weeks later.' She dropped her eyes and began to twist the handkerchief she clutched. 'Two, maybe three – no, it was two weeks later. He came to the room I was cleaning and said I was to come to his office when I finished, that he had business with me. I was very frightened. I didn't know what he meant, what business he meant.' She stopped. 'Oh Misha, Kola, I'm so sorry,' she sobbed. 'Bobby, couldn't you, please?'

'No, Sis,' her brother said, all harshness gone from his voice. 'You're doing fine, go on.'

Mariya wiped her eyes with the hankie and began again. 'When I got to his office, he told me the authorities were going to send my mother to a labour camp in Siberia called Kolyma and that hardly anyone, especially women, ever came back from there. He said that maybe they wouldn't send her, if I helped him. I told him I'd do anything to help my mother but I didn't know how I could help him. He said … he said I could watch Professor Salenko for him, tell him what he said and what he did. He would tell the authorities I was helping and they wouldn't send my mother away.'

She dropped her head into her hands, crying. 'I didn't want to. I honestly didn't want to. I didn't know what else to do.'

For several minutes the only sound in the small apartment was a young girl weeping.

Her brother stared out of a window, thinking of a world where fifteen-year-old girls went to school and sang in choirs and played softball; where they weren't coerced into betrayal and treachery.

Kola sat silent, a hand covering his eyes, thinking of the father he might never see again.

Misha felt himself turn to stone. Hard. Pitiless. He stood stock-still in the middle of the room, staring at Mariya, until finally he asked the question that was breaking his heart: 'Why didn't you tell me?'

She looked up, her face streaked with tears. 'He said if I told anyone that he would know and he'd tell them I wasn't helping and they would send her away. Don't you see?' she pleaded. 'I didn't have a choice. I had to do what he said.'

'There's always a choice,' Misha said quietly and walked to the far end of the room.

'What did you tell him, Mariya?' asked Kola. 'What did you know that you could tell him?'

'I told about his criticisms of Stalin, how he called him names like Old Moustache and said he was crazy, and about how he thought Stalin was wrong to arrest traitors like Alknis and Tupolev.' Mariya's cheeks were pink, but her voice carried a trace of rebuke. 'I think your uncle *was* wrong, to say such things.'

'Anything else?' Kola asked. 'Did you tell him anything else?'

'I said I thought he was religious.'

Kola shook his head but said nothing. He leaned back in his chair and closed his eyes.

'How did Yelenchuk know my uncle would be alone, Mariya?' Misha knew his voice was harsh – that it sounded cruel. It mirrored how he felt. 'How did he know that, Mariya? Did you tell him?'

Mariya cowered in her chair. When she answered, her voice was barely audible. 'He said if you weren't there you wouldn't be arrested – you and Kola.'

For a time, no one spoke. Finally, Kola opened his eyes and looked at her.

'You knew they were coming to arrest my father?'

She nodded, her eyes on the floor.

'And you said nothing?'

Bobby went to his sister's side. 'Come, Mariya. We have to go now.'

After they left, Misha and Kola remained silent for several minutes. Outside, a dog barked again and again, defending his master or chasing cats? Overhead, a neighbour in noisy shoes clattered back and forth, back and forth, cleaning perhaps or preparing to leave for the day. From the kitchen came the sound of a ticking clock. Misha looked at his watch. It was not yet eleven. *How could it still be morning? Yesterday at eleven we watched Chkalov command the skies. Today… today…* he covered his face with his hands, trying to hide his tears.

His cousin spoke: 'She didn't say anything so very awful, did she? I mean, calling Stalin an old moustache – they can't send you to the camps for that or for saying Papa's religious. I mean, he doesn't go to church or pray or anything like that.'

'It isn't what she said, Kola, it's that she said it.' Misha's voice pulsated with anger. 'I knew she was very young. I didn't know she was wicked.'

'Oh, Misha, she's not wicked. The situation is evil, not her. He was threatening her mother – that's evil, not her.'

Misha shook his head but said nothing, thinking of their times together, how happy he'd been, when all the while she was watching, listening, waiting for him to say something about Uncle she could report. There's always a choice, he told himself; his grandmother's admonishment still ringing in his head. He shuddered. I thought she loved me.

A few minutes later there was a knock at the door. Kola and Misha looked at each other, suddenly alert, unable to keep hope at bay. But it was Zvi, fresh from the University. He'd pretended he needed to see Orest – Professor Salenko – to discuss an assignment he was having trouble with. This allowed him to ask several students and one of the other professors if they knew his whereabouts. No one had seen him or knew anything certain, but all of them had heard he was one of those who'd been arrested. Altogether, five history professors and two assistant professors had failed to deliver their lectures as expected that morning, and six students were missing.

Zvi went on: 'He's known to oppose the new Russified history curriculum and was overheard saying that the required emphasis on the happy, brotherly ties between Ukraine and Russia was bunkum. Apparently, this was enough for Yelenchuk, who hates him – or so the rumour goes – something to do with Orest humiliating him in front of his boss. No one knows the details, but it sounds like Yelenchuk engineered his arrest.'

'At least that's a better reason than calling Stalin an old moustache,' Misha muttered under his breath.

'What's that?'

'Nothing important. We know he's been taken.' Misha told him about Mariya and how she'd been threatened and what she had done.

While Misha spoke, Zvi grew increasingly agitated; his cheeks flushed, his eyes bright. Finally, he burst forth: 'Misha, Kola, this is my fault. I am so sorry. I don't know what to say. I should have said something. I don't know now why I didn't. I saw her, Mariya, coming out of Yelenchuk's office, the day I bought the Rum Baba for Misha's birthday. I was late, trying to catch Orest before he left, to give it to him. I took a short-cut through the so-called *Cheka-Corner*. I was determined not to miss him. Oh, God, let me sit down.'

All three sat and Zvi began again. 'As I approached Yelenchuk's office, a woman came out and hurried down the

183

corridor ahead, pulling a headscarf around her face. I froze instantly. She looked just like Mariya. But there was no reason for Mariya to be there at that time of the day. I hurried after her, telling myself I was probably wrong but when I got close enough, I called her name. She stopped and slowly turned around. She smiled as if she was happy to see me, but I thought she looked confused, maybe even frightened, definitely more alarmed than pleased. I asked her if everything was alright.'

Zvi smiled sadly. 'I kept my voice gentle, almost playful. I didn't want her to think I was interrogating her – she looked worried enough. She said there was nothing wrong, that Yelenchuk had a meeting or something earlier in his room and had asked her to come later than usual to do her cleaning. That was all. Nothing to worry about. She asked if I was coming to Misha's birthday party, said she'd see me there, and disappeared down the corridor. I watched her go, not completely convinced by her explanation. But I decided not to say anything. I might have been imagining things, or plain wrong. She was most likely worried about her mother or something. So I didn't tell you. I'm sorry – so, so sorry.'

Somehow the cousins got through the rest of the day. Meals were prepared and eaten, dishes washed; Orest's years of training had not disappeared with him. Each hour felt endless and both were relieved when the day was finally over and it was time to turn in. Kola decided to sleep in his father's room, saying he'd feel like he was still there, somehow; leaving Misha alone for the first time since he'd heard Mariya's awful story.

Lying in bed, he was unable to sleep, unable to push her image from his mind – smiling, laughing, weeping Mariya – unable to stop blaming her for the loss of his uncle. *There is always a choice – always.* His thoughts were harsh. His heart cold. *I should never have met her for coffee, never walked with her in the garden,* he told himself, *never, never, never.* Soon, he was overwhelmed by grief, by the pain of loss, by memories. He was thirteen years old again, crying in the darkness of a house empty of life; a house filled with the dead. *Am I never to have anyone? Am I always to be like a tree shorn of its branches, a dead, bare trunk?* He lay in the darkness and wept, convulsed by shuddering, heart-wrenching sobs, and knew that through the wall at his side, Kola also lay in the darkness and wept, alone like him and bereft.

The days of May disappeared one by one as the cousins waited for Orest to return, anger vying with despair, hope dwindling hourly until it was gone. Bobby no longer came to the apartment. He and Kola had met at the Aviation Institute and come to an understanding. Mariya was gone from Kiev to a factory job in Chernihiv and Misha supposed that her dream of returning to school would wither and die. Zvi was a frequent visitor, often bringing his cousin Rachel with him. Misha watched the attraction between Kola and Rachel grow beyond friendship, as he turned to her for succour, as she consoled him. He watched and resented them, even though he knew he was being unfair; resented the happiness he saw rising from the ashes of his love for Mariya. The cousins were not estranged, not quite, but the weeks after Orest's disappearance were difficult.

Misha spent more time with Fedir, taking comfort in the company of someone who did not daily remind him of his absent uncle; who had not been some part of the love he'd shared with Mariya. Over coffee at Kudlyk's one afternoon, he told Fedir, rather shame-faced, that when Orest disappeared, he'd thought at first that he – Fedir – might have known something about it. He did have some odd friends, after all. Fedir had laughed, saying he was many things, perhaps, but not a sneak.

At month's end, he and Kola volunteered early for harvest; extra workers for extra months were always welcome on the collective farms. Kola headed west towards Vinnytsia while Misha travelled east towards Kharkiv; from there they would be sent to farms where and when they were needed. In previous years, they had travelled together and worked together, as cousins and comrades. This year, unsaid and unacknowledged, each wished to be away from the sight of the other, away from the pain of remembering with every look the uncle/father who was not there. So they parted, each to seek alone the solace of solitude and anonymity.

Chapter 16

Misha was awake in bed, listening. At one o'clock he had heard heavy footsteps, booted, he thought, on the stairs leading to the apartment, in the corridor outside the door, then nothing. Silence: five seconds, ten seconds; until the man or woman continued upwards. At two o'clock, a car door had slammed on the street below. He'd waited. No voices. No one on the stairs. No insistent knocking. A deep breath again. Now it was three. He had to sleep sometime but wasn't it four o'clock when they usually came?

He'd arrived home from harvest physically fit but nervous; not quite frightened, but not comfortable. He lived behind locks and chains. He'd been alright in the countryside, one farm worker among hundreds. No one knew who he was – who his uncle was – no one cared. As long as he did what he was told and kept his mouth shut, he was invisible. Since coming back to Kiev, he'd been uneasy. Thinking they'd come for him or Kola or Zvi. When he was a child, he'd thought his uncle was the funniest person in the world. As a young man, he knew he owed his life to him. Even so, he hadn't realised the strength he drew from Orest until he was no longer there; hadn't known that his uncle had been a wall – a bulwark – between the grown-up Misha and the frightened, starving child who'd lost everyone he loved. He wished Kola was back. He'd…

'Misha! Open up.'

A yell came from the other side of the door. Someone rattled the doorknob. It was daylight outside. Without knowing it, he must have slept after all. Another shout.

'Misha, it's me, Fedir. I know you're in there. Open up.' The doorknob rattled again, more vigorously this time. 'I'm not leaving till you do.'

'Wait!' Misha yelled at the closed door. He stumbled out of bed and put yesterday's clothes back on, unchained and unlocked the door, and stood back for Fedir to enter. He hadn't seen him since May.

'Locks won't keep them out if they want to come in,' Fedir said, walking through to the sitting area.

'How did you know I was back?' Misha asked peevishly.

'I've been checking for lights. Harvest is done. Classes start soon.' Fedir peered at him. 'What's the matter with you?'

'Nothing.'

'Well, that's good, because we're going on a trip. Do you want coffee or tea?'

'Vodka.'

'From the way you smell, you've had plenty already. The whole apartment stinks.' He crossed the room and opened a window. 'That's better. Now coffee.'

Fedir paired the drink with some stale cake he found in a cupboard, handed both to Misha and sat. 'So, talk to me. Why wouldn't you answer the door? Why all the locks? You haven't let the bastards get to you, have you? You look healthy enough.'

Misha grimaced. His clothes were dirty. He was dirty – unshaven – on edge. He felt as if he was shrinking into himself. 'Kola's not back yet,' he said.

'He will be soon, I expect. But how are you? That's what I want to know.'

'The locks – I keep the door locked because Kola's not here.' Misha looked sideways at Fedir. 'You asked.'

'So I did. Have you heard anything more about your uncle?'

'No.'

'And Mariya – what about Mariya?'

Misha held up a hand, palm flat, as if to stop Fedir's words reaching him. He'd spent his harvest summer drinking too much vodka trying not to think of Mariya – and failing. He had not known until those weeks how love continues to thrive, to grow slowly and inexorably, whether the beloved is present or not. He knew it now but was damned if he was going to talk about her.

'She's gone. Okay?'

'Okay. But listen, Misha, you can't let them win, Stalin and his Russian henchmen, they're not worth it.'

'Yelenchuk is a Ukrainian,' Misha said.

'He's still one of Stalin's henchmen, bastards looking out for themselves. If that means corrupting fifteen-year-old girls, they'll do it. If you let yourself be afraid, then they win. From what I've heard about your uncle, I'll bet *he* wasn't afraid.'

Misha winced, as if slapped. He opened his mouth to speak, then dropped his head into his hands and stayed silent. After a few moments, he sensed Fedir sitting down beside him.

'I'm sorry, Misha, I shouldn't have said that. It isn't true,' Fedir spoke quietly, putting an arm around Misha's shoulders. 'We're all frightened, all of us: me, Kola, even your uncle. Only stupid people aren't frightened.' He stood and began pacing the room, still talking. 'The thing is – Misha, look at me – the thing is, you can't just give up. You're young and strong and healthy. You can't just let them win without a fight. Anyway, I need you to go on a trip with me. So cheer up!'

'What trip?' Misha asked, his voice querulous.

'Good! I knew you'd want to come.' Fedir sounded triumphant. 'We're going on a journey, young man, from Kiev to Kherson and from Kherson to Kiev. Six hundred miles round trip, in a car with a driver, all in the name of agriculture. How does that sound?'

'Don't you know they banned cannabis three years ago? You sound like you've been smoking something you shouldn't or having funny dreams… pipedreams perhaps?' The hint of a smile flitted across Misha's face.

'A joke! He's made a joke!' Fedir chuckled and sat down again. 'It's not a dream, Misha. It's a real trip, with a real purpose. Remember when Khrushchev gave that speech at the Institute? You can't have forgotten. His old peasant shoes made of bark – *lapty*.'

'I remember. He must have really hated them, because he said –'

They shouted together, grinning. '*No more lapty*!'

'Well, someone must have done something right,' Fedir went on, 'because he's hired one of the university research staff as an assistant, Oleg Krylenko, and Oleg has hired me. It seems Stalin told Khrushchev not to spend all his time in steel mills. So he's decided the collective farm planning system needs looking at and he wants us, well, Oleg, to do the looking. Oleg's going to the farms east of the river and we're going to do the west. What do you say to that?'

'What's it got to do with me?'

'You can't expect me to go by myself, can you? Anyway, it'll be fantastic experience.'

'But Khrushchev?' Misha's voice echoed his disbelief. 'You'd really work for Khrushchev, Ukraine's head bastard? You know he thinks Lysenko's a miracle worker – the man you say is ruining Soviet agriculture. How do you square that?'

'I haven't joined the other side, Misha. I know what he's like, what he's done, and that Lysenko is his pet biologist. But it's a brilliant opportunity for me – for us. With luck, we might have a chance to undo some of the harm

Lysenko is doing. How many others in the Institute could say that? Anyway, we'll be working for Oleg, not his boss.'

'You forgot to mention it would be good for your career.'

'Okay, it'd be good for my career. But don't get me wrong. I really do think we could do some good. So, will you come?'

Before Misha could answer, Fedir spoke again. 'Oops, I almost forgot my trump card,' he smirked. 'On the way back, we could stop in Hovkova. *Now* will you come?'

Misha sat perfectly still. *Hovkova – we could stop in Hovkova.* He pushed Khrushchev into the shadows, stood up, stretched, rubbed the stubble on his chin as if noticing it for the first time. He let a few more moments pass remembering the village of his childhood, but already knew his answer. 'On one condition,' he said. 'We don't leave until my cousin gets back.'

'Easy.'

Kola returned five days later. He bounded through the unlocked apartment door and hollered for Misha. Within seconds, they were hugging and laughing and exchanging playful punches; frolicking like bear cubs newly released from hibernation. Like Misha, Kola had come back from three months' farm labour physically fit and healthy. But where Misha had been fearful, Kola was full of stories he was eager to share, of people he'd met and places he'd seen. In exchange, Misha told him about his impending trip with Fedir, barely able to contain his growing excitement; the terrors that bedevilled his return to Kiev seemingly banished. They talked about Orest: how they were certain he would survive and how pleased he'd be to see them getting on with their lives; and how they missed him, how very much they missed him. Thus the breach that had appeared in the wake of Orest's arrest, the breach that wasn't quite a rift, was healed, feelings of resentment forgotten, and the grief that drove them apart, however briefly, now drew them together in a deeper understanding of the ties of blood and love.

Chapter 17

Two days later, on a beautiful September morning, Misha was packed and waiting. It was almost nine o'clock and he'd been ready since eight.

'Perhaps the assistant's assistant decided he doesn't need an assistant,' Kola said, grinning at him.

'Ha-ha – very funny. He's only fifteen minutes late, maybe the driver was late or had problems or something.'

Minutes later, a knock on the door announced Fedir's arrival. He came into the apartment radiating high spirits and apologies. 'We started late, then had to take an enormous detour. Dovzenko's making a film – you know, the guy who made *Earth* – well, this one's about Mykola Shchors and the whole of Volodymyrs'ka is closed, and Bohdan, he's our driver, he wanted to go via the Khreschatyk and I said no, go west and then we got lost.'

'At least it was only a Civil War hero that delayed you and not anything important,' Kola said, laughing. 'Poor Misha's been waiting for hours.'

'Only because I want to get away from you, big boy. See if you can stay out of trouble while I'm gone. I'll be back in three weeks.' He hugged his cousin, picked up his bag, and followed Fedir out of the door into the sun.

'He's not waiting for us, is he?' Misha's eyes gleamed as he spotted a chubby man dressed head to foot in brown standing beside a scrupulously clean black Ford.

'He most certainly is. Come and meet Bohdan, who knows everything there is to know about his car – and will tell you at great length – but not quite enough about driving in Kiev.'

Misha was delighted. He put his case alongside Fedir's in the trunk and climbed into the back seat. Bohdan settled himself behind the wheel, eased the car away from the curb and headed down Pan'kivs'ka street, muttering. In the back, the two young men judged it to be in their best interests to remain silent while their driver fought his way through the streets of the city. After a time, the battle was won and Kiev dropped away, replaced by the first of seemingly endless fields golden with wheat. On their left was the Dnieper, which they would follow, sometimes near, sometimes unseen, until their arrival in the early evening at Cherkasy, where they would spend the night. Misha remembered visiting the town with his family years before and wondered if he'd recognise it. He vaguely remembered a funny building with turrets and a giant cone sitting on its roof, but wasn't sure they existed or were simply a small child's fancy.

'What's that?' he said, his daydreaming interrupted by Bohdan speaking over his shoulder to his two charges in the back seat.

'One hundred kilometres an hour top speed, comrades,' their driver repeated for his benefit. 'That's what we'd be doing if this road was paved. Covered with dust in summer and undriveable most times in winter. One good thing, though, no ditches. Once you're in a ditch, comrades, you can't get out, can you now? Not without help.'

'Why are the car wheels painted red, Bohdan?' Fedir asked, nudging his companion lightly with his elbow.

'For the Party, comrade, for the Party. This here's a 1933 Model A Ford sedan, built right here in Ukraine, in Kharkiv. It took some Yankee help to get us going, but this here's a Socialist car through and through; red wheels, that's why.'

'I wonder if Bobby's papa made it,' Misha whispered to Fedir.

In the front seat, Bohdan was rambling. '…three-speed gear shift and reverse of course but not synchronised, so it gets a bit noisy if you're not careful changing gear…'

They followed the road through dusty villages, between fields and alongside patches of woodland, always heading south. At noon they stopped atop a hill near Kaniv, where Bohdan surprised them with a basket of sausage, black bread and apples which they ate watching the Dnieper drift by. The real work of the trip began the next day and today was warm under a blue sky filled with birds. From somewhere, beer appeared and they drank and dozed as the sun dipped towards the horizon.

The idyll soon ended and not long after six o'clock Cherkasy came into view. Bohdan stopped the car in front of the Hotel Dnieper, retrieved their bags, dropped them unceremoniously on the pavement and without warning, set off rapidly down the road, shouting back to them: 'Tomorrow morning, eight o'clock, here!' before scuttling around the corner.

The travellers watched him disappear, bewildered.

'What's he up to?'

'I've no idea.'

'Very strange.'

'Fedir, look, the hotel, it's got turrets –'

The next morning began warm and grew hotter with each bump and twist in the road. By ten o'clock, the arid south wind had covered them with a fine, burning dust. By eleven, heat waves shimmered over the wheat fields and above the road ahead, robbing the land of air. Then, in the half-minute before Misha knew he had to get out of the car instantly or die, Bohdan pulled off the road into the shade of a small copse.

'Off you go,' he said. 'Rozumivka's around the next corner. The boss of the farm is Borys Fedorenko and he's expecting you. I'll be here when you're finished.' With that, he leaned back and closed his eyes.

If Misha was surprised to find himself on foot heading down a dusty road, Fedir appeared quite nonchalant. 'It's Khrushchev's idea,' he said. 'Makes us look like men of the people – which we are, of course – arriving on foot rather than by car.'

Thus began the routine that would everywhere be the same as they traced an ellipse from Kiev: Bohdan would stop the car out of the sun and out of sight within a half a kilometre or so of the *kolkhoz* they planned to visit, and snooze until their return or take up that day's edition of *Bolshevik* or *The Communist* to replenish his stock of news and scandals, ready for the next leg of the journey. Fedir and Misha would walk into each farm, dust-covered on arrival but laden with enough cigarettes and loose tobacco to make certain of a comrade's welcome. They'd talk about the weather, the harvest, the new machines being made in Kirove and the old ones still in use on the land. They'd walk the fields and meet farmers and farmers' wives and share glasses of cold tea on hot days. Once everyone's strangeness was overcome, they would ask the farmers about making their own plans for the collective farm instead of waiting on Moscow. What would they grow? Why that? Would it work? Would they want it to work? After a time, two or three hours usually, they'd return to the car and write down all they'd been told, out of sight of the village so as not to intimidate, and add their impressions about the farmers' aptitude and willingness to plan for themselves. Their work done, they'd continue down the road to the next town for the night, only to begin again early the next morning.

'Where do you suppose Bohdan goes after he dumps us at a hotel?' Misha retrieved his bag from the pavement where their driver had dropped it before disappearing down the road yet again.

'I haven't the faintest idea,' Fedir replied. 'But we're in Kherson tomorrow, which is big enough to hide in. We could try following him.'

'Yes, why not? He says he's got a surprise for us, after the farms. Perhaps we can surprise him too. Did you know he's from Kherson? Apparently there's some monument or grave he wants to show us, something most people miss.'

'I can't wait.'

The following day they visited two smaller collective farms before Bohdan finally turned the car towards Kherson, on the delta of the Dnieper. The summer-hot sun beat down hour after hour, without relief, scorching, silencing, as they trudged village roads, inspected barns and circled fields. All thought of following their mysterious driver or visiting unknown tombs had fled long ago. It was hot. Misha was hot; hot and tired and reeking of filthy sweat. All he wanted was the dark quiet of an anonymous hotel room on a back street in Kherson and some cold water to bathe in. But Bohdan had other plans.

'I suppose you know most Ukrainians are crazy enough to believe good always triumphs over evil?' he asked from the front seat. Undeterred by the ensuing silence, he continued: 'That in the eternal struggle against evil, man is far superior to the devil, even if he offers to sell him his soul? That the simplest peasant can find a loophole somewhere and end up in Paradise?' He turned around to ensure his charges were still awake. 'Well, I'm taking you to the grave of one of the best men who ever lived, but who nevertheless got beat by the devil himself.'

Not long after this extraordinary announcement, Bohdan brought the car to a halt in a village some four miles from Kherson. There, enclosed within a small, walled cemetery, was a large monument of marble surmounted by a sun-dial. Bohdan beckoned them to follow and upon reaching the grave, read its inscription aloud. 'Johannes – that's Ivan to you and me – Johannes Howard, *Ad Sepulchrum Stas, Quisquis es, Amici*, 1790.' He smiled. 'That's Latin and means here's his tomb, whoever you are, you're a friend. 1790 – that's when he died. All because he was trying to beat the devil and lost.'

'And who was this Johannes Howard?'

'A great English philanthropist and a prison reformer, who came here to show the world the misery and disease running wild in the Tsarina's prisons and hospitals and to tell her, Empress Catherine, to clean 'em up. He travelled for six months visiting pest-houses and glory holes and quarantine stations across Europe, examining people with jail fever and typhus, trying to find a remedy for the Black Death. Then one day here in Ukraine, in November 1789, he rode out to visit a young lady ill with fever, got caught in a storm, and died of typhus two months later.' Bohdan shook his head at the injustice of the great man's death.

'Well, perhaps he should've worn heavier clothing when he went horseback riding in winter,' Fedir said in an unsympathetic tone. 'But what the devil does the devil have to do with it?'

'Ah, I thought you'd ask that,' Bohdan retorted triumphantly. 'He was a deeply pious man, this Johannes Howard. But he tried to get rid of the devil's own disease, the plague, and the devil struck him down. The devil needs the Black Death, you see. Without it, he'd have to leave it up to us humans to wipe out thousands of people at a stroke, wouldn't he? And that's not always so easy.'

'Bohdan, I'm beginning to believe you're a man of hidden depths.'

'Oh, no, not me. I'm just a driver. That's all. Just a driver.'

The heat that enveloped them daily, redolent more of high summer than the cusp of autumn, finally broke that night in a crescendo of thunder and heavy, driving rain that beat ceaselessly on the hotel window. They failed to follow their mysterious driver, enticed by thoughts of supper and a cold bath. Refreshed but sleepy, Misha lay on the narrow hotel bed in the dark and imagined John Howard riding across the steppe in rain such as this, lightly clad, not knowing his act of kindness to an unknown lady would be his undoing. *The work of the devil? Not likely.* He smiled and fell asleep.

It was still raining late the next morning when they arrived at Mykolaiv, a small town at the mouth of the Bug estuary. Expecting Bohdan to drive on without stopping, Misha was surprised when he pulled up in front of a small cafe on the embankment overlooking the river and ordered them out of the car.

'Have a coffee or more breakfast or a walk in the rain.' He pointed down the street to their left. 'Over there, the dockyard where the great Battleship Potemkin was launched. Go have a look – it's history. I'll be back in 30 minutes.' With that, he drove away, leaving them bemused and rained upon.

'Have you ever thought Bohdan looks exactly like what Khrushchev will look like in another ten years: rotund, bald, and twinkly?'

Misha looked doubtfully at Fedir. 'I'm not sure about the twinkly. Have *you* ever thought he might be one of

209

Khrushchev's spies and when he disappears it's because he's reporting on us?'

'Only since yesterday. The day before, remember, we stayed overnight at the farm and he was never out of our sight. Then yesterday we were back in a town and off he went. And the difference – '

'Collective farms don't have NKVD offices.'

'Precisely. And for the next week we're stopping overnight every night on farms, so Mykolaiv's his last chance to report in until Uman, and by then we're nearly home.'

'And to think I almost liked him.' Misha shook his head in disgust. 'I should be used to it by now.'

'Forget it,' Fedir said. 'Can't be helped. So – what's it to be, coffee or a battleship?'

A week of work followed: mile after mile of unpaved roads, uncounted glasses of tea and slices of almond tart, but not quite enough vodka to mask the sameness of the stories they were told of misguided planning schedules, impossible grain quotas, out-dated equipment, and rogue officials demanding payments in kind, in money, in favours. At week's end, the homeward journey beckoned.

Since rounding the corner at Kherson and heading towards Kiev, an overwhelming longing to see the village of his childhood had sprung up within Misha. He'd not been back since leaving. He had told himself there was no reason to go. He was too busy getting on with life. The past was long ago. But now, knowing he'd be there soon, if not the next day, then the one after that, he understood for the first time that a part of him had stayed behind when he'd left Hovkova, when Orest and Kola rescued him from almost certain death, perhaps even the best part.

They travelled through Uman, bypassing Sofiivka Park with its Greek statues, pergolas and waterfalls, and headed across country to Hovkova. Once there, Fedir and Bohdan sought out the leader of the collective farm, leaving Misha free to wander the village alone. He stopped first outside the schoolhouse, his home for thirteen years. He didn't see the peeling white paint on the outside walls or the cracked lintel over the front door. He didn't see his sister Nataliya lying dead across their father's desk, winter garlands at her head. Instead, he remembered the once happy boy he'd been, sitting side-by-side with Zvi on a double wooden bench behind a double wooden desk, slates at the ready. He remembered his father, in front of the class, telling them wondrous things. He'd been proud to be the teacher's son; the teacher-father who knew everything and didn't mind – usually – that Misha wasn't as clever as Zvi. His eyes smarted as love for his long-lost father filled his heart.

He walked up the main street towards the old church. He saw no one he knew and was surprised to pass small groups of women chatting in Russian. He only remembered Ukrainian being spoken in the village of his childhood. Reaching the square, he sat on a bench under a linden tree facing Dudyk's store, except it wasn't Dudyk's anymore and hadn't been since 1931 and the expulsions. He'd loved coming to the store when he was little. He'd laugh at the stacked bags of grain and flour standing like sentries guarding the door to the private rooms beyond the shop floor, and peer

212

in vain at the locked cabinet with its mysteries hidden behind frosted glass. Best of all were the shelves behind the counter, filled with exotic, multi-coloured tins hiding sweet-smelling spices, foreign teas and roasted coffee beans. If he'd been particularly well-behaved, his father would lift him up high so he could watch the shopkeeper tip tea leaves into the copper measuring bowl, knock the side of the bowl gently, and put the counter-weights in place one by one, slowly, carefully, knowing he had an audience. He shivered despite the warm weather. Those times seemed long, long ago.

Then, in his mind's eye, he saw a frightened little boy, dog by his side, watching his father and his teacher at the head of a gang of thugs encircling Dudyk's store, bent on evicting the supposed kulaks from their rightful homes: he saw himself. He remembered watching with his sister Nataliya as the shopkeeper, his wife and daughters and son Yuri were driven from the village: her grief at losing her special friend Yuri; his shock at their father's actions.

Many years passed before Misha discovered what became of the Dudyks, but Nataliya never knew that Yuri was one of thousands to die digging a canal to nowhere; that his sisters perished during their first winter in the camp. She knew soon enough, as did Misha, of the millions of others who shared their fate, as the land around them filled with columns of poor peasants, mildly-prosperous farmers, and shopkeepers fleeing – or forced to flee – collectivisation. That day, however, all she knew – all he knew – was that a young man she might have loved had been unjustly and violently driven away by their own father.

Pushing the unhappy memory away, Misha walked across the square to a bench facing the old church. Seeing it again, he remembered Mama and Grandmama, clubs raised against soldiers, fighting to save the church bells. He'd been about two minutes away from home that day, when coming down the road straight at him was a gang of twenty or more village women carrying rakes and staves and scythes. Seconds later, his mother and grandmother, wooden clubs in hand, had dashed around from the back garden to join them. The boy couldn't believe what he was seeing. He had no idea where they'd found clubs or what was happening. He followed them down the road, keeping hidden behind the trees, listening to them chanting as they marched towards the soldiers: *The church must be saved. The bells must be saved. One day, God willing, the Devils will go*. But then shots rang out and three women fell to the ground. No one moved. No one spoke. Misha had bolted from his hiding place and pulled his mother away, insisting she and Baba came home with him.

I was brave that day. The thought brought a smile to his lips. It faded quickly, his heart caught in his throat. Images of half-dead villagers and village children flooded his mind. He remembered his last days with his beloved mother, her dying, shrivelled body; remembered Baba, Nataliya. They were all gone, and the child he once was gone with them. *I loved them and they loved me. I was happy and then I wasn't*. He sat without moving, listening to the wind in the trees overhead, tears wetting his face.

After a time, he got up from the bench, looked around the square one last time, and walked back up the main street towards the farm. They left an hour later, headed northeast towards the Dnieper. He sat silent in the back of the

215

car, watching the fields surrounding Hovkova slip away. As mile added to mile, he thought that for all his eighteen years of age, he'd arrived in the village a boy and was leaving it a man; that a burden had fallen away and he had learned to love his childhood, despite its unforgotten horrors.

Chapter 18

Misha was looking forward to getting home. He was eager to talk to Kola and wondered how Rachel was, sorry he hadn't asked his cousin about her before leaving. And Zvi – he hadn't seen Zvi for weeks. Perhaps they could come for dinner. He'd cook something simple. He smiled: it would have to be simple, given his meagre culinary talents. He leaned forward and tapped Bohdan on the shoulder.

'How long before we're back in Kiev, Bohdan?'

'Sorry, can't say.'

'Not even a guess?'

'Nope. Can't say, sorry.'

Silence permeated the car. Fedir read through the copious notes they'd made day after day. Misha looked out the window. Bohdan drove.

After a time, Bohdan said, 'The boss wants to see you.'

'The boss?' asked Fedir. 'Do you mean Comrade Khrushchev?'

'Yup. The boss.'

Fedir and Misha exchanged looks of mutual bemusement. Fedir went back to his notes and Misha leaned back in his seat. He hadn't thought, when he agreed to come on this trip, that he'd end up meeting Khrushchev. He wasn't too happy about the idea. He remembered when Khrushchev – newly appointed First Secretary of the Ukrainian Communist Party and Head of Kiev – had first arrived in the city with NKVD Commissar Yezhov in tow. Day after day his picture had adorned the front pages: not handsome but compelling, his dark, almost hooded eyes and full, fleshy lips deflecting attention from his prematurely thin, greying hair, swept back, receding, cropped too close over his ears. Misha had laughed aloud when he saw the pictures; laughter that his uncle Orest had stopped cold. Funny-looking Khrushchev might be, Orest had said, he was also a zealous Stalinist-in-Ukraine, ready to repress and purge his way back to Moscow.

A so-called man of the people, he had a temper to stay clear of, however much he liked a joke or looked like a comedian.

'Almost there.'

Bohdan's words cut through his musings. He glanced through the car window. It was early evening. They were following a narrow, twisting track climbing through woodland. A sharp bend in the road led to an opening between high stone walls; behind these, a two-storey A-framed dacha and Oleg Krylenko – Khrushchev's assistant and Fedir's boss – waving them in.

'Welcome to Mezhgorie! You must be Mykhailo.' Oleg shook his hand, then turned to Bohdan. 'Put the car in the garage and take the bags inside. You may join us later.' He clapped Fedir on the back. 'It's good to see you again. You must be thirsty after your drive. Nikita Sergeyevich has ordered cold drinks for you. He's swimming and will join us soon. Come, this way, to the terrace.'

They passed through a narrow gap in a hedge of clipped yew trees that extended thirty feet on either side of the dacha before curving in and down towards the river. Hidden behind was a wide stone terrace sitting proud above grassland that sloped gently downhill to a sandy beach at the river's edge. In the centre of the terrace, a rectangular oak table large enough for a family of six and six of their friends; in its centre, an ice-filled jug of lemonade, another of kvass, and pretzels. They helped themselves, sat at one end of the table and gazed at the Dnieper below, glinting in the rapidly dissolving evening sun.

Misha sipped his lemonade gratefully: it had been a long journey. 'You said Comrade Khrushchev is swimming?'

Oleg nodded. 'Every day when he's here, sometimes twice a day. He makes his bodyguards swim as well.' He laughed. 'They don't like it much, especially when it starts to get cold.'

'Our trip went well,' Fedir said. 'And we've got stacks of notebooks.'

'Good. Me too. You're staying the night, Nikita Sergeyevich will insist, and we'll work on them in the morning. He sees Comrade Stalin in about ten days.' He stood and waved in the direction of the river. 'That's him now: the one in the white robe.'

A group of five men was climbing the slope. Within minutes, they'd reached the terrace and Khrushchev was striding towards them, hand outstretched. 'Fedir Maksimovich, *laskavo prosymo*! Mykhailo Oleksandrovich, welcome! I hope Oleg Pavlovich has made you comfortable?'

'Yes, Comrade Khrushchev,' Fedir answered for them. 'Very comfortable, thank you.'

Their host chuckled, 'Good, good, but you must call me Nikita Sergeyevich – I insist.' He waved them back to the table. 'Go, sit, drink your drinks. I have things I must do but then I will cook a worker's supper to delight you. Sit – enjoy the view.'

Dinner was an hour later in a room whose wooden walls were lined with the trophies of long-dead hunters. They ate Ukrainian *borsch*, beet soup with pork, beef, tomatoes and garlic, together with dark rye bread. Khrushchev held forth on the many variations of the dish: how the Ukrainian version differed from the Russian, when it was made without meat, where it was made with chicken, and where some crazy peasants made it without beets. Plain steamed fish followed the soup, followed in turn by plump *varenyky* dumplings stuffed with plums, picked – so he said – by Nikita Sergeyevich only that morning from a tree not fifty yards from where they were sitting. Much vodka and many toasts accompanied the meal, to the visitors, to the host, to absent friends.

When the dinner, but not the vodka was finished, Khrushchev turned to the purpose of their visit. For nearly forty minutes they discussed their various journeys: where they'd stopped, who they'd seen, what they'd heard. Finally, Khrushchev asked Oleg to tell him the single most important thing he had learned from all the *kolkhozy* he'd visited. The one thing he wanted Stalin to know. Oleg replied without hesitation: it was the farmers' overwhelming desire to do their own crop planning, including what to grow from year to year and season to season.

'Excellent!' said Khrushchev, nodding. He looked at Fedir. 'And you?'

'I agree with Oleg Pavlovich absolutely. I would add that they show a strong aptitude for planning, bred from many generations of experience, which would be unlikely to lead to imbalances in food production.'

'Excellent also, and well said.' Khrushchev turned to Misha. 'And you, Mykhailo Oleksandrovich, what would you add?'

'Of course I agree with everything my comrades have said. I would want Stalin to know also that past shortages and gluts too often happened because of inappropriate central planning, based on fashionable biology rather than sound practice.'

'*Niet*,' Khrushchev said, waggling his index finger. 'Stalin does not want to know that. Not in the Report.'

'But –' Misha began again.

'*Niet,*' Khrushchev repeated. 'I said, not in the Report.'

'But – '

Khrushchev sat without speaking, his face sombre. At length, perhaps taking pity on the naivety – the artlessness – of youth, he smiled. 'Misha – I may call you this? Misha, let me tell you a story. Not so long ago, at a great gathering of the Party in Moscow, Comrade Stalin told me to dance the *gopak*. Now, can you imagine me, with these short, stubby legs, on my haunches, kicking my legs out in time to the music? No?' He smiled again. 'Well, neither can I. But let me tell you something else, Misha, when Stalin says dance, a wise man dances.'

Khrushchev's smile disappeared. His eyes grew cold, hard, half-hidden under hooded lids. 'Do you understand now, my young friend, that when I say no, I mean no?'

Fear coursed through Misha. His heart battered his chest. He couldn't breathe. He hoped he didn't look as frightened as he was. 'Yes, Comrade Khrushchev, of course. Thank you. I understand most clearly. Yes. Thank you. Not in the Report, no.'

Misha returned to Kiev in better spirits than when Fedir had goaded him into travelling. Revisiting Hovkova and remembering the love he'd known there had revived him; given him strength, as well as peace. He picked up the routine of everyday life but if no longer uneasy or frightened, he was nonetheless more heedful of circumstances and the possible unwanted outcomes of his words and deeds. He'd been naturally inquisitive from childhood but also, he now realised, naïve, and Khrushchev's words had struck home. Power calls the tune.

He'd met power before – Petro Dmytrovich, an unimportant teacher in an insignificant village – but not like this. Not like Khrushchev's. He understood now its ubiquitous cunning and potential for tyranny; how evil in power might drip down through seemingly infinite layers to harm – or starve – the people one step below, and below, and below; and in this way, destroy a nation. It wasn't only success that might depend on understanding this now-obvious truth, but life itself. The realisation did not comfort him, but he hoped it might help him survive.

His return to Kiev coincided with the beginning of the end of mass terror. The Head of the NKVD in Ukraine went first. Ordered in the summer to shoot a thousand people in five days, and under threat of arrest by autumn, he faked his suicide in November and disappeared.

Stalin's NKVD Commissar Yezhov was next. He had failed to notice that in a world of denunciations, one arrest quickly became three, three became nine, nine became twenty-nine, until finally there was no one left to denounce or arrest or shoot. Who was arrested had not mattered to him for months. *When you chop wood*, he said, *chips fly; better a thousand innocents die than one traitor escape*. Quotas were there to be filled and quotas were filled, and over-filled: two million arrested; one million shot.

Too many people being arrested, Stalin said. *Not a good strategy for war: it had better stop*.

Thus it transpired that it was the NKVD who had been at fault; who would take the blame. The NKVD who had perpetrated a policy of mass arrests, spread discontent, and masterminded a reign of terror, the *Yezhovshchina*, so called after their leader, the Capitalist Spy and Wrecker, Nikolai Yezhov. The NKVD Commissar. Not Stalin.

Yezhov was gone by December 1938. Then, in the cold middle of the month, Valery Chkalov, the man Misha, Kola, and Bobby had watched swoop and roll and twist in the sky over Kharkiv, crashed while testing the latest jet fighter. *A great tragedy*, the newspapers said. *He told Stalin no too many times*, the whisperers said. Thus, all probable – and improbable – enemies were now dispatched; no fifth-columnists or nay-sayers were left to stand between Stalin and his war. On the streets of Moscow, Kiev as well, came the songs of a new cantata, Prokofiev's *Hail to Stalin,* marking the leader's 60th birthday:

> Never before for us
> Has life been so joyous…
>
> This light, warmth and sun
> Stalin has brought us…

Misha's nineteenth birthday came and went in January. They didn't celebrate. Not without Uncle Orest. The weather grew colder and the first filigree, feather-like snow fell mid-month. Bobby came to the apartment again, and from time to time joined the cousins, Rachel, and Zvi for an impromptu meal. He never talked about Mariya, and Misha never asked.

In February, the Aviation Institute was purged. Kola and Bobby escaped unscathed but professors, instructors, and engineers were arrested and accused of sabotage. Someone had to take the blame for Chkalov, Kola told Misha: nothing was ever an accident.

In time, spring arrived and the river thawed. In their favourite café in a small lane off Varoslaviv Street, Fedir and Misha debated travelling to Moscow to see the All-Union Exhibition, with its two hundred pavilions spread across six hundred acres.

'Will you go?' Misha asked.

'I don't know. It's Khrushchev's big thing. If Oleg invites me, I'll go. What about you?'

Misha chuckled. 'How could I stay away? Having seen the real thing on our trip last year, how could I possibly miss the official version of the modern collective farm? Changing the subject, have you heard about Lysenko's latest?'

Fedir shook his head. 'Do I want to?'

'Oh you do,' Misha continued, grinning. 'It seems he thinks we should mobilise chickens to kill a weevil eating the sugar beet.'

'You're joking.'

'I'm not. He wants a great chicken army, roaming the fields, chomping up beetles. And when his plan was mocked by experts across the land, Comrade Khrushchev stepped in and corrected their views.'

Fedir reached across the table for Misha's empty cup. 'More coffee?'

Summer came at last, bringing days of seemingly endless sunshine, outdoor concerts, and rumours of war; rumours that swirled through the streets of Kiev, carried on the wind, leaving no one untouched. Fear and bravado grew hand-in-hand: fear of the conquering German; conceit in the all-powerful Red Army. Then one day, the rumours were wrong. There would be no war. Germany the enemy was now Germany the friend. Ribbentrop and Molotov had signed. Stalin had smiled. Time had been bought, to make tanks and guns and bullets, to patch up an army and sew warm clothes for soldiers in winter. If anyone was surprised, if anyone remembered the many thousands of traitors, spies for Germany, lost in camps across the nation or dead, no one said so now.

Summer ended suddenly on the first day of September 1939 when Germany invaded Poland. Two days later, Britain and France declared war on Germany. Two weeks later, Russian troops entered Poland, in collaboration with their new-found German allies.

One day not long afterwards, Misha was returning home earlier than usual after a lecture had been unexpectedly cancelled. He hoped Kola would be there. He hadn't seen much of his cousin in recent weeks. He was always off somewhere, doing something, but when Misha asked what, he brushed the question away or said he had extra work at the Aviation Institute. Misha missed him. Fedir was a good friend, but Kola was his family. If he was at home, perhaps they could go to the market or find somewhere new to eat. Misha was restless and looking for company.

As he entered the building, he heard Kola talking in the corridor above. He couldn't make sense of the words and he didn't recognise the second voice. As he climbed the stairs, two heavy-set men with sunburned complexions and several days' growth of beard passed him, heading down. Dressed for outdoors in heavy boots, rough trousers and plain jackets, they looked like farm workers. Misha thought they were unlikely friends of his cousin.

'Hi, Kola, I'm home,' he called out as he came through the door. 'Who were the men you were talking to?'

Kola came out of the kitchen but waited a moment before speaking. 'No one you need worry about, Misha,' he said at last. 'No one at all.'

20

Part Three

War

Germany's invasion of Poland in September 1939 was swiftly followed by the declaration of war on Germany by Britain, India, Australia, New Zealand and France. By June 1940, Denmark, Belgium, Norway and France had all surrendered to Germany. One year later, Hitler ordered the invasion of the Soviet Union, with Kiev captured and occupied within months.

22 June 1941

Misha nearly missed the beginning. He was deeply asleep, dreaming he was lying awake in his funny cupboard-bedroom next to the school rooms. It wasn't quite light in his dream and he could hear Mama and Baba chattering in the kitchen, rattling pots and pans. Soon, Mama would bring him a cup of tea because it was his -

'Misha, wake up. Misha. Can't you hear it? Wake up.'

Kola was shaking him – too bloody hard. He waved an arm to fend him off. 'Go away. It's still night. Leave me alone.'

'It's the Germans, you idiot, they're bombing the airport.'

Instantly awake, Misha bolted upright. 'What?'

'It's the *Luftwaffe* – they're bombing the airport. Come to the window. You can hear them.'

They stood at the open window and listened to the muted explosions coming from Kiev's eastern suburbs. Kola's excitement was palpable. His words poured out in a torrent of approval.

'It'll be war now and about time too. It's been almost two years since Poland. We thought they'd come in May but Yugoslavia and Greece slowed everything down. But they're here now. It won't be long now.'

'What the hell are you talking about? Look at me.' Misha yanked his cousin around to face him. 'What won't be long now? You sound like you want a war. You can't possibly mean that.'

'I can and I do, if it'll get rid of the Russians, which it will.' Kola twisted away from Misha's grasp; a braggadocio strutting. 'The Germans have a bigger army and a better army. They'll win, and they'll win fast. And when they do, Ukraine will be free.'

Misha was stunned. When he found his wits again, he was furious; his voice harsh. 'Those two men, the ones who were here, what, eighteen, twenty months ago, they were underground, weren't they? Is that what you've been doing? Why you're never around? You've joined the bloody Nationalists. Tell me, which section did you sign up to? The ones who like killing Jews or those who prefer Mussolini's friendly fascism?'

'I'd join anyone who'd get rid of the Russians, and if it takes war with Germany, so be it.'

'You can't possibly believe that.'

'How could I believe anything else? How could you? There's nothing the Germans can do to me – to us – that the Russians haven't done already and worse. They'll give us back our country and we will build a world where fifteen-year-old girls don't denounce innocent men.'

Misha flinched. 'That's cheap. If your father was here, he'd say you're forgetting your history. He'd tell you not to trust German promises.'

'I think he'd be proud of me.'

The sound of gunfire drew them back to the window. Three small planes were overhead, chasing a fourth. Fires burned in the distance, adding unnatural streaks to the early morning sky. They stood side-by-side without speaking, their argument postponed, spellbound by the spectacle unfolding before them. After a time, Kola turned to Misha and smiled wryly. 'Well, Cousin, I don't think they'll be opening the new football stadium this afternoon, do you?'

Later that morning, the pair slipped into the flood of Kievans pouring into the city centre. Along the main street, the Khreschatyk, people huddled in small, still, whispering groups, watching and waiting, as if the city and everyone in it was holding their breath. *Is it war? Will the planes return? What will Stalin do?*

Kola spotted some of his fellow students from the Aviation Institute outside the Red Army enlistment office and the cousins joined them. They were young men now. Misha had turned twenty-one in January; Kola would be twenty-two next month. Kola's pilot training had one more year to run. Misha would graduate from the Institute of Agriculture in mid-September and start work there as a researcher the following week. He'd gained weight – a bit of muscle, too – and the cousins once again looked like twins.

'So, Kola, enlisting already?' A would-be flight engineer Kola had known from childhood jostled him playfully, nonchalant in the face of war. 'Shouldn't you wait until you get your wings? Learn how to fly maybe?'

'Don't worry, Borys, I've no intention of enlisting, so I won't be dropping bombs on you yet.' Kola grinned at his old friend. 'I guess you're waiting for the doors to open so you can sign up – get yourself something to do instead of sleeping through classes every day.'

'Well, maybe tomorrow or perhaps the day after that. I need to check my diary first!'

As they laughed, overhead loudspeakers – fixed to telephone poles, lamp-posts and buildings – crackled into life. Along the street, talk stopped in mid-sentence as eyes swivelled upwards. Kola nudged Misha. 'This'll be Stalin. I bet Hitler gets his war.'

But it wasn't Stalin. Instead, the voice of the People's Commissar Vyacheslav Molotov thundered through the air.

'Citizens of the Soviet Union! The Soviet Government and its head, Comrade Stalin, have instructed me to make the following statement. Today at four a.m., without a declaration of war, German troops attacked our borders and bombed from their airplanes our cities of Zhitomir, Kiev, Sevastopol, Kaunas, and some others, killing and wounding over 200 persons. This unheard-of attack upon our country is perfidy unparalleled in the history of civilised nations…'

As Molotov's rant continued, Misha watched the upturned faces around him. Kola looked satisfied, almost pleased. His friend Borys less so, perhaps thinking not of enlistment as an officer-airman but of conscription as a foot soldier. A few feet away, a woman lifted a small, fretful child into her arms, apprehension draining the colour from her cheeks. An old man sat on steps leading upwards, slowly shaking his head at the thought of yet another war. Misha turned back to Molotov, who was outlining what would happen next:

'Now that this attack on the Soviet Union has taken place, the Soviet Government has ordered our troops to repulse this brigand-assault and to drive the German troops from the territory of our country…'

So it was war. Kola was right. Misha's eyes stung; his face flushed. He wanted to howl in despair: *Haven't I had enough grief already? Must there also be war?*

At length, patriotic music replaced Molotov. Misha was startled to hear cheering coming from the end of the street, but a quick glance around showed most people were quiet, too used to public silence to say much. He started to leave and signalled Kola to follow: 'I've got a lecture, let's go,'

'So, where was Stalin?' Kola asked as he caught up, then answered his own question, a smirk in his voice. 'The master of deception, deceived. Hiding in his dacha, I'd guess. Probably wondering how the hell he's going to win a war with hardly any generals or admirals or tanks that work or planes that fly or –'

'Why don't you just shut up? War is not a joke, okay?'

'I was just –'

'I know. Forget it. Let's go.'

Misha missed the lecture. He hadn't the heart to go. It was the summer solstice. The sun had seemingly stood still hour after hour in the clear blue sky of a beautiful day. He'd been in Kiev for seven and a half years. He was healthy and enjoying life in the city, his classes at the Institute, his friends. But today, all the fears of his childhood came rushing back: soldiers, deaths, riots and violence, no food; everything war would bring again.

Almost worse than all of those things was Kola. Sometimes – like this morning – he felt that he hardly recognised his cousin. When they were children, it would not have been too far wrong to say that Kola was his hero, his idol. Certainly, he'd loved his cousin more than anyone else, excepting his parents; he still did. Kola had always been his other side – sometimes his braver side. He'd once thought he could read Kola's mind, like people say twins do. But now – now he no longer knew what his cousin was thinking, no longer knew what he was doing or about to do. They no longer fit together.

Chapter 21

Twelve days later Stalin spoke to the Soviet nations. That day, Kola and the others were in Café Lypky, a place they usually avoided, thinking it too close to Communist Party headquarters. From the beginning, they had met in public places, cafés usually, while being careful not to frequent the same location too often. The rapidly-advancing German invasion increased the threat of police surveillance. House-to-house searches were underway for private radios and weapons, and anything else deemed useful to the Red Army – or to traitors. People with German surnames were disappearing, and so-called 'unreliable elements' – which would include Kola and his friends if caught – were being deported north. Keeping a low profile until the Germans took Kiev was key to the Nationalists' plan and getting harder by the day.

Kola, along with Viktor, Moise and two others, Ivan and Dmytro, had been recruited to membership of OUN, the Organisation of Ukrainian Nationalists, in 1939, about two months before Germany invaded Poland. Misha had all but interrupted a meeting with Viktor and Ivan a few weeks later when he'd returned home unexpectedly. Kola had brushed off his questions about the pair and hoped Misha would forget them. His cousin's angry remarks on the night Germany invaded made it clear he had not. Kola didn't understand Misha's animosity towards the Nationalists. The Russians had killed their grandparents and starved – murdered – Misha's parents and sister. They took Kola's father. How could he not want an independent country?

As the group of earnest young men debated possible safe places to meet in future, the café loudspeaker coughed into words.

'Comrade citizens, brothers and sisters, men of our Army and Navy! It is to you I am speaking, dear friends…

243

'Shit!' Kola jumped to his feet, sputtering and spewing coffee on himself, the table and the floor. He winked at Viktor sitting opposite and quickly offered an explanation in a loud, cross voice. 'Damn bug. There was a bug in my coffee!' He sat down again and only Moise, sitting next to him, could hear him muttering *Dear friends, my ass*.

Viktor, promptly and loudly, told him to shut up as he, Viktor, and everyone else in the room wanted to hear what Stalin was saying, and then winked back.

'The war with Fascist Germany cannot be considered an ordinary war... our war for the freedom of our country will merge with the struggles of the peoples of Europe and America for their independence, for democratic liberties...'

Kola leaned back in his chair, his coffee forgotten, his hands still. He gave every appearance of listening carefully to Stalin's words. Inside, he seethed: the man's a lunatic. Independence! We'll give him independence alright. Then we just might get some democratic liberties, and some freedom too – from him.

'All our strength for the support of our heroic Red Army and our glorious Red Navy! All the forces of the people for the destruction of the enemy! Forward to victory!'

Kola leaned forward and whispered so that only Victor could hear: 'Not if we have anything to do with it.'

A few days after Stalin's speech, the group settled on the Far Caves of the Perchersk Monastery as their new meeting place, where they could gather with other like-minded men and receive updates on Germany's march towards victory. The Perchersk Monastery had been shut down by the Bolsheviks when Kola was a child and its grounds turned into a museum quarter, only for the museum itself to be abolished eight or so years later. Its paintings, artefacts, and relics had long ago been dispersed and the monastery's buildings and churches boarded up or turned to commercial use. In the limestone caves below, labyrinths of tunnels, cells, and catacombs had also been emptied, but here and there the mummified remains of a monk or saint still rested in its burial niche, giving testimony to nine centuries of religious life.

'This place gives me the creeps,' Dmytro said. 'Look, those are hands. Shit, I almost touched them.'

Moise told him to shut up. 'It's a dead saint. There's dozens of them down here. They did the hands like that, stretched out of the coffin, so pilgrims could kiss them and ask the saint to intercede on their behalf to get their sins forgiven. Maybe you should try it.'

'No thanks. How about you, Kola?'

Kola was a non-believer. He was nonetheless deeply touched by the sights and silence of the catacombs, their barren underground chapels with still-visible streaks of wax coursing down rough-hewn walls, spilt from long-ago tapers that had once lighted the way of martyrs to their windowless cells. He didn't believe in saints, but he thought they should not be mocked; should be left in peace.

'Forget it, Dmytro,' he said. 'We've got more important things to talk about. Apparently Zhukov told Stalin that Kiev is a lost cause and should be abandoned in order to

246

save the troops and tanks defending it. Stalin told Zhukov he was talking rubbish and fired him – sent him to the front lines – and named himself as Supreme Commander of the Soviet Armed Forces.'

'Bloody hell,' Ivan chuckled. 'If they weren't already losing, I'd say they were done –

'You're right about them losing,' Dmytro chipped in mid-sentence. 'I've heard that over 800,000 Red Army soldiers have been captured and another million killed. Minsk, Smolensk, Zhitomir. They'd be in Kiev already if Hitler hadn't sent the Wehrmacht the other way. I guess it helps to pick a country with miles of flat land to invade.'

'They'll be here soon enough. The plan is –'

'What I want to know,' Dmytro interrupted again, 'is which one of us is going to raise the flag after they get here?'

'Dmytro, what *are* you talking about?'

'What I'm talking about, *Kola*, is the Great Lavra Bell Tower. As soon as the Germans get here, they'll want to put their swastika on the top. Well, I think there should be a yellow and blue as well and I want to be the one to fly it up.'

247

'You don't think maybe you're counting chickens before –'

As Kola was speaking, the fifth member of their group, missing until then, stepped quietly into their cell meeting place.

'Viktor, it's about time. Where've you been? We've been waiting for you.' Kola peered at his friend. 'Are you alright?'

'No, I'm not. I need a drink.'

'Ivan, have we got anything to drink? Get something for Viktor, will you?' Kola pulled up a chair. 'Here, sit.'

Viktor took the glass of vodka offered and drank half of it before speaking. 'My cousin, the one in the Red Army, has run away. I had to find him somewhere to stay.' Viktor's voice trembled. 'He's been through hell. Fucking hell. They're all dead – thousands, dead.'

'Dead? Who's dead?'

'Ukrainians, Russians, Georgians. It didn't matter. They're all dead. Whoever was there.' He shuddered, then fell quiet. The others waited. After a few moments, he took a deep breath and began again.

'You know that four days ago the German Sixth Army captured the hill overlooking the main Moscow road, and to get to the German position Red Army troops had to cross the small river at the bottom and then climb the hill – right? So, all the Germans did was to wait at the top of the hill for them to get close enough, and then fire. My cousin said it was like shooting fish in a barrel but much, much worse, because with fish you eventually run out of targets.' He swallowed the last of the vodka and handed his glass to Ivan for a refill.

'However many died, the Red Army were ordered to keep climbing: wave after wave of soldiers in formation, twelve men across, each row two hundred metres in front of the one behind. They marched towards the machine guns, carrying rifles with bayonets attached – bayonets, for Christ's sake – and when the first row was dead, the second row and then the third continued up the hill past their comrades' bodies. When they died too and the fourth row started up the hill, they were easier to kill because the piles of dead bodies slowed them down and made them clumsy.' He paused, swallowed more vodka and began again, his voice cold with anger.

'The thing is, even if they'd wanted to stop, they couldn't.' He laughed harshly. 'They've got *blocking detachments* – that's what they call them – blocking detachments: armed bastards who stand behind the troops to keep order, to make sure that our good Soviet soldiers do their duty, to make sure they don't give up, whatever the cost. My cousin said it went on for three days and nights before they were allowed to retreat. That's when he ran away.'

No one spoke.

Kola remembered the words Misha had said after Molotov's speech: *War is not a joke*. Images flooded his mind of terrified soldiers clambering over the bodies of their blood-soaked comrades, knowing they were only minutes, perhaps seconds, from their own deaths. He shuddered. It was not supposed to be like that.

'I said they were losing.' Dmytro broke the silence. 'Good for Germany.'

'Shut up, Dmytro.' Kola didn't bother to keep the disdain from his voice. He looked at Viktor, sitting rigid, staring at nothing, as if it was he who'd escaped death, not his cousin. 'That's enough for today. Come on, Viktor, let's go.' He helped his friend to his feet and they left together.

The two would-be-liberators of their country walked through the surrounding parkland, heavy at heart and silent. From time to time, Kola caught sight of the river, empty of its pre-war, late-summer boats. Overhead, starlings darted back and forth across tree tops in the failing light. There was a gentle, warm breeze. The beauty of the evening could not have made a greater contrast with Victor's report.

After a time, Kola spoke, 'I didn't think it would be so bloody. I thought, when it was obvious they were losing, they'd surrender.'

'My cousin says he won't go back. I don't blame him. He didn't want to go in the first place.'

'Poor bastard.'

They walked on for a time without speaking. Kola's mind played and replayed Viktor's story. 'So, what do we do now?'

'Finish what we started, I suppose.'

Stalin's speech to the people shattered the pretence of life carrying on as normal. Cafés and shops fell quiet, concerts were cancelled, the picture-house closed, and the city began to empty.

The family of Nikita Khrushchev was among the first to go, at the head of a swelling cavalcade of elites panicked by their leader words into fleeing the German onslaught. Trucks and cars choked the roads north and east, piled high with anything and everything portable and valuable – expensive furniture, art work, jewellery. People who couldn't or wouldn't leave filled their larders and cellars with food. As yet there was no looting, only endless queues for the diminishing stocks of grain and salt and oil.

Tensions heightened when the mass evacuations began: all key workers were to be sent to the Urals, Siberia or Central Asia. Among the first to go were University of Kiev departments capable of contributing to the war effort, such as physics and mathematical mechanics. Less important institutes like Misha's would wait until the westward movement of troops eased, and space on the railways freed up. Unless, as Misha feared, the Germans got to Kiev first.

It was mid-morning on the last day of July. Misha and Zvi Rosen were sitting at a window table in Zoya's, Podil's oldest café, watching Kola and Rachel outside on an apparently unending circuit of Kontractova Square. Misha was worried about Zvi. Rumours of the widespread slaughter of Jews by SS mobile killing units – *Einsatzgruppen* – had reached Kiev within days of Stalin's speech. Although the thought of losing Zvi for a second time pained him immensely, he hoped to persuade his friend to join the flight from the city. He'd just told him about the massacre of ten thousand Jewish men, women, and children in Kishinev by German and Romanian troops.

'Kola doesn't believe it, but apparently it happened in Lvov as well, and Zhitomir. I think the rumours are too similar to be false. You need to go and take Rachel and her family with you. It won't be safe if – when – the Germans get here.'

But Misha was not telling his friend anything he didn't know already.

'They say it went on for three days in Lvov,' Zvi said. 'They had lists: who was Jewish, where they lived, where they worked. After they'd worked through the lists, they started grabbing Jews off the street. They say two thousand died.'

Zvi gazed into his coffee cup for a long moment, as if hoping to find an explanation for the killings. He looked back at Misha, his friend since childhood.

'But it isn't just Germans, Misha. It's Ukrainians, too, doing the killing. The worst stories say the SS shot the men and the Ukrainian police shot the women and children.'

'I heard about Ukrainians lining the streets to welcome the German convoys, but not about them shooting Jews. All the more reason why you must go. The same thing could happen here. There are boats crossing the Dnieper. You could cross over.'

'And go where?' Zvi shook his head. 'Besides, Rachel's mother and father refuse to leave, and if they won't go, she won't go, and I can't leave her to cope alone.' He smiled sadly. 'Believe me, Misha, I have tried to convince them. But there was a meeting in the synagogue soon after the invasion. The elders decided they would stay and that's that. The general view appears to be that life under the Germans couldn't be any worse than under the Bolsheviks, so why go.'

Misha didn't know what to say. He waved through the window at Rachel and Kola, whose latest circuit had brought them within sight. He nodded in their direction. 'I doubt he's trying very hard to convince her to leave, since he thinks it's all Soviet propaganda, put out to make monsters of the Germans. He thinks the Germans are going to liberate Ukraine and we'll all live happily ever after. I can't make him see sense at all.' He shivered, despite the warmth of the day. 'I wish my uncle was here. He'd know what to do.'

'Don't blame yourself. Kola's a good person inside. He'll come straight – I know he will.'

'I hope you're right. Sometimes I'm not so sure.'

Misha watched Kola and Rachel as they walked arm-in-arm, looking content with each other and the warm morning sunshine. They passed the elegant Contract Building, for which the square was named, jostled through the crowded market stalls and turned a corner at the battered fountain of Samson and his lion Misha had shown Mariya so long ago. When they came close to the café again, he beckoned them inside.

In almost the same instant as he sat down, Kola piped up: 'So, Zvi, has Misha convinced you that Kiev isn't safe and that you and Rachel and her folks should join the exodus?'

'I suppose it's still possible the Soviets might win.'

'The war's been lost since the first German soldier crossed the Bug – that's why Stalin kept quiet for so long. Why he left it to Molotov to break the news. But all that stuff about killing squads – that's rubbish. There'll be lots of room for you, and Rachel, in a free Ukraine.' He smiled broadly. 'Guaranteed.'

Misha was sure his cousin was hopelessly misguided, but he didn't want to quarrel with him again. He was saved from deciding what to say next when Rachel got to her feet, saying she had promised to meet her mother. She kissed Kola lightly on the forehead, said to stay where he was, and left. Kola suggested they go as well and invited Zvi to walk back to the apartment with them. Within minutes, they were on the funicular headed to the Upper Town.

Back at the apartment, they found Bobby waiting on the doorstep and invited him in for coffee.

'No coffee. I've got something much better.' He drew a small bottle of slivovitz and a large bag of pretzels from the satchel at his side. 'Four glasses, please.'

'Plum brandy!' Misha's eyes gleamed. 'Who's getting married?'

Bobby held up his hand, imperiously. 'Wait. All will be revealed.'

Kola quickly assembled glasses and a bowl for the pretzels. 'Okay, we're ready. What's up?'

Glass in hand, Bobby saluted them. 'Congratulations! You, Kola, are now a pilot, and you, Misha, a full-fledged agronomist.' He emptied his glass. 'Of course, I'm now a pilot as well, so I deserve congratulations also, and that calls for another drink.' With his glass refilled, he turned to Zvi. 'I didn't expect you here, Binyamin – sorry, Zvi – but you also deserve congratulations. You are now a historian. Salut!'

Kola and Misha spoke at the same time, both dumbfounded. 'What on earth –? '

'It's the war,' Bobby interrupted. 'They've graduated the lot of us, all across the country. We're now qualified – finished – done.' He smiled at Kola and raised his glass. 'Well done, flyboy!'

'Well done yourself. Have a pretzel.'

The four young men spent several happy minutes drinking and eating and marvelling at the sudden end to their studies. Too soon, reality slipped back into place. Misha was the quickest to realise the potential consequences of early graduation.

'I suppose the bad news is we're now more likely to end up fighting, especially you two, as pilots.'

'Maybe,' Kola said. 'But I'm not going to make it easy for them to find me.'

Bobby nodded in agreement. 'Me neither, although in my case, it'll be doubly hard.' All trace of his earlier merriment vanished. 'I had another reason for coming today, and for the brandy. I'm leaving Kiev tonight, while it's still possible. I'm going to Chernihiv to find Mariya. I can't leave her alone there, not any longer, not now. As far as I know, Chernihiv hasn't been bombed. I'll head north through Oster and just keep walking until I get there.' He turned to Misha. 'You understand, don't you, why I have to go? Why I can't just leave her there, alone.'

Mariya. Misha hadn't heard her name for a long time. The pain of her betrayal wasn't quite so sharp but the memory of his cruelty towards her – a fifteen-year-old child – still stung. There is always a choice, he'd told her. What easy words they were. What choice does a daughter have when her mother's life is threatened? He was filled with longing to see her face one more time, to touch her skin one more time, to hold her.

He assured Bobby he was doing the right thing. 'Do you need any money? How about food?'

'No, I've got both. But what I would like before I go, is a bit more plum brandy.' He took a key from his trouser pocket and handed it to Kola. 'To my apartment. Use it if you want. I don't know how long it'll stay empty, but it's mine until the end of December, or yours now.'

Misha tipped the last of the brandy into their glasses. '*Bud'mo*! he said, raising his glass in salute. Let us be!

'*L'chaim*!' added Zvi, raising his. To life!

'DON'T TAKE ANY WOODEN NICKELS,' Bobby said in English, and drained his.

'*Na konya*!' said Kola. On your horse! He embraced his fellow pilot. '*Au revoir*, Bobby.

Take care of yourself.'

Bobby embraced Misha and Zvi and headed for the door. '*Do pobachennya.*' I'll be seeing you.

Abruptly, Misha put his half-empty glass on a nearby table. 'Bobby, wait. I'll walk out with you.'

On the street, Misha hesitated. 'Let's walk a bit,' he said. After a few minutes, he put his arm through Bobby's and kept walking, still without speaking. Finally, the words came.

'Bobby, when you find Mariya, will you tell her… will you say I understand – say I was wrong to be so cruel; that I forgive her and wish her happiness?' He entreated his friend, the once-upon-a-time American. 'Will you do that for me?'

'Of course I will, Mykhailo.' Bobby enveloped him in a hug. 'There's nothing I'd like better.

Chapter 23

The people of Kiev rallied to the defence of their city. Misha became a firewatcher and spent three nights and two days of each week on the roof of his apartment building watching for German fire bombs. Only once so far had he been called upon to act, when a twin-engine Junkers returning home after a night raid on the port saved one last bomb for the railway. Two bomblet incendiary sticks landed near enough for him to scoop up and drop into his water bucket where they hissed into obsolescence. The bucket, a pair of heavy gloves, a helmet, some sand, and an odd-looking hose plus pump-fitting for the bucket were his only weapons of war, and he hoped the demands upon them would be few.

In truth, though, he loved being a firewatcher, particularly at night when the darkness let him think of times and people he barred from his thoughts during the daylight hours. He'd sit with his back to a wall, watch the stars brighten, the clouds glide across the face of the moon, and remember. He'd think of his mother and how desperately sad he'd been when she died, so weak and so sorry to leave her young son alone. He'd look at the small silver spider he still wore around his neck, Mama's last present, and think back to the stories she'd told him about her and Papa's life together before he and Nataliya were born.

Or he would call to mind his sister and how she had made him laugh sometimes and scolded him other times, and how she had blushed when he teased her about liking the shopkeeper's son, Yuri. He could still hear her bossing Kola and him at Christmas as they helped her set the table for Holy Supper: 'Put the hay on the table first,' she'd say, 'to remember the Manger where Christ was born and make sure you spread it carefully. Then the cloth – it's the one grandmother embroidered many years ago, so remember not to spill anything on it when you are eating. Next, we set the places where we will sit – you, Kola, you may lay one in memory of your mother. Then the braided bread, the *kolach,* goes in the middle of the table. When we're ready to eat, Papa will put a candle in its topmost loaf and light it, while Mama will light candles in the window as a welcoming sign to passing strangers.'

Misha could still see himself and Kola exchanging smirks as she gave them their orders – they had heard it all before – but they said nothing, simple nodded and did what they were told. He'd always hoped she'd forget the small dish of kutia she put at each place, and told her so every year. And every year, she ignored him.

Sometimes, when the sky was especially laden with stars, he'd let himself think of Mariya and the short time they had together. Mariya, not many miles away but lost to him. He would wonder if she was looking at the sky too and if she ever thought of him. He hoped Bobby had found her safe and well; that he'd delivered Misha's message.

That day, however, Mariya and the others were far from his mind. Dusk was falling and he was watching what he guessed were the death throes of four bridges crossing the Dnieper. Flames and black smoke billowed into the air above parts of the city where the bridges were – or had been, probably. He'd seen no planes overhead, which likely meant they'd been blown up by retreating Soviet troops. He hoped they'd left the Kissing Bridge by the football stadium; he liked it. The new electric power station in Podil had gone up in flames not long before the bridges, and he supposed they'd destroyed the water tower and the cannery as well. *To keep them out of enemy hands*, Stalin would say. A pity about those of us left behind, he thought.

The sound of artillery and gunfire, hour after hour, provided the soundtrack to the panorama surrounding him: the German 6th Army fighting its way methodically, street by street, through the suburbs, moving inexorably toward the centre of Kiev. He wasn't frightened and wondered if that was because he had yet to see any actual fighting or German soldiers. He laughed this morning when the street loudspeakers advised all men aged between sixteen and fifty of their imminent conscription into the Red Army. So far, neither he nor Kola had been called up. He was glad. He didn't want to be a soldier. He wouldn't mind marching or rain or even the bitter cold of winter, if the war lasted that long. He didn't know if he could kill anyone. How could he

266

know that? He'd never fired a gun or been in a serious fight or owned a knife. He knew, though, that if it came to it, he'd do whatever was necessary. *I'm not a coward – not with a hero for a grandfather.* But he'd have to have food. He'd heard too many stories of soldiers going without eating day after day and he knew he couldn't do that. He promised himself when he left Hovkova, when Orest had come for him, that he would always have enough to eat. No matter what happened, he'd never starve again; not that.

He wondered what Kola would do if he was drafted. He hadn't seen much of his cousin since he became a firewatcher. They didn't argue about the Nationalists anymore, which was both good and bad: Their arguments had at least given him some inkling of Kola's activities but now he knew nothing, except that his cousin spent a lot of time away from home. He almost, but not quite, wished Kola would be called up, but was also afraid he'd be shot as a deserter for refusing to go. He smiled: with German troops surrounding the city and Soviet troops fleeing it, conscription was unlikely to happen to either of them any day soon. He wasn't frightened, though, which pleased him. He knew he'd fight if he –

The roar of three low-flying planes crashed into his thoughts. He whirled around to watch them head towards the port, catching sight of the black crosses painted on their underbellies. Suddenly there were three more. Then another five. Then too many to count. It was as if the whole of the Luftwaffe was in Kiev and over his head. Bombs exploded across the city outskirts, in the west, the south, the north. Flashes surrounded him. Everywhere but the centre: the bloody Krauts were saving the best buildings for themselves.

'Christ!' He flinched as an explosion in the streets behind the university rocked the building beneath his feet. 'The railway,' he said, unaware he had spoken out loud.

He headed for the door, then caught sight of a single Soviet fighter with its distinctive red wingtips headed towards a cluster of German Stukas circling over the western edge of the city. Almost immediately, one of the German planes spotted the Soviet defender and wheeled to confront it, dots of smoke from its machine guns signalling its approach. The

Soviet pilot didn't try to evade the attacker. Instead, weaving gently from side to side, he headed straight for the circling enemy planes.

'Can't you see them?' Misha shouted at the sky, unable to take his eyes away from the impending disaster.

Somehow, the Stuka missed. It swerved upwards to turn for another try. In that instant, the Soviet fighter doubled its speed, climbed slightly upwards, and rammed its propeller into the tail of the enemy plane. Misha stopped breathing. The two aircraft hung motionless in the sky, then the small Soviet plane exploded into nothingness, while its enemy twisted and tumbled to earth.

Misha leaned back against a wall, still watching the sky, astounded by the drama he'd witnessed. Kola had told him about air ramming – *taran* – the same word for a battering ram, but until now he hadn't quite believed him. Slowly, terrifyingly, the meaning of the sky battle spread through him, stripping him of any sense of excitement. 'If that's all we have left,' he told the night sky. 'We really have lost.'

From behind a screen that imperfectly concealed two couches squeezed tightly together in a space barely big enough for one, Kola called to Rachel to come back to bed. 'I'm lonely by myself,' he moaned.

When Bobby lived there, only one couch hid behind the screen. His sister Mariya's had been kept in tiny room off the kitchen, where she'd slept. It was from there, after Rachel agreed to meet him, that Kola dragged the second couch, to make a place for her beside him. They could have made the space larger or removed the screen altogether, if they'd chosen, because the apartment was theirs alone. But they didn't. They cherished the tiny hidden world behind it, the sense of being unseen; perhaps because their love-making was new or because it was secret, unsanctioned. Perhaps they simply liked the slightly-battered grey screen and its unnaturally colourful, painted birds. For whatever reason, the screen stood where it always had and separated the joy of being together from the everyday acts that took place on the other side: making tea, eating a sandwich, washing dishes.

Kola lay half-buried under blankets, drowsy, contented, like a cat in sunshine. He stayed that way when, out of sight on the other side of the screen, Rachel answered him.

'No, you come here.'

'Not until you say you'll marry me. You say you love me – why won't you marry me?'

'Oh, Kola, we've been through this. It's not the right time to be getting married. There is a war going on.'

'What better time? Let's get married tomorrow.'

'No.'

'It's not the war, is it? It's your mother, she doesn't like me.'

This time, Rachel stayed silent and it seemed to Kola that the blessing of the screen – that it could not be seen around or through – had become a drawback. When she didn't answer yet again, he faced a dilemma: he could call once more or he could get up. The thought that he might just turn over and go to sleep didn't enter his mind.

She was standing at the window, dressed only in a slip, her hair falling loose across her shoulders. She turned when she sensed him beside her, a sad, half-smile on her lips. 'I knew if I didn't answer you'd eventually get up,' she said quietly. 'My mother loves you, although she always hoped I'd marry Zvi. But she's so glad you're not *that American*, that she has decided to forgive you for not being Jewish. She was convinced for a time I was in love with Bobby. But forget that – look, there.'

She pointed out the window to a sky red with flames. 'It must be Syrets', on the other side of the Jewish Cemetery.' She leaned back against Kola, as if for warmth. 'Good friends of my parents live there. I played with their daughter when I was little.'

She turned away abruptly from the window and crossed the room to retrieve her robe, lying in a heap by the bed.

'The leaflets said they wouldn't bomb the city centre,' Kola said, still watching the fire burning no more than three miles away. 'They seem to be keeping to that.'

'Oh, Kola, how can you defend them? It's okay if they bomb the outskirts as long as they leave the centre alone? You can't mean that.'

His cheeks reddened. 'No, of course I don't mean I want them to bomb Syrets' or Podil or anywhere. It's just – '

'It's just you think they're helping your friends, the Nationalists, and what's a few bombs compared with that, yes?'

'Don't you be angry with me too, Rachel,' he said, pulling her to him. 'Misha is angry enough for both of you.'

'I'm not angry, not really. But you being involved with them is so dangerous, and I can't help thinking it'll all come to nothing.' She smiled sadly. 'We'll get the Germans, lots of people will die, lots of Jewish people, and the Nationalists will get nothing. Zvi says they're terrible anti-Semites.'

'The Nationalists? Not the ones I'm with. But even if only half the stories about the other ones – the Banderites – are true, then Zvi's right. I wouldn't go near Bandera's lot. Here in Kiev it's mostly followers of Andriy Melnyk and I've never heard anyone say he's anti-Jewish. I'd never work with anyone anti-Jewish, Rachel. How could I, when I love you?' He drew her hair away from the side of her neck before bending to kiss it gently.

'Don't kiss me, Kola, not now. We need to talk.' She slipped out of his arms. 'Do you want tea?'

'What about the Germans, Kola?' Rachel asked, after they were settled at the table. 'The pogroms in Poland and Lithuania and Bessarabia? And now more killings in Ukraine. They say that 17,000 Jews were killed by the SS last week, near Chernivtsi. You can't just pretend these things aren't happening.'

'It could be propaganda put out by Moscow to make the Soviets keep fighting.' He hesitated. He wanted to tell her, to confide his dreams, but was afraid she'd think him a fool.

He took a deep breath and then the risk. 'It's not the Germans I want, Rachel, even if I do think they couldn't be much worse than the Russians and even some Ukrainians if it comes to it. The Germans will make Ukraine independent, something the Bolsheviks would never do in a thousand years' A look of chagrin crossed his face. 'I told Misha I hate the Russians and that I'd do anything to get rid of them. Well, that's not completely true. I do hate them, that part is true. But I love my country more, much more, than I hate either the Russians or the Germans. From the time I was little, I listened to my father's stories about Ukraine, about its history and about the land: *our destiny is the soil; forsake it and you are lost, cling to it and it will develop all your powers and draw out your soul…* I don't remember the rest.'

He got up from the table and walked back to the window where he stood looking out without speaking. After a minute, perhaps less, he turned to face her.

'You won't laugh at me?'

She shook her head very slightly. 'Of course not.'

'A free Ukraine – that's what I want, for my Papa, if he's still alive, for Misha, for you and me' He paused almost imperceptibly. 'For our children.'

'But Kola –'

'No, you see, there's a plan.' He interrupted, his voice full with excitement. 'They're here already in Kiev, waiting to act. I've met the leaders. There's two hundred here and another thousand coming with the Wehrmacht. After the Germans drive the Soviets and the Red Army out, but before they take control of the city, the Nationalists will set up a new Council, a *Rada*. They will govern alongside the Germans for a while and then … after a time … they –' He faltered, then stopped.

'After a time what? The Nazis will fade away and let the *Rada* run the country?' Rachel held out her hands to him. 'Oh, my darling sweet Kola. You don't really believe that will happen, do you?'

Three months after the Luftwaffe bombed Kiev, the German Army occupied the city. Misha watched their tanks drive up the Khreschatyk in triumph; witnessed small clusters of fellow citizens offer bread and salt and cheers to the troops who'd turned their city's suburbs to rubble. Two days later, he joined the masses heading into the countryside to bargain for food. He'd stockpiled only a few days' supply before the city fell and refused to join the looters roaming the streets under the indifferent gaze of German soldiers. He didn't have much to exchange for food – a few books, some embroidered linens, a not-particularly-valuable St Basil icon, two brass oil lamps, and his sister's fur hat – remnants of his childhood. The rest of the apartment, the furniture, plates and glasses, bits of decoration, were Orest's and he reckoned it all now belonged to Kola. He hadn't seen his cousin since the Germans took over. Too busy putting up Ukrainian flags, he supposed.

He took the lamps and the icon into the countryside, where they turned out to be worth more than he'd thought they'd be, and returned home with a chicken, a dozen eggs, and two kilos of potatoes. The Ukrainian militiaman controlling re-entry into the city, swastika on his armband and club by his side, gave his bag only a cursory search before sending him on with a peremptory wave, no doubt hoping for better pickings from the people coming up behind.

By the fourth day, the rules governing the occupation were clear: a curfew from eight at night until six in the morning, with violators shot on sight; registration of all adults and no work without registration; house-to-house searches for proscribed goods and people; no fraternization, and Germans to the head of each queue and the centre of each sidewalk.

As the first week of occupation ended, Misha accepted that he had to register for officially recognised work if he wanted to survive. Five more minutes in bed first.

Misha left home just before noon. Despite the onslaught, Kiev had yet to lose itself as a city. Its best streets and its best buildings remained unscathed. Men and women still hurried up and down its avenues going about their personal business, although the hubbub came now from people jostling to register, queuing to buy bread, scrambling to get home before curfew. There were no cars or trams, only rickshaws and walking: rapid, heads-down, walking.

He headed up Volodymyrs'ka Street, passed the university and the Opera House before turning into Prorizna Street from where he could join the Khreschatyk. He didn't hurry. It was mild, if a bit windy. The autumn rains were not many days distant and he was inclined to dawdle and enjoy the sun when it made an appearance from behind passing clouds. Turning into Prorizna Street, he instantly regretted his ambling. There was an enormous queue for the Labour Office, snaking down the street and around the corner into the Khreschatyk. He berated himself: *It'll be hours before I get to the top. Why the hell didn't I come earlier?*

At the same moment, an immense explosion ripped through the air. Black smoke slashed through by leaping orange-red flames poured across the top of Prorizna Street. Whatever had blown up was on the Khreschatyk. Heedless of the terror-stricken crowds streaming away from the explosion, Misha ran up the road toward it and rounded the corner. Dozens of people – Kievan and German, soldiers and civilians – lay in the road, covered in debris and blood, limbs askew or missing. Some were crying for help, from God or Mama or any passing stranger. Others would never speak again. Misha ran toward a woman pulling at jagged planks of timber covering the body of a young man.

'I'm sure he's alive,' she wailed. 'He must be alive … you –' she said, looking at Misha. 'Help me… please.'

He tried to lift the timber but couldn't. Telling the woman he'd be back, he ran towards a small group of men who appeared to be doing nothing more than watching the chaos. Surprised to see Fedir Wendelko among them, he called out and beckoned for him to follow. Starting back towards the woman, he heard Fedir shout loudly for him to stop. He hesitated, puzzled, and in that instant, a second bomb exploded, sending the ruined building crashing down on the injured and rescuers alike. The blast flipped Misha into the air. He landed badly and lost consciousness. As he came to, Fedir and a stranger were lifting him from the rubble. They carried him to safety and bundled him into a rickshaw. He heard Fedir tell the driver where to go, then passed out again. When he surfaced, he found himself on the sofa at home. Later, he learned a third bomb had gone off about ten minutes after he'd been carried away, destroying the nearby Grand Hotel, headquarters of the German military government.

While Misha recovered, Kiev burned. The fire that began with the first explosion spread rapidly, whipped by strong winds, unfettered by attempts at control. It took three days to set up an effective water supply. By then the Khreschatyk had all but disappeared, as one landmark building after another exploded. People living in adjacent streets, like Fedir, were evicted by German soldiers searching for bombs. Streets were cordoned off. Residents were ordered not to return. Before the last

flames died down, most of one square mile of the inner city –
the heart of Kiev – had been destroyed and twenty thousand
people were homeless.

Rumours instantly flooded the city of three hundred –
five hundred – a thousand bombs found and made safe: in
Government House, the National Opera, the Central Bank, the
Cathedral. It took longer for word to spread that it was the
NKVD and Red Army who had placed the bombs; who had
expected the invaders to occupy the best and most prominent
buildings; who didn't care how many ordinary people died in
order to scorch the city they were abandoning.

After the fire had burnt itself out enough to make the
streets safe, Fedir and Misha walked into the centre to see the
devastation. The air was rank with the stink of charred wood,
burnt rubber and worse. A pall of black smoke hung
overhead, robbing the day of sunlight, burning their eyes.
Barely ten days had passed since German troops marched
triumphantly up the Khreschatyk. Now the street was
destroyed. City residents and German soldiers had fought the

flames side-by-side. Now both were looking for someone to blame.

Chapter 26

'Misha, damn you, wake up!'

Misha opened his eyes. 'Kola? What the hell?' His cousin was shaking him roughly. 'What are you trying to do, finish the job the bomb started?'

'You must come with me – now.'

Misha shook himself awake, suddenly alert to the anxiety in Kola's voice.

'It's Rachel. The Germans have said all Jews must report this morning and I can't stop her going. She won't listen to me. Zvi's going too. You must hurry, we haven't much time.'

While Misha dressed, Kola told him about the notices in Ukrainian, Russian, and German that had appeared the day before, ordering all Jews to report to the corner of Mel'nykova and Dokterisvka streets, near the old Jewish cemetery, by eight o'clock the following morning. They were to bring documents, money, valuables, and warm clothing. Failure to comply would be punishable by death.

The cousins ran the short distance to Shevchenko Boulevard, hoping to grab a rickshaw that would get them to Mel'nykova Street more quickly than walking. The boulevard was deserted and they kept making their way north on foot, cursing the Soviet soldiers who'd knocked out the city's electricity supply as they left, stopping the trams.

'Why didn't you come yesterday? I could've tried reasoning with Zvi, if I'd known.'

'She didn't tell me until just before curfew.' Kola's anger slipped out as he spoke. 'She obviously planned the timing meticulously. When there was just enough time for her to reach her parents' home before curfew but not enough for me to get to you, she told me about the notices – I hadn't seen one – that her mother and father were determined to report as instructed, that she was going with them, and that she was going home immediately, to help them get ready so they could all leave first thing in the morning.'

'Didn't you try to tell her, explain to her, it was bound to be a –'

'Of course, I did,' Kola interrupted angrily. 'I tried everything to make her stay with me; believe me – everything.' He kept walking without speaking for a few moments, then stopped, despair written across his face. 'You've been right all along, Misha. I know it now. The Germans – I shouldn't have believed them. They're going to be sent away somewhere awful, to a camp or a ghetto or…'

'Let's not worry. Let's just get there.'

They heard the tumult long before they saw the confusion of men, women, and children pushing and being pushed along Mel'nykova Street: black-hatted Orthodox Jews, ringlets dangling, their wives behind them, wigs half-hidden under dark headscarves, shepherding half a dozen children or more. Elderly Jewish men with long tangled beards, arm-in-arm with fragile elderly Jewish women, struggling to keep upright, helped by anxious grown children. Modern young Jewish mothers carrying babies, husbands beside them, suitcase in one hand, two small children trailing from the other. Thousands upon thousands, dressed in their best, for travel to a new place: some straining to get through the crowds, some wishing to turn back; none wanting to die that day.

'Oh God, we're too late. There's too many. We'll never find her!' Kola wailed, his distress heightened by the flood of people filling the street below them.

'We'll find them. Come on, down the hill.'

Within minutes, they joined the moving throng. There was just enough room for the pair to walk in the road alongside the procession without having to thread their way through the ghouls watching from the opposite sidewalk. Had either one been a linguist, he'd have been captivated by the fragments of Polish, Yiddish, Hebrew and German that marbled the passing hum of words rising from the queue. The angry shouts and taunts from the sidewalk were all too understandable, though, as Russian and Ukrainian Kievans gave in to ingrained hostility towards their Jewish neighbours.

'There she is – I see her.' Kola ran ahead, waving his arm and shouting: 'Rachel – wait, it's me, Kola. Rachel.'

Within moments, he was by her side, smiling broadly, his arms enfolding her. 'It was the red coat, I saw your red coat.'

He turned to his cousin who'd caught up. 'I saw her red coat. Her father brought it back for her from Germany years ago, but she hardly ever wears it – it's too good. Oh, Mr Chovnik, Mrs Chovnik – I'm sorry. I didn't see you. Good morning.' He smiled again. 'I saw the red coat – that's how I…'

'Kola, stop.' Rachel said harshly, but then softened her tone. 'I told you not to come, Kola. You shouldn't be here.'

'But –'

'Well, we're here now,' Misha intervened, walking alongside Rachel's parents who continued to be swept forward. He smiled at her younger sister, Zoya, and nodded a greeting to Zvi. 'I'm Kola's cousin Mykhailo, Mr Chovnik, Mrs Chovnik. I'm sorry we haven't met before. It would be nice to go somewhere to talk, to sit awhile, perhaps have some tea?'

'No, it would not. We would lose our place in line. You must see that.' Rachel's father spoke without looking at Misha, his eyes not wavering from the line in front.

'But Mr Chovnik, I'm not sure you should believe the promises Germans make.' Misha spoke gently so as not to offend the older man. 'It might not be safe here for you or your wife and daughters. Won't you come away, just for a little while?'

'I'm sure you're a nice young man... Mykhailo? Is that your name? But you are talking nonsense. The Germans have not made any promises, as you say. It is simply a census. They will count us, then we will be sent to a new place.' He paused for a moment. 'You think I would endanger my wife or my children? Pah! You know nothing. I have always obeyed the law and I will continue to do so. It is a census. That is all.'

'But Papa, perhaps we could come back tomorrow? I mean, since Kola has brought Misha here to meet you, it would be nice to sit and talk. You think so too, don't you, Mama?'

'No, Rachel, Mama is not strong enough to do all this again tomorrow. We stay.'

The caravan inched forward. Rachel handed her bundle to her younger sister and put her arm around her mother, as if to imbue the older woman's spare frame with some of her own strength. Kola hovered at Rachel's side, saying little, his silence unmarked in the cacophony that engulfed them. Zvi and Misha dropped back a pace or two.

'Zvi –' Misha began, his tone pleading.

'No, Misha, there's no point. I know what's waiting. You know I can't leave them to take this journey by themselves. Remember the eleven-year-old waif they took in, without question? I was not just penniless and friendless, but the son of my father, as well; a political exile. They didn't turn me away then and I can't abandon them now. Neither would you, if you were in my place.'

They moved forward with the queue, briefly silent.

Then, without giving Misha a chance to try again to convince him, Zvi handed his friend a small but thick leather-bound book he'd pulled from the small satchel he was carrying. 'This is for you,' he said, his smile bittersweet. 'It's Papa's copy of *War and Peace*. I haven't quite got to the end yet – perhaps you could finish it for me?'

Clutching Zvi's book, Misha lost the fight against tears.

Zvi took his arm. 'Come on, my friend. Cheer up. We had a few extra years together, didn't we? I never really expected us to meet again, did you? And who knows, cousin Isaac might be right – maybe it *is* a census. In which case, I'll want my book back. See you take good care of it, okay?'

Misha nodded, but could find no words to express the love he felt for his childhood friend or his pain at losing him once more, this time without hope. They quickened their pace enough to rejoin the others. Then Zvi stopped and pointed to the front of the queue, to a line of German soldiers and Ukrainian militia stretching across the roadway.

'That is as far as you go, Misha. Once we're through there, it won't matter what or who we are or what we believe. You must take Kola and leave.'

'I'll miss you, Zvi, more than I can say.' Misha paused, trying to smile. 'I promise to keep your book for you.'

They hugged for moments Misha wished would never end, and drew apart without further words. Zvi went to help the Chovniks through whatever was to come. Misha told Kola he had to come away now; that he had to be brave for Rachel's sake, so she could do what she felt she must. Rachel and Kola clung to each other until, with the briefest of kisses, she pulled away and walked with her family towards the human barricade blocking their way.

Kola and Misha made their way slowly back along the road they'd followed only a short time before, past the unending procession in the roadway, past the watchers on the sidewalk. They said little as they struggled to comprehend what was happening. At the turning where the road to Podil joined Mel'nykova Street, Kola halted.

'I can't go with you, Misha, not yet. I need to go to the apartment. Where we were. I'll come later, a few days maybe. I don't know.'

Misha looked at Kola's tear-streaked face, knowing it was a mirror image of his own. If the words existed that could take away his cousin's pain and his own, he didn't know them. He clasped Kola tightly. 'Come home when you're ready,' he said. 'I'll be there.'

Kola stumbled through devastated streets, his eyes blinded by tears. Somehow, he managed to get back to the apartment where he'd shared so many hours of joy with his beloved Rachel. He felt her kiss on his lips. He smelt her skin. He wanted to die with her. Inside at last, hidden from the sight of others, he gave way to his grief and howled. In his mind's eye, he followed his love, caught in that heaving mass of human bodies rancid with fear, pushed from behind, pushing those in front, struggling to protect her mother and father. He heard again the soldiers barking orders: *Hopp! Hopp! All belongings here, food to the right, other to the left.* Then a gate opened and she was gone.

The fates were kind to Kola. They spared him the sight of Rachel's fear as she watched the soldiers at the gate count each man, woman, and child as they passed through, stopping when some number known only to the guard was reached, sending some forward, holding others back, separating parents from children, husbands from wives. He didn't hear her pray that her family would not be torn apart or count it a blessing that they were still together when they entered a wide corridor forged from facing rows of soldiers, shoulder to shoulder, Alsatians by their side.

The pressure from behind Rachel never abated. Her only course was ahead, into the flailing blows meted out by jeering, laughing soldiers wielding heavy rubber truncheons; soldiers who cared nothing for age or infirmity or dignity. To her, they looked drugged or drunk; perhaps they were simply evil. She tried to stay near her mother and young sister but was pulled away, pushed forward – *nein, nein, bewegen* – no, no, move. She stumbled onward, weeping. Kola, her beloved Kola. What would he do, when he knew for certain she was never coming back? She would be dead. She would feel nothing, but what about him? What would happen to him, without her?

The brutal corridor ended in a small grassy field, filled to overflowing with bruised, bloodied, naked people. A soldier shoved Rachel's staggering mother forward into the field, shouting for her to undress quickly, hurry up, hurry up. Rachel helped her mother. Zvi helped her father. Their shame hung from them, like shredded cloaks, hiding nothing. Then, one by one, they were forced through a narrow gap in high sand walls at the field's edge to the side of a deep ravine. *Babi Yar.* In front of them, across the ravine, rows of soldiers holding machine guns; beside them, each other, hand-in-hand: Issac and Leah, Rachel and Zoya, Zvi. She looked upwards, saw the sun one last time, felt its warmth one last time, and then, nothing.

Chapter 27

A few days later Misha was alone in the apartment, sitting in his uncle's chair, Zvi's last gift in his lap. He brushed his fingers gently across the embossed lettering on the cover, *Leo Tolstoy War and Peace.* He turned to the ornamented flyleaf inside, where he found Yakov Rosen's signature, with Kharkiv, 1919 written below. The book was in Russian and as Misha held it he felt daunted, not by the language, which he could read well enough, but by its length. No wonder Zvi hasn't finished it, he thought, almost smiling.

A piece of paper, folded over and over, fell from the middle of the book as he leafed through. Picking it up, he opened the folds to find an essay entitled 'What is a Jew?' *This question is not as strange as it may seem at first glance*, he read, scanning quickly to the end … *the nation which neither slaughter nor torture could exterminate, which neither fire nor sword of civilizations were able to erase from the face of the earth, the nation which first proclaimed the word of Lord... such a nation cannot vanish. A Jew is eternal; he is an embodiment of eternity*. Leo Tolstoy, 1891.

Misha refolded the paper, taking care to match the creases – to fold it exactly as Zvi's papa had folded it – and replaced it in the book where Zvi had kept it. He put the book on the table beside him, straightening it carefully. Then, his composure cracked and, not for the first time, he leaned back in his chair and wept.

In time, Kola came home. Unshaven, his clothes rumpled and dirty, he smelled like a sewer.

'My God, you stink,' Misha said. 'Go and wash. I'll heat some coffee. Do you want food?'

'No food, just coffee.'

While Kola cleaned up, Misha restocked the stove with wood, lit an oil lamp and a few more candles, cursed the Red Army yet again for destroying the electricity plant, and put some not-quite-stale bread and cold chicken on a plate, in case his cousin changed his mind. When Kola returned, Misha told him that Fedir's building had been caught in the bombing and that he was staying in the apartment until he could find somewhere else. Kola surprised him by suggesting Fedir could take over his bedroom if he wanted.

'I won't be here much, so he might as well stay. He's not going to find anywhere else. This is good, by the way, thanks,' he said, waving a drumstick in the air.

'Where will you be, in Podil?'

'No, that's gone. I've passed the apartment key on, never mind who to.'

Misha raised his eyebrows, but didn't ask.

'Let's just say it will be put to good use. No, I'm going to fight with the UPA and I want you to come with me.'

'UPA?'

'You were right about the Germans making promises they don't keep – probably never had any intention of keeping. And it's not just Jews.' – Kola stopped speaking for a moment – 'Not just Jews they're killing. They've started on Ukrainian Nationalists as well and God knows who else. Bandera's in prison in Germany and about two thousand of

299

his supporters in Poland have been shot. I don't care much about them – anti-Semitic bastards – but it looks like they're about to start on the Kiev people. So we're setting up an underground army to fight both Germans and Soviets. Well, Germans first, as far as I'm concerned. The Soviets can wait until we finish the bloody Krauts.'

'So the UPA is a partisan army?'

Kola nodded, then grinned, his eyes bright. 'Come with me, Misha, into the marshlands. We may not be able to get the bastards who… who killed Rachel and Zvi, but we'll get others. Lots of others.' He reached across the table and put a hand on Misha's arm, once again a boy tempting his younger cousin into adventure. 'You'll come, won't you?'

Before Misha could answer, Fedir came into the apartment, shedding water like a long-haired dog left outside too long. 'It's bloody awful out there. Isn't it too early for it to be raining this hard? Mind you, it won't do the German tanks any good.' He took his drenched coat to the kitchen to dry and returned with a cup of warmed-up coffee, grimacing as he drank some. 'This tastes like it was made before the war. But never mind, I've solved the problem of how we survive until the Krauts lose.'

Fedir smiled at Kola before continuing. 'It's good to see you again, Kola. You're going to be grateful to whichever ancestor gave you your beautiful blue eyes. You too, Misha – or, I should say, Michael – and Nicholas – very grateful indeed.'

Misha had no idea what Fedir was talking about and neither, apparently, did Kola. They gawked at him, mute.

'Good, I've got your attention. Now listen.'

Fedir reminded them of the system the Germans were using to discriminate between people in occupied territories, with its four categories – castes, he called them. At the top of the pyramid were *Reichsdeutsche*, or Germans from Germany, who could do anything they wanted. Just below them came *Volksdeutsche* who, narrowly defined, were Germans living outside Germany or in German colonies. They also had privileges, but fewer. The general population came next: expendable labour to fuel the German war machine. At the bottom, awaiting eventual destruction, were enemies of the Reich: members of the Communist Party, Commissars, regional officials and the like and, of course, Jews and gypsies.

'But you know all this,' Fedir said, shuddering slightly as he drank more coffee. 'Ugh. Haven't we got anything better than this?'

'Fuck the coffee. Get on with it,' Kola snapped. 'As you say, we know all that, so what of it?'

'Well, there are at least two things you don't know, probably three. First, because Stalin deported thousands of ethnic Germans, let's call them *Volksdeutsche*, to the gulags in the run-up to the war, the ones left in the cities are mostly former farm labourers, itinerant factory workers, that sort of thing. That means there aren't many around who the Germans can use to help run their new paradise. So what they're doing now is changing – *softening* – the definition of who counts as *Volksdeutsche*. Which brings me to the second thing you don't know, and that is I'm a *Volksdeutsche*, maybe even according to the older, stricter definition.'

Fedir stopped speaking and smiled at Kola and Misha as if they were a theatre audience whose attention he'd once again succeeded in capturing.

'How does Fedir Maksimovich Wendelko, with his dark hair and dark eyes, turn into an ethnic German?' Misha asked, bemused.

'Easy,' he replied. 'By being the great-grandson of a Mennonite who fled to Russia from Prussian-occupied Poland in the early nineteenth century, looking for religious freedom. Most of those who came didn't assimilate – they stayed German at heart, and probably made up a sizeable proportion of the ethnic Germans deported to the gulags in the thirties. My people did assimilate and changed their name in the process. If we hadn't, I'd be Theodor Maximilian Wendel, Wendel being my German great-grandfather's last name.' He smiled. 'Rather appropriately, it means 'wanderer' in German and it used to refer to migrant Slavs in the sixth century. More pertinently, I've got the papers that link me back to Herr Wendel.'

'Which, presumably, you can take to the German authorities and, with the snap of a finger, become a *Volksdeutsche*, privileges and all.' Kola's face darkened as he spoke. 'Is that the idea?'

'That's the idea.'

Misha heard the rising tension in Kola's voice and intervened quickly to prevent an argument. 'What's the third thing we don't know?'

Another smile. 'The DVL: the *Deutsche Volksliste* – the German People's list – which you join by having Aryan characteristics, like your blue eyes, and by being willing to be germanised. So, tomorrow, you come with me to the German civil headquarters, present yourselves as Michael and Nicholas Salenko rather than Mykhailo and Mykola and say you've always believed you had a German great-grandfather long ago and you'd like to work for them.'

'Not possible. I couldn't – *we* couldn't.' Kola flushed with anger. 'Those – those bastards just murdered thousands of people, simply because they were Jewish. People I loved, that Misha loved. You sit there and suggest we should *work* for them? You're out of your fucking mind. I'd rather starve.'

'Which you will, if you stay in Kiev and don't work for them.'

'Well, we're not staying in Kiev, are we, Misha? We're going into the marshlands, as partisans, to fight the Germans, not work for them. Tell him, Misha. Tell him we're going, maybe even tomorrow.'

Before Misha spoke, Fedir began again: 'Well, you'll probably starve as partisans as well, if you're not shot or don't freeze to death.' He paused for a few seconds, before turning to Misha. 'You haven't forgotten Khrushchev, have you? You didn't want to work for him either, but we were able to do some good, weren't we? We helped Ukrainian farmers, didn't we? Well, it'd be the same working for the Germans: we'd wreck their plans and help Ukrainian farmers.' He leapt from his chair, agitated. 'It's all about food now, Misha, food for German soldiers and for Germany: Ukrainian food. At least until the Germans are driven out – if they're driven out. Did you know they blockaded the city today? No more going into the countryside to bargain for chickens, which will mean starvation here in Kiev. Food is for Germans, not us.'

Kola broke in. 'As partisans we'll bomb the trains and the food will never get to Germany.'

'Maybe,' Fedir sat down again before going on. 'But I'm not sure that'll be much help to the people living here. Working on the inside, we can fudge the figures so that less food gets on the trains in the first place and more stays with the farmers – Ukrainian farmers.'

Fedir turned to Misha. 'It's up to you, Misha. You can become a partisan and go to the marshlands with Kola and get mighty hungry, starve maybe. You can stay in Kiev and find whatever work there will be for non-Germans, clearing rubble if you're lucky, corpses if you're not, and definitely starve. Or you can work with me *against* the Germans, but from inside, and have enough to eat.'

Misha hadn't spoken since Fedir had told them about the DVL – the German People's list. He looked at Kola, full of passion and anger, so hopeful Misha would go with him, fight alongside him; then at Fedir, calm, invitingly sensible, with his plan to sabotage the Germans. Both were convinced his way was the right way. Misha wished he shared their certainty.

'Well, Misha?' Kola broke into his thoughts. 'Are you coming with me?'

It was the middle of the night. Misha was alone and awake, lying on his back in bed, still wrestling with the awful choice facing him. He'd put off answering Kola, told them both he needed time to think, not that thinking had done him much good during the last few hours. He wanted to be like Kola, brave and foolhardy, dynamiting German trains, killing German soldiers, helping to win the war from behind enemy lines. It's what Prince Andriy would do – he told himself, half-smiling and picturing the hero of *War and Peace* – and Papa and Grandpa, and Uncle Orest. It's what I must do as well. It's the brave and right thing to do.

Then, unbidden, an image surged into his mind of a frightened, starved boy with spindly legs stuck below an

307

empty, swollen belly and stick-like arms lacking the strength to scrape the ground in hope of finding a forgotten potato. The boy he had been.

He turned to face the wall alongside the bed, trying to escape himself.

It's not fair. Kola will leave and I'll have no one.

He wanted to believe Fedir. He wanted to believe that Rachel would understand. He wanted to believe he could help subvert German plans to strip the county of food; that somehow it would be no different than working for Khrushchev. Khrushchev – hah! He'd worked for him because he thought they'd be helping modernise Soviet agriculture and maybe they'd even undo some of the harm – the havoc? – caused by Lysenko. He had believed Fedir then. He would like to believe him again. But what had they actually achieved? A small, temporary relaxation of central control that disappeared almost as quickly as it happened. No, what he really learned from working for Khrushchev was that telling truth to power is dangerous, especially when power is corrupt. Power wins.

The Germans held the power now and he had no doubt they were corrupt. Would they win?

He was finding it hard to convince himself that he and Fedir could do the Germans much harm and thought it all too possible they would end up helping them by default. Once more he resolved to join Kola and become the brave warrior of books and ballads. He wasn't a coward, after all. But then the fearful image returned and he knew that he could not starve, would not starve, ever again – and once more turned his face to the wall.

Chapter 28

The Marshlands

Kola left Kiev a few days later, after a long and acrimonious argument. *Fedir's Fantasy*, he'd called the plan to work with the Germans. Fedir won the argument and Misha stayed in Kiev.

He met his fellow-nationalist, Viktor Fodchuk, at the edge of the city. Together, they headed north to Chernobyl, a small town on the outer fringes of the Pripyat Marshes; a journey that would take two days of walking broken by a night of rough sleeping.

When almost within hailing distance of their destination, they came across a field of corpses. Towering over the clearing were ten or twelve trees shorn of all branches, with cross-bars and braces nailed high up each trunk. Suspended from the cross-bars, one at each end, were the remains of men, partisans according to their placards, arms hanging loose by their sides, their faces black and eyes glass-like. The field was muddy from a day of endless, dripping rain and evening mist swirled up and around the once-trees, now-gallows, as if nature itself was trying to conceal the horror men had done. Kola tasted bile and swallowed hard in an unsuccessful attempt to stop the sick pouring out.

'It's bad,' Viktor said. 'But probably not the worst.'

At Chernobyl, they met Viktor's cousin, Roman, who would guide them into the marshlands. Kola had to disguise a smile on meeting Roman, who was as far from his image of a freedom fighter as Stalin was from a Sunday school teacher. Short and podgy, with thick glasses and sparse hair, he looked like a draper's clerk down on his luck. But he was Kola's avenue to the partisans and so he expressed his gratitude and nothing more.

They left for the marshes once it was dark, walking rapidly to get free of the small town. After a time, they joined a narrow river, turned northwards and walked its bank in the intermittent light of a three-quarter moon that flitted in and out of passing clouds. They cut through dense woods and crossed open moors, skirted reed-laden swamps and small, barely visible ponds. From time to time, Kola caught glimpses of distant water reflected in the moonlight. He'd never before been to the Pripyat Marshes and only now that he was here, in their midst, did he appreciate Roman's value as a guide. Swallowing a vast area of northwest Ukraine and Belarus, the wetlands stretched three hundred miles from west to east, and a hundred and forty miles from north to south. The few roads that crossed it were narrow and unpaved, rendering the area all but impenetrable to anything larger than horse and cart. Partisans were safer there than almost anywhere else and Kola could think of no better base for harassing Germans. While partisan fighters could leave and return on foot, neither seen nor followed, German Panzers floundered in the bogs and German infantrymen feared it as a no-man's land dividing their armies in the south from those on the road to Moscow.

No one spoke as they walked. Sometime earlier Kola had asked Roman what would happen when they met the partisan band they were joining; if any attacks were planned; how soon he'd get to fight; if they had any weapons. Roman had grunted and shook his head, muttering 'all that's for Ruslan to decide'. Kola thought it highly improbable that anyone was eavesdropping, but kept his own counsel and walked on like the others without speaking.

Ruslan proved to be the partisan leader. A long-limbed, burly man in his late twenties with thick curling hair and dark recessed eyes, he greeted his new recruits with a speech of welcome so rapidly delivered Kola thought he must have made it many times. After walking all night to reach the encampment, he had been hoping for a few hours' rest, but Ruslan kept him back after the others were sent to one of the sleeping houses.

'Why are you here?' Ruslan's voice commanded instant attention.

'I want to fight Germans,' Kola responded, somewhat surprised at being asked to state the obvious.

'There's an army doing that. Why not join them?'

'Because I hate the Russians almost as much as I hate the Germans,' he said, again thinking this should be obvious to a nationalist partisan leader. Why else would he be there?

'Why?' Ruslan barked.

Kola paused before speaking again, suddenly aware that this was not simply idle chatter. He was being tested – interrogated. He'd assumed Viktor's say-so would establish his *bona fides*. Clearly, it had got him only as far as the door.

'The Soviets starved my uncle's family to death and sent my father to the gulags, or killed him, I don't know which. The Germans murdered the woman I wanted to marry and threw her in a pit.' He stared at Ruslan as he spoke, his eyes bright with anger and defiance. 'Is that enough for you?'

'It's enough.' Ruslan clapped him on the shoulder. 'Go,' he said. 'Sleep now. We'll talk tonight.'

A day or two later, Ruslan admitted he'd known Kola's history long before he'd arrived in camp; that he'd spoken the way he had *to take his measure*, as he put it, laughing, *to see if I could bully you a bit.* Having passed muster, Kola was launched into a round of training which would turn a brave city boy into a cunning fighter able to slip through woods unheard and unseen and cause great damage in the Wehrmacht's hinterland. He loved the transition from Kiev's city streets. On all-day hikes, he laughed at grouse scrambling across his path in terror and confusion, listened to woodpeckers hidden in the branches of hundred-year-old aspen trees, and admired the economy of beaver dams. He learned that moss doesn't grow on white birch bark, but on the side of oak trees it will tell you which way is north; that you must never eat snow without melting it first or your tongue will swell and your mouth hurt long before your thirst is quenched. He became a good marksman; not the best, but good enough. He went on foraging trips to local farms and ate kasha for breakfast, lunch and dinner. After ten days, he was ready. He would go with Roman, Viktor and Pavlo – the youngest member of the band, barely seventeen, but its best climber – to Zlobin, thirty miles north, and blow up a train.

They left camp the next day during a break in the cold autumn rain that had drenched the previous two weeks. Their destination: a single-track wooden bridge over the river Druc. A dozen trains a day crossed there, travelling north to Germany loaded with oil from the Donbas and grain from the southern steppe, and south to Ukraine, bringing fresh German troops and armaments.

They made their way towards the bridge through a landscape shrouded in mist and semi-darkness. Roman took the lead armed with a submachine gun, listening for sounds that shouldn't be there. Close behind, Pavlo and Kola, rifles in hand, their backpacks enclosing four small bombs re-fashioned from unexploded German shells; and Viktor, carrying a second submachine gun, watching where they'd been.

They were not expecting the bridge to be guarded because as yet there had been little partisan activity in the area. Their plan was not simply to destroy the bridge. Bridges were easily and quickly repaired. Instead they would rig it to explode moments after a train began its traverse, causing the engine and second carriage to topple into the water, while leaving the remaining carriages on land, overturned and twisted across the tracks. They reckoned this would immobilise north-south rail passage for a substantially longer period. In the absence of timing devices or a remote detonator, they would use layered tripwires. Two small bombs set high under the upper struts of the bridge would be linked to each other by wire stretched across the tracks and to two bombs farther along the bridge's underbelly. When the engine passed over the tripwire, it would trigger the first two bombs which, on exploding, would discharge the second two.

Timing was critical. Since the bombing of a major supply train on the Minsk-Moscow line six weeks previously, all trains in the occupied territories were preceded by a two-man motorised railcart checking the line for sabotage. The explosives and tripwire would have to be put in place between the passing of the railcart and the train's arrival. They counted on about ten minutes to get the job done.

As they waited in nearby woods for the railcart, the rain began again. Not the hard, wind-driven downpour of previous days, but a drizzling, soaking, misty rain that crept through the thickest clothes and overran the widest brims. The four men stood without speaking, almost without breathing, as if by being still, the dripping sodden rain might miss them and fall on their neighbour instead.

After a time that felt forever, the railcart came into view and disappeared out of sight. While Roman and Viktor stood guard, Kola and Pavlo quickly climbed the undercarriage of the bridge and, with one on each side, worked their way along its length until they were over the river. They strapped the first two bombs to the wooden struts, about ten inches or so below the iron rails. Pavlo threw the trip wire to Kola across the top of the rails, and working slowly in the wet, they each attached one end to the bombs. Edging their way farther out over the river, they repeated the process with bombs three and four. Kola then unwound the longer tripwire, tossed one end across the track to Pavlo and, holding it in such a way to ensure it remained slack, worked his way back to bombs one and two. He watched as Pavlo inched his way across the wooden struts to attach it to the wire connecting the second pair of bombs. Suddenly, far too soon, he heard the sound of the train whistle, signalling its approach.

'Kola, Pavlo!' Roman hollered from the side of the river. 'Forget the rest – get off the bridge, now!'

Pavlo was crawling towards the centre of the bridge. Kola shouted at him, echoing Roman's words, then quickly made his way back to the ground, reaching the safety of the woods just moments before the train thundered past onto the bridge.

Roman, Viktor and Kola watched from the obscurity of the trees as their first partisan mission together unfolded almost as precisely as planned. Slowing slightly to cross the bridge, the engine passed over the tripwire and triggered the first two bombs. As its momentum carried the engine forward, these bombs exploded under the second carriage; while at the same time, the now-exploding second pair of bombs ripped the struts from under the engine. But the dull *crump* of the small bombs on the bridge was soon forgotten in the screech of iron wheels braking on iron rails and the roar of carriage after carriage smashing into and over one another. The engine and second carriage plummeted into the river, as the carriages following twisted and bucked, ploughing up tracks and land before coming to a stop in a mangled heap.

The three partisans grinned at each other in triumph. The wreckage was much more spectacular than even the seasoned Roman had expected. 'Well, the bastards won't forget this bridge in a hurry,' he said. 'But now we've got to go, quickly.'

Kola and Viktor looked at each other, alarmed. 'What about Pavlo? We can't just leave him.'

'We can. He's either alive and he'll catch us up, or he's not, in which case we can't help him. Either way, it won't do him any good for us to be killed.' Roman turned and plunged deeper into the trees, away from the clamour surrounding the crash.

Kola shuddered at the uncompromising harshness of Roman's words; all the same, he turned and followed him through the woods.

They headed almost due south, following an unpaved country road not yet rendered impassable by German tanks churning the roadway into a river of mud. Travelling by road made their journey longer, but quicker. As he walked, Kola's mood swung between elation at the success of their mission and anxiety about Pavlo. There's a chance he jumped clear, he told himself. I didn't see him do it, but he might have. He was only seventeen, too young –

'Pssst, Kola.'

Roman's hushed voice brought him out of his thoughts. He saw his two companions, half-crouching, moving off the road and into a thick pine grove running parallel. Roman pointed down the road in front, silently offering him an explanation. They had just passed the village of Recyca and were less than a half mile from the main road to Gomel. There, in the distance, at or near the crossroads, was what appeared to be a dozen Wehrmacht soldiers pulling a car, headed east along the main road.

'They must be stuck in the mud,' Viktor said once they reached the safety of the wood. 'There's probably some bigwig in the back who doesn't want to get his boots dirty.'

Kola grinned. 'Well, there's three of us and only twelve of them or thereabouts. They'll all have nice German rifles. Shall we go and get them?'

Roman looked at him doubtfully. 'Are you crazy? Four against one? Not the best odds.' He paused for a moment. 'What do you think, Viktor?'

Before Viktor could respond, a voice came from behind: 'How about three against one: does that sound better?'

The three men wheeled around to see Pavlo emerge from behind a tree. Amid muted expressions of delight, he told them he had jumped off the bridge just before the engine tripped the first wire and swam downriver out of sight. 'I was pretty cold and I ran most of the way, trying to dry off and warm up. I spotted you a few minutes ago, just before you decided to plunge into the trees. I figured you had to have a good reason, so I did the same and here I am. Shall we go get the Germans?'

Roman looked at the three eager faces in front of him. 'Well, I guess I'm crazy too. Here's what we'll do…'

The pine grove petered out about fifty metres from the crossroads, well within the range of the submachine guns Roman and Viktor carried. As they got closer to the end of the trees, it became clear that the soldiers were focused entirely on the quagmire into which they and the car were sunk. On each side of the vehicle, soldiers pushed and pulled; rifles slung across their backs. Inside the car a single passenger remained. No one stood guard. No one watched. The enemy today was mud. So nobody noticed when Roman and Viktor emerged from the pine grove, at least not until they began to fire. In less than a minute, before they could pull their rifles off their backs, twelve soldiers were dead.

'*Schiess nicht!* – don't shoot.' The passenger in the back seat tossed his pistol out of the car window and slowly opened the door. He got out, hands raised above his head in surrender. A single shot rang out, holding him suspended, startled, sending him lifeless into the mud. A few feet away Kola lowered his rifle, his face unreadable. He stood still, saying nothing, looking at the dead German sprawled in the mud, thinking of Rachel. He could almost hear her schoolteacher's voice admonishing him. *Two wrongs have never made a right, have they, Kola? Killing him won't bring me back.* He shuddered. It might not, he told her, but it's made me feel a whole lot better. He waved at his comrades gathering their bounty. 'Hey, I'll help. How many rifles did we get?'

Chapter 29

Kiev

Misha was standing at the window overlooking the street, scratching pictures in the ice that coated the inside. Working for the Germans brought benefits, but heating at home was not always among them and came and went as it pleased. He etched a long-legged spider in the thickest part of the ice, a twin to the small silver one he still wore around his neck. 'You'll last a while,' he told the ethereal creature.

It was January 6th, his twenty-second birthday and he was alone. He didn't know where Fedir was, or Kola. He missed his cousin. There hadn't been many birthdays-cum-Christmas Eve they'd spent apart. He stared through the iced window, trying to see, something, anything. There was only darkness. Footsteps. He heard footsteps. He froze; waited motionless: there were footsteps in the corridor. Kola? Risking capture to say happy birthday? Within seconds, whoever it was continued past his door, heading elsewhere, and he went back to scraping shapes in the ice on the window.

He hadn't seen Kola since his cousin left to join the partisans last October. He hoped he was safe and somewhere warm. He'd heard stories about German soldiers freezing to death in uniforms wet with sweat from marching. The partisans were smarter than that, he reckoned. They should be, they'd grown up with Russian winters.

He'd started working for the Germans a few days after Kola left, alongside Fedir. The District Commissar had jumped at the chance to employ two trained agronomists, especially ones with field and research experience. Many of the Volksdeutsche applying for work were of no use, he said, and he readily accepted Fedir's claim to be an ethnic German with barely a glance at his papers, agreeing that Misha's blue eyes, putative German great-grandfather, and aspiration to be German proved that he, too, was Volksdeutsche.

They were assigned to the Department of Nutrition, Farming and Supply, or NFS for short, on Bankova Street, under the supervision of Herr Dr Karl-Jürgen Bäcker, an agricultural specialist from Bonn. His job, and theirs, was to increase the supply of food to Germany and the Wehrmacht, and not to worry about feeding the citizens of Kiev. Fedir was sure they'd soon be doing the opposite, once they learned the ropes and a few tricks.

Working for the Germans yielded immediate and tangible benefits. The building where they worked was heated and had its own dining room, with canteens whose fare was calibrated for every level of the pecking order. They were paid in roubles rather than the charming-looking, if not-very-valuable *karbovanetsi* – banknotes – issued by the Germans, with their bucolic scenes of peasant life. They had cards that permitted the purchase of double rations from ethnic German shops selling meat, salt, and butter. They were exempt from taxes and forced labour requisitions. And for all this, Misha reminded himself, all I had to do was sell my soul to the devil – if I have one.

He thought about his cousin every day. He had long ago forgotten his anger with Kola for joining the Ukrainian Nationalists and helping the German invaders. Rachel's death had changed everything. A partisan army was the right place for Kola: he'd always been brave and reckless. Misha wasn't sure why he'd been so upset in the first place.

The Nationalists had done well in the beginning. They set up a *Rada* – National Council – as the starting point for a future government and gained control of the police. They published one hundred issues of their own newspaper, *Ukrainian Voice*, advocating independence, which soon became Kiev's largest paper. The Ukrainian flag flew side-by-side with the swastika and people talked openly of the day when it would fly alone.

But they went too far. Germany did not conquer Ukraine in order to free it from the Bolshevik yoke. They came, according to Herr Bäcker, quoting Hitler: *first to dominate, second to administer, and third to exploit*. Ukrainians would work for the benefit of Germany or be destroyed. After little more than two months – fulfilling, unbeknownst to Misha, Rachel's prophetic words to her lover – the National Council was disbanded and forty political leaders executed. The newspaper was closed and its editors executed. The Chief of Police was executed. The few Nationalists who escaped death disappeared. At the time, Misha was glad that Kola was far away.

The Nationalists weren't the only ones who died in the autumn and winter of 1941. After a stream of successes, Hitler ordered an autumn attack on Moscow – despite the lessons of history, despite losses amounting to one in five of the invasion force. Operation Typhoon, Herr Bäcker told them, *pace* Herr Hitler, would be *the last large-scale decisive battle of the year* and it would *shatter the USSR.* As Fedir commented when they were alone, perhaps the Führer didn't know that the danger of a typhoon lies not only in its lightning speed but in the rain as well. On the seventh of October, five days after the Germans launched their drive on Moscow, the *rasputitsa* – the quagmire season – struck and constant heavy rains turned every road, every field, into a sea of mud. Within a week, Operation Typhoon was stymied, travelling no faster than a gentle breeze, advancing little more than five miles a day.

329

Throughout the debacle, announcements of the previous day's executions punctuated the daily broadcasts over Kiev's street loudspeakers. To Misha, it was as if German setbacks could be assuaged only by Kievan deaths: seventy-five so-called arsonists shot in mid-October; a week later, a hundred Kievans chosen at random and shot after the former Duma was bombed. Another hundred picked off the streets in early November and shot in punishment for the killing of two German soldiers. When the Assumption Cathedral exploded in December during a Christmas service attended by high-ranking German officers, killing or injuring scores, the authorities declared it an act of *bandenkreig* – partisan warfare – arrested five men and two women, called them partisan leaders, and hanged them. For days afterwards, as he walked to work, Misha passed their bodies twisting and swaying in the wind, a lesson to others, until gradually, thankfully, they disappeared under a blanket of snow.

The announcements, the shootings, and the public hangings finally began what the slaughter of Jews had failed to do: turn lingering support for the occupiers into hatred and fear; both soon made worse by reports filtering into the city of torture and mutilation among Red Army PoWs. Stories of captured soldiers with their eyes put out, their hands cut off, their ears, legs or arms burnt by red-hot irons; of twenty-five hundred deaths each day in the camps, from lack of food or shelter.

But more than the deaths of soldiers, more than the slaughter of random citizens, the ultimate threat that turned the people of Kiev resolutely against the Germans and into themselves was that of starvation. There was no solidarity, no coming together in the face of overwhelming adversity. Those who could find food, ate. Those who could not, starved. Armed blockades on bridges and roads kept the countryside closed. Canteens opened for people with roubles or those who were useful to the Germans. The Red Cross fed feral children hot soup and bread at mid-day. Looters scavenged diminishing sources. People helped themselves and their own families as they tried to survive on weekly rations of four hundred grams of hard yellow bread made of millet and chestnuts. Helping others was a fool's game. Help the wrong

331

person – a Jew perhaps – and the Germans would shoot you. Help a friend and they would likely as not take the food you offered and steal the rest you had. In a little over three months, thousands died. Some in full sight, sitting on the pavement; most hidden in their homes. The Germans watched and did nothing. And the population of Kiev shrank.

Misha recognised the bitter irony of his situation. He had chosen the city over the marshlands because of his fear of starvation, and now the city was starving. This didn't only strike him as cruelly absurd. The city's hunger shamed him. He was ashamed to be eating while others went without; ashamed to be safe while others fought. While Kola fought. But when he faced himself in the dark of the night, he knew that he would make the same choice again, that the horror of Hovkova caught in famine was still too close, that the memory of hunger still too strong. He moved away from the window where he'd been keeping watch. *Perhaps I am a coward after all –*

Chapter 30

The Marshlands

While Misha waited in vain for his cousin on the night of his twenty-second birthday, Kola was one hundred and fifty miles away, safe from German soldiers in the midst of the Pripyat Marshes and protected from the coldest winter in a hundred years by the thick log walls of a Russia *izba*. When the quagmire season gave way to frost, Ruslan had ordered a change in tactics. They now operated exclusively inside Ukraine, south of the marshlands, disrupting communications between German Central and Southern Army Groups, hindering the delivery of troop reinforcements and supplies. Kola had become an expert in cutting telegraph and telephone lines. He could teach anyone who asked how to lay all-but-invisible mines under rail tracks. But for weeks, nothing he'd done had matched the thrill of seeing the train plunge into the river, of listening to the railcars crash. Compared with many partisan bands, theirs was well armed. Kola was only sorry there hadn't been much call upon their firepower.

He was in camp with Ruslan waiting for the return of a group sent to re-mine a section of track the Germans had repaired after a previous attack. It was early afternoon on a clear winter day.

'There's a barracks and ammo dump ten miles north of Zhitomir,' he said. 'Two towers, two guards in each tower. We could go in at night, take the guards out, and then machine gun the Krauts in their beds.'

Ruslan was unable to hide his laughter. 'Kola, that's the worse plan I've heard in a long time. If I listened to you, we'd all be dead in a week.'

'What's wrong with it? We've got enough guns and plenty of men – what the hell is *that*?' Kola jumped to his feet at the sound of a motorcycle apparently landing on the roof over their heads.

Ruslan laughed again. 'Relax, it's probably Evgeniya. You haven't met her yet. Well, you're in for a treat, especially if Masha's with her.'

Ruslan headed outside, signalling Kola to follow. There, in the clearing their camp ringed, was a small, green, wooden bi-plane, out of which two women were climbing.

'Evgeniya! I've been waiting weeks for you to come back. Where have you been?' Ruslan enfolded the newcomer in a hug that would have smothered a bear, before turning to her companion. 'Masha, come and kiss me quick. I've been missing you every day.'

Kola watched with great amusement and no little envy. The woman Ruslan called Evgeniya had deep-set dark eyes and a halo of black curls escaping her pilot's leather cap. She strutted a little when she walked and had a raffish, devil-may-care manner that put him in mind of the pilot Valery Chkalov. 'Wouldn't mind flying with her,' he muttered quietly to himself.

Dressed in identical canvas overalls and leather jacket, Masha lacked the other's reckless air but was the most beautiful woman Kola had ever seen. Her pilot's cap had hidden pale blonde braids that crossed and re-crossed the crown of her head. Her skin seemed to glow; her eyes somewhere between blue and green. He knew he still loved Rachel but looking at Masha, he thought for the first time that someday he might care for someone else. In the meantime, he chuckled to himself, it's a pity Misha isn't here: Misha and Masha, the perfect pair.

'Kola!'

Ruslan's bark pushed the silly joke from his mind.

'Grab the parachutes and take them inside.'

Kola followed them indoors where they were soon joined by others eager to hear news of the war. Masha told them about the tragic loss of fifty thousand Red Army soldiers in the encirclement of Bryansk; how the *rasputitsa* brought the Wehrmacht's progress towards Moscow almost to a standstill; and how half a million women, children and old men had needed only four days to dig 5,000 miles of troop trenches and sixty miles of anti-tank ditches and to lay nearly two hundred miles of barbed wire.

'Then Stalin,' she said, 'after sending the Government and all of the foreign embassies five hundred miles east to Kuibyshev, decides to stay in the Kremlin and declares it a fortress! To cheer everyone up, he parades the army through the streets of Moscow for his October Revolution speech: *The enemy is not so strong as some frightened intellectuals picture him ... the invaders are straining their last efforts...* Everyone was freezing – I'm sure this is the coldest winter *ever* – but they all cheered madly.'

Evgeniya took up the story. 'Then, after the ground freezes in mid-November, the Krauts head for Moscow again. They are crazy. Their soldiers don't have winter uniforms so they freeze. Their guns freeze. Their trucks and tanks freeze. Their supply dump is at Smolensk, three hundred miles away, so they are probably starving as well.' She shook her head in disgust. 'So, they get to thirty miles or so away from Moscow in about a week and to the suburbs in early December, only to find almost a million fresh Red Army troops waiting for them.

'Stalin, wily bastard that he is, had refused to send reinforcements to any armies anywhere for weeks. Instead, he'd been secretly gathering together hundreds of thousands of reservists. These guys were added to the ranks of the Red

337

Army and at three o'clock in the morning on December fifth: *Wham!* They attacked in the north, the south, and the centre, all at once. It was bloody minus thirty degrees! The Krauts didn't know what hit them.'

Masha took the story back: 'We heard nothing but guns and cannon for more than a week. Then on the thirteenth, Radio Moscow crackles into life and announces the Germans are retreating. Operation Typhoon is *kaput*! It was amazing! Now they're all huddled under ten feet of snow somewhere.' She shivered despite the warmth of the fat Russian stove in the middle of the room. 'I'm surprised you've got so little snow here. It's why we were able to land. It's much colder in the north.'

Ruslan turned to the woman sitting beside him. 'Evgeniya, you said you had some special news?'

'Better than news, I have congratulations! From Comrade Khrushchev himself!' She smiled broadly, managing to include all of the twenty men now gathered around her. 'Listen to me, *khlopchyky* – boychicks – the Krauts sent seven hundred trains to Ukraine in October and

November with troops and supplies for their armies in the south, but not even two hundred got through and most of those were ones they'd had to hold over from September. Your smashed train was not only among the biggest, it was one of only two that destroyed a bridge at the same time.' She raised her glass in tribute. '*Za vas*!' Here's to you!

Evgeniya's words sparked an outbreak of laughter, chatter and back-slapping. Kola noticed her take advantage of the distraction to speak quietly to Ruslan. He unashamedly tried to listen. 'I'm sorry *miy druh* – my friend – but I have bad news for you. Your sister has been taken.' Evgeniya paused briefly, giving time for the meaning of her words to sink in. 'There was an order – they say directly from Hitler – to pick up as many Ukrainian girls as possible, to be servants for Nazi families in Germany. I've heard he wants half a million, no younger than fifteen and no older than thirty-five. They took Kateryna last week, from a bread queue. I am so sorry.'

Ruslan's head dropped to his chest. 'But she is the youngest,' he mumbled, as if her youth should have saved her. 'The baby.' He said nothing for a time, then shook himself, hard. 'I should have been there, to protect her. I should have been there.'

'You couldn't have saved her, Ruslan.' Evgeniya took his hand in hers. 'They would've shot you if you'd tried.'

Kola heard most of what passed between Ruslan and Evgeniya and guessed the rest. 'Tell me about your plane,' he said to Evgeniya, hoping to divert Ruslan, at least momentarily. 'Is it one of those things they call a *kukuruznik*? Are you and Masha night witches?'

'Well, you're a clever boy, aren't you? Yes on both counts. Although we're not part of the 5-8-8,' she flashed a smile his way. 'Too many women for my liking.'

'The 5-8-8?'

'So you don't know everything? The all-woman 588th Night Bomber Regiment. They're amazingly brave and scare the living daylights out of the Germans. Or maybe I should say 'nightlights' as they mainly fly at night. I trained with them for a while.'

'She's being modest.' Ruslan said quietly. 'It makes a change. She was one of their best before she decided –'

'Hush, that's enough out of you.' Evgeniya rubbed Ruslan's arm. 'Kola – that's your name, right? Kola doesn't want to hear my history. But tell me, boychick, how do you know about planes and night witches?'

'I'm a pilot.'

Her eyes lit up. 'You're a pilot? Mmm, how interesting.'

Kola couldn't interpret her tone of voice. 'Yes, or at least I have been since they graduated us all a year early. I haven't flown much yet.'

'Tell me, have you ever flown at night?' She paused, and then turned to Ruslan. 'You don't mind if I take this young lad for a walk, do you?' She got to her feet. 'Come along, Kola. We won't be long.'

A few hours later, after a short lesson in take-off and landing, Kola was sitting at the controls of the Polikarpov U2, flying tree top height, heading south, with Evgeniya left far behind, comforting Ruslan in her own way. Sitting behind him, in aviator's cap and goggles, was Masha, in charge of a machine gun, a sack of grenades, and getting them to their destination: the same German barracks near Zhitomir that he'd earlier tried to cajole Ruslan into attacking on foot. The plane carried six fifty-kilo bombs which, along with the grenades, they planned to drop on two hundred sleeping soldiers.

'The best part,' Masha told him with a laugh before they took off, 'is that they can hear us coming but too late to do anything about it. Apparently just knowing about us gives some of them insomnia.'

The little plane flew through the dark without lights, hiding from ground troops on the move. After they'd been in the air for about an hour, Kola felt a tap on his shoulder. He turned slightly to see Masha pointing downwards, with the fingers of her left hand splayed, letting him know they were about five minutes away. He let go an exhilarating laugh. He'd almost forgotten how much he loved flying, and now there he was, up in the air, at the controls – albeit of a *wooden* plane – flying to bring death and destruction to Rachel's

342

killers. He laughed again. He was an avenging angel, striking from the sky. Dozens would die! Hundreds! Hurrah!

On their first pass across the German camp, Masha dropped grenades into each of the two watchtowers. Kola wheeled the little plane back over the camp as quickly as possible. He spotted four wooden buildings bunched together, no doubt to defend against ground attack. While Masha fired the machine gun at startled, half-dressed Germans tipping out of their barracks, he skimmed the camp about twenty feet above ground and when directly overhead, opened the bomb carriage and let go all six bombs at once. Increasing his speed as quickly as he dared, he guided the plane up and over the trees and headed for home, with the whoomph of exploding bombs ringing in his ears.

Early the next afternoon, he and Ruslan waved farewell as the rattling wooden plane carried the two night witches to their next assignment farther south. 'It'll be spring before we see them again,' Ruslan said, still looking at the sky after the little plane had disappeared. 'Pity.'

It began to snow heavily that night and continued throughout the next day. When it finally stopped, the camp was buried under three feet of heavy, powdery snow so beautiful it made you glad to be alive, but which clung relentlessly to clothes and boots, chafing exposed hands and faces. Skis and snowshoes became essential and travelling long distances burdensome. As the temperature plunged, Ruslan planned excursions that grew ever closer to the local villages, greatly increasing the risk of German retaliation against the people living there. It was Roman who first crossed swords with him about this change in tactics.

'You know bloody well they won't follow us back to camp in the marsh!' he bellowed, during an exchange that was growing ever more heated. 'It's too bloody dangerous for them here and they know that, so they kill villagers instead: men, women, children, they don't care, just so they can say they punished the partisans.' He jumped to his feet and walked to the end of the room and back, visibly making an effort to calm himself. 'Ruslan, it's okay for you. You're not from here. But I am. These people in the villages are my people. We can't just let the Germans shoot *them* to punish *us*. We must keep our operations well away from them. You know we must.'

Ruslan shrugged. 'It's too dangerous for us to go farther than I've planned, that's what I know.'

Roman stood looking at Ruslan without speaking, as if unwilling to believe what he'd heard. He spun on his heels and headed towards the door, calling to Kola over his shoulder. 'Hey, Salenko, come with me. We need to get food.'

Hastily, Kola grabbed his coat and fur hat, strapped snowshoes over his boots, and caught up with Roman on the trail leading west. The older man was gesticulating and talking to himself in agitated tones, evidently still angry. 'I'm going to bloody join Verestyuk. Someone else can guide everyone in and out of the marshes. I'll join Verestyuk.'

'Who's Verestyuk?'

'Huh?' Roman looked startled to see him. 'What're you doing here?'

'You told me to come with you to get food, remember? Who's Verestyuk?'

'Verestyuk? He's special. Used to be a Melnyk nationalist but now he's got his own group, not hooked up with any of the others. He never does stuff that hits back on peasants or townspeople, or at least he tries not to. He cares about them.' Roman laughed. 'He might even want a free Ukraine with room for Jews and Poles, maybe even a few Russians as long as they don't try to run the country. Not keen on Bolsheviks though.'

'He sounds good. Where are we headed?'

'A kolkhoz near Petryka village. I heard they've got chickens to sell.' He smiled. 'And there's a very pretty girl in Petryka I used to know.'

The two men travelled the rest of the way in silence and soon arrived at the collective farm where a bit of haggling and some ersatz coffee shared between friends led to agreement on the price for six chickens and two dozen eggs. They were soon on their way again, headed back to camp after a detour through nearby Petryka; a typical marshland village with a single straggling road running between twenty or so small, tin-roofed, single-storey wooden houses, one shop, a boarded-up church, and a small square ringed with trees. Roman stopped at a house at the end of the street, indistinguishable from its neighbours. The curtain on the left-hand window twitched and the door was opened by a hunched, elderly woman, her head covered even indoors. She beckoned Roman to enter and Kola followed him inside.

Roman kissed the old woman on both cheeks. 'Hello Babtsia, is Olena here?'

'No, she's gone. Gone with the others.' She wailed. 'They're gone now.'

'What's this, Baba? What's happened?' Roman led her to a faded sofa and sat down with her. 'Tell me what happened.'

The old woman's story was soon told. German troops had come to the village after partisans attacked a convoy on the road to Gomel, about five miles away. They lined up the boys and men on one side of the square and the women, girls, and small children on the other side. They told the women that if they didn't point out the perpetrators, the men would be shot and the village burned. Of course, there was no one for them to point to, since none of the villagers had taken part in the raid. This didn't matter to the Germans. They shot first one man and then another, before pointing a rifle at the head of a twelve-year-old boy standing at the end of the line. The boy's mother cried out for them to spare her son – he'd done nothing wrong. A woman stepped forward and pointed to her own husband and named him a partisan. The Germans killed him and his wife, then left, only to return minutes later and abduct three of the youngest women, including her daughter, Olena.

Roman tried to console the old woman without success and at length they had to leave. They trekked back to the compound, knowing they would tell Ruslan about the encounter, in the hope their attacks could be moved farther away from the marsh villages. But when the day was nearly at end and they had reached the camp, their meeting with the partisan leader was bitter and changed nothing. As they left him, Kola turned to Roman. 'Tell me more about Verestyuk,' he said. 'Tell me where I can find him.'

Chapter 31

Kiev

'Beethoven's 9th. It must be Wednesday.'

'What's that?'

Fedir nudged Misha and pointed to the loudspeaker on the telephone pole across the street. 'Beethoven, every Wednesday. Mondays and Fridays, Wagner. I particularly like The Valkyries. Bruckner on Tuesdays. Ukrainian folk songs on the weekend.' He paused for a moment. 'To keep us peaceful perhaps?'

'What about Thursdays?'

'German military music – haven't you noticed?'

'Can't say I have.'

Misha walked on for a time without speaking. They were headed to work at the District Commissariat on Bankova Street. It was June. The morning was warm and he relished the feel of the sun on his face. Winter had lasted too long, with temperatures barely creeping above freezing until the end of April. The horse chestnut trees were only slowly coming into blossom. There were no pigeons. Misha only half-believed the stories about them being shot by the Germans to stop partisans using them as messengers. Perhaps they'd all been eaten, like the cats and dogs, like Arkadiy. He shook away the memory; focused on the missing pigeons. A bit of both, he reckoned, but either way, he missed their silly courting.

'Our Germans are nothing if not methodical,' he said, thinking back to the music.

Fedir laughed. 'They are indeed. One could almost like them if they were just a little bit less so.'

'I think that's probably the least of their faults.'

'Well, yes. You're right, of course.'

Misha studied Fedir out of the corner of his eye. He'd always admired his quick-wittedness. His instinct for survival. He couldn't quite put his finger on what was bothering him, except that perhaps Fedir wasn't always what he seemed to be. He'd doubted him once before about Uncle

Orest's disappearance but had been proved wrong. Now, though, he wondered if his friend was falling under the spell of the Germans. He wasn't anti-Semitic; at least Misha had never had reason to think so. Perhaps it was because they spent their days being devious, trying to mislead their German masters, that he'd begun to think his friend was getting rather too slippery, too good at deception and manipulation. That taking him at face value might—

'Wake up, we're here.' Fedir prodded him for the second time that morning. 'It's 'Michael and Theodor' time again.'

Misha was surprised to see the bleak, grey building where they worked looming in front of them. 'Have we a plan for today?'

'We do. Just follow my lead.'

Before they started up the front steps, someone in the street caught Misha's eye. He grabbed Fedir's arm. 'Look, there, in the road.' He pointed to a shabby old man, with rags for shoes, pushing a wooden cart laden with corpses. 'I'm sure that's Professor Davydenko, from the University. He used to have dinner with my uncle. I met him quite often.'

He walked toward the road calling to the old man. 'Hey, Professor, Professor Davydenko, wait!'

Fedir pulled him back. 'Shut up. He's not your professor and even if he was, you can't be seen talking to him. A colleague of your uncle, you say, which would make him a historian, right? In German circles, completely useless. Why do you think he's collecting corpses? Historians, philosophers, linguists: none of them have any economic value. Why do you think they shut down the university? I'm surprised he's still alive. If it even was him.'

Misha watched the old man manoeuvre his terrible load down the road, recognising the fate that could have been his. He thought it probably wasn't his uncle's friend. He didn't answer to his name or turn around or stop. He just kept going. Maybe he looked a bit too old. Almost certainly it wasn't him. He watched a moment or two longer, turned away and followed his friend into the building.

'Theodor, Michael, come in.' Their tall, thin German boss beckoned them into his office. 'What can I do for you?'

'*Guten morgen*, Dr Bäcker. Michael and I have been thinking about next year's wheat harvest and we hoped you would have time to speak with us about it.' Fedir hesitated near the open doorway.

'Come in and sit down, please, both of you. And you must call me Karl-Jürgen, I have told you this many times before. Please, sit there.' Waving them towards a trio of chairs surrounding a small table under the windows overlooking Bankova Street, he buzzed his secretary. 'Three cups of coffee, Greta, thank you.'

'So, what is this you want to say about next year's harvest?'

'Tell me, Karl-Jürgen, have you ever heard of Trofim Lysenko?'

'Yes, of course, Theodor. He is the crazy professor who thinks Darwin is wrong.'

'That is almost true. In fact, he is the professor who everyone in the *West* thinks is crazy. You've heard of black propaganda?' The German nodded, looking interested. 'Well, the stories in the West, especially in universities, about the failure of Lysenko's new agro-biology were just that – stories; spread by Soviet agents in the West to deter capitalist scientists from investigating his methods and discovering for themselves the excellence of his work. The truth is Lysenko developed a way to create frost resistant wheat; just as he earlier managed to grow peas in winter. For this, he was awarded the Stalin Prize.' Fedir smiled. 'You probably did not hear of the award because it was given last year, when Germany was thinking of other things.'

Fedir drank some of his coffee and waited for the story he had told to germinate.

The German sat still and erect in his chair, without speaking. His small, bright eyes jumped from Fedir to Misha and back to Fedir again. If what the young man said was true, more grain could be produced, more quickly. The constant conflict between food for the people of Germany and food for the Wehrmacht could be resolved. 'So,' he said after a few minutes, 'Tell me how this frost resistant wheat is grown.'

Got you Misha said to himself, smiling inwardly.

'It is quite simple and that is its genius,' Fedir explained. 'The seed is soaked and chilled in snow for several weeks before planting. This process, which Academician Lysenko calls vernalization, allows us to grow winter wheat in just one season, much more quickly than before.' He paused. 'Michael and I were fortunate to attend a lecture given by Academician Lysenko where he explained the process in great detail; indeed, that is where we first met.'

'And you, Michael, do you agree with what Theodor has told me? Are we to believe in this man Lysenko?'

'Most certainly, Karl-Jürgen. Trofim Lysenko saved collectivization.'

Once back in their office with the door safely closed, Fedir smirked at Misha and said, 'Trofim Lysenko saved collectivization – I don't know how you said it without choking up!'

'It was good, wasn't it?' Misha beamed. 'But what's going to happen when he finds out it's all hogwash? When his frost resistant wheat freezes?'

'It will be well over a year, almost two, before that happens, I reckon. These days anything can happen in a year. Who knows, maybe they'll lose the war by then.'

'Maybe pigs will learn to fly?'

'Only if Lysenko gets to teach them!' Fedir retorted, laughing. He went to his desk and sat down. 'Onto serious things: how's the double-bookkeeping coming along?'

'Do you mean the double, or the double-double?'

'The double. Karl-Jürgen says the food quota's gone up again for delivery to Germany. He's worried the army is taking too much and *der vaterland* will suffer, not to mention his career prospects. He wants us to check the books he shows *Oberstleutnant* Müller to make sure they look okay; that they don't show any more grain than he says there is, at least none the Lieutenant-Colonel can spot. And while we're at it, if we can think of any ideas like the last one, he'd be grateful …

very grateful.' Fedir rubbed his thumb against his first two fingers, mocking the German's implicit offer of a bribe.

'He liked that one, didn't he?' Misha said; 'and it was so simple. We offer the Wehrmacht twice as much grain as they can use or store. They have no option but to refuse the shipment because it is far too much – for which we cannot be blamed – and we get to send it to Germany instead. Hey presto! quota filled and the army suffers. I'm not sure I can think of another one quite as easy as that one. Couldn't we just do it again?'

'Probably, but we should wait until Müller is replaced, to be on the safe side which might not be that long, given the turnover in officers. But if Herr Dr Bäcker is showing the army the books, we need to check that his figures and our figures match, that there isn't any more *official* grain than you and I say there is. Can you take the latest batch home tonight and go over them?'

Hearing a knock at the door, Misha nodded his agreement but said nothing. He called out for whomever it was to come in and was surprised to see Karl-Jürgen's secretary, Greta, looking flushed and excited, come into the room.

'Please, Dr Bäcker says, will you please come now to his office.'

They followed Greta down the corridor and were ushered back into the office they had only just left. Karl-Jürgen and a man in a grey uniform were examining the large map of Ukraine covering the wall. Karl-Jürgen was listening intently to his visitor as the newcomer pointed here and there on the map, drew imaginary circles, and gesticulated broadly while pouring out a rapid stream of German; to which Karl-Jürgen nodded his apparent agreement. A third man, dressed in a plain brown suit, sat at the table under the window, seemingly indifferent to the discussion taking place in front of the map. As far as Misha could tell, the focus of attention was Zhitomir about ninety miles west of Kiev, but his smattering of German – he understood a few words but not enough to make sentences – meant he gleaned next to nothing of what the two men were saying. After a short time, during which he and

Fedir waited by the door, the uniformed man finished speaking and with Karl-Jürgen moved away from the map and back into the centre of the room.

'Ah, Michael, Theodor, there you are. Come in.' Karl-Jürgen waved them forward and turned back to his visitor: '*Reichsführer Himmler, hier sind die beiden Agronomen ich ihnen erzählt habe. Es tut mir leid, dass sie kein Deutsch sprechen können, aber ich habe einen Dolmetscher, wenn Sie mit ihnen sprechen möchten.*'

Misha's ears pricked when he heard the name Himmler. A smug-looking bastard, he thought, with a weak chin and weaker-looking eyes – probably why he wore such a fancy uniform. He wondered why the German shaved what little hair he had so high over his ears. He sniggered inwardly: he looks like he's wearing a brown doily on top of his head. The Hitler moustache isn't very impressive either. Maybe if you're in charge of the nastiest organisation in the Third Reich, it doesn't much matter what you look like. The shock of Fedir speaking German brought him sharply back to attention.

'*Guten tag, Reichsführer. Wilkommen in Kiew. Ich freue mich sehr sie kennen zu lernen. Es tut mir Leid aber ich spreche kaum Deutsch.*'

Himmler laughed. '*Gut gemacht, junger Mann. Ich freue mich auch sie kennen zu lernen.*' He turned back to Karl-Jürgen: '*Dieser ist ziemlich schlau. Wir können junge Männer wie ihr benutzen.*'

'*Ja, mein Reichsführer.*'

The two Germans continued their conversation for several minutes. Misha wondered why they'd been summoned, apparently, to meet Himmler. He also wanted to know how much German Fedir knew and what else there was about his friend that he didn't know.

Eventually Himmler and Karl-Jürgen appeared to come to some agreement. They shook hands and Himmler took up his peaked cap from the desk in preparation for departure. Before leaving, he spoke to Fedir again. '*Sie sind ein kluger junger Mann. Darf ich Sie zum Mittagessen einladen?*'

Karl-Jürgen translated: 'He wants to take you out for lunch – yes? He will pick you up here tomorrow at noon.'

Misha's eyes widened as Fedir nodded his agreement. 'Yes – *Ja, danke.*'

With a brief '*Auf Wiedersehen*' from the doorway, Himmler left.

'But Dr Bäcker, my German, it's not… it's not good enough,' Fedir stumbled over his words.

'That will not be a problem.'

'What does the *Reichsführer-SS* want with me?'

'Tomorrow, Theodor. Tomorrow's soon enough for that discussion.' Karl-Jürgen went back to his desk. 'Now, what about those figures I need to show Müller?'

Back in their office, Misha closed the door carefully and then turned on Fedir, consternation mixed with anger: 'So what was that all about? Since when do you speak German?'

'I merely welcomed him to Kiev and said I was pleased to meet him.' Fedir sat down at his desk and casually began to sort through some papers, as if encounters with top

Nazi brass were something that happened every day. 'Oh, and I told him I don't speak much German, which I don't.' He looked up. 'I don't know why you're so irked.'

'You don't know why I'm so irked?' Misha went to his desk, jerked out the chair and sat. 'You fawn over a Nazi mass-murderer and you don't know why I'm *irked*? You cannot possibly be thinking of going to lunch with him!'

'I don't know how I can possibly *not* have lunch with him. I don't imagine too many people say no to Himmler. I can't see it'll do much harm anyway, just to listen to what he has to say, find out what he wants from us.'

'From you, you mean. Come off it, Fedir. You're not so naïve to think you can pick and choose from whatever the Head of the SS suggests. If you go to lunch, you're in for it – whatever *it* might be. You know that.'

Fedir got up from his desk. 'Well, we'll see tomorrow, won't we? I've had enough for today. How about a drink at that café on Mikhailovskaya? I hear they've got Dutch waitresses.'

'They're not waitresses, Fedir. No thanks.'

363

Misha used to love walking through Kiev, before the war turned it into a city of beggars, where clearing rubble or collecting the bodies of the starved was the only employment for hundreds of Russian and Ukrainian inhabitants; before looking the wrong way at a flag or a man in uniform could get you shot. Since the occupation took hold, he always walked quickly, always took the shortest route possible. Just as he tried not to think about working for the Germans, he tried not to see the damage they had wreaked on his city; his country's new capital. But that day, for the first time in a long while, he wanted to walk slowly.

He had been badly shaken by the meeting with Himmler and by Fedir's obsequious attention to the Nazi leader. 'His bloody boot-licking,' he muttered. It was one thing to work in NSF, giving Karl-Jürgen bad advice, helping him to short-change the army, misrepresenting harvest yields – not just to the Wehrmacht but to Karl-Jürgen himself. He could just about live with that, just about convince himself he was harming the German war effort. But if Himmler entered the picture?

His wandering took him to the Bessarabka covered market at the end of the burned-out Khreschatyk. He remembered the day he'd seen Zvi there, pretending to be someone else; remembered the last time he saw his childhood friend. He shivered, despite the warmth of the day and decided to skip the market. The Botanic Garden had reopened at the end of May. He'd head there instead.

He turned up Shevchenko Boulevard, surprised by the number of open shops and cafés. He passed a barbershop full of men, none in uniform; then a hairdresser's with two or three well-dressed women inside. Many people had settled into the occupation quite comfortably. It simply hadn't been visible until the Germans relaxed the rules a bit, eased the curfew and travel restrictions and – surprise of surprises – announced they were going to finish building the new football stadium. That would have won over half the city by itself, he thought, at least the male half. Trying to convince them life is better under Herr Hitler than Comrade Stalin. They're clearly right for some people. *For me as well?*

For him as well? It was a question he didn't want or didn't know how to answer. One of the *what if* questions he tried not to think about: what if there had been no famine; what if Papa hadn't disappeared or Uncle; what if the Germans hadn't invaded. His father used to tell him that he had once dreamed of sailing away from Odessa and seeing the world, but fell in love instead and had a family and a different life. Then he'd say: *We all just get along somehow, Misha.* He supposed that was what he was doing, getting along. He sighed. I just wish it didn't feel so empty.

He crossed over the boulevard into the Botanic Garden. As always, he looked up at the University Red Building, to where his uncle's office had been and then walked down the path to the bench where he'd sat with Mariya and made such a fool of himself. Pistachios. He shook his head: so many memories and so few happy ones. Perhaps, like the market, walking through the garden was also a mistake.

He headed across the grass, aiming for the exit onto Pan'kivs'ka Street. As he passed a magnificent yew with branches draping the ground, he heard a whimpering noise coming from the bower created by its pendulous boughs. Thinking an injured dog or cat might be inside, he pushed his way into the middle. Inside, a small boy, perhaps seven or eight years old, jumped to his feet and tried to flee through the branches on the other side. He wasn't quick enough and Misha caught him by the arm and held tight.

'Hey, relax, I'm not going to hurt you.' He smiled at the boy. 'I promise. Okay?'

The child nodded, but said nothing.

'Are you living in there?'

He nodded again.

'What's your name? Come on, you can't answer that with a nod. I won't hurt you, honest. My name is Mykhailo.'

A few moments passed before the boy finally stammered: 'My name is Iss – Ivan.'

Misha smiled at him again. 'Well, Ivan, you're pretty dirty and I expect you're hungry too. Would you like to come home with me and have some food? There's no one there to harm you, I promise.'

The boy nodded once more, followed Misha out of his hiding place inside the tree and through the streets to the apartment, silent but seemingly unafraid.

Once at home, Misha gave him the choice of food first or a wash and clean clothes. Not surprisingly, the child opted for food, and was in the bathroom some time later washing himself when Fedir arrived back from the café. Misha told him they had a visitor, Ivan, and explained how he'd come across the boy in the Gardens.

Fedir laughed. 'You're a real guardian angel, aren't you? I hope the little scallywag isn't a thief. I don't suppose he'll stay forever. I'll go say hello.'

He returned instantly. 'That's no Ivan,' he said, all trace of humour gone. 'That's a little Jew-boy you've brought home, and they don't call them Ivan.'

'What are you talking about? He's a child. He said his name is Ivan. That's good enough for me.'

'He's circumcised. He's Jewish. They shoot people for helping Jews. They'll shoot us if you let him stay.

Misha said nothing as seconds ticked by. His mouth soured. He wished Fedir was anywhere but there, in front of him. Finally, he said: 'This is my home, Fedir, and you are a guest in it, just like Ivan. The boy stays.'

Fedir shook his head. 'Don't say I didn't warn you. You'll get us both shot.'

In keeping with their normal routine, Misha and Fedir left home early the next morning. Ivan was left to fend for himself in the apartment. Misha told him it would be safer to stay inside, and thought that the invitation to help himself to whatever food he could find would readily persuade the child, given that he'd been scavenging for food since the Red Cross children's canteens shut down. The child had spoken of the canteens as if they had been heaven-sent. For one *karbovanets*, which he usually managed to beg, he'd had hot soup and one hundred grams of bread every mid-day. The Germans had killed his family, but missed him because he'd hidden in a cupboard under the sink. 'Lucky I'm so small, eh?' he'd said, almost smiling.

Fedir and Misha spent the morning in their office until a knock on the door announced the arrival of Himmler's driver. Until that moment, they had pretended Fedir's lunch meeting with the Reichsführer-SS wasn't about to happen, and his cheery *wish me luck* elicited nothing more than a slight shrug and a shake of the head from Misha. Since his friend's departure, however, Misha had done little more than brood, waiting for him to return. He owed Fedir a great deal. Perhaps he wasn't always to Misha's liking but he had saved his life when bombs rained down on the Khreschatyk and goaded him out of fearful self-pity after Orest disappeared. Misha hoped he had not bitten off more than was good for him.

'Michael, Michael, wake up – you're not concentrating.'

'What? Oh, I'm sorry, Karl-Jürgen. What were you saying?'

'I was saying,' the German's voice conveyed his impatience, 'that the announcement is next week, on the first anniversary of the invasion, and we need to discuss what comes next. You told me some time ago that you and Fedir conducted research among farmers on collective farms. I asked if this would help us.'

Misha had the good sense to look chagrined. He had reluctantly come to like his German boss, almost. Karl-Jürgen was dour, keen to do his best for his country as well as protect his own prospects, of course. He wasn't at all like Orest or Misha's father, despite being of a similar age. He certainly lacked his uncle's sense of humour. If anyone, he reminded Misha of Dr Rosen, who had himself been serious, upright, and proper in all that he did and said; in Misha's boy-memory, at least. If only he wasn't German.

'Yes, of course, please forgive me. Our research trip may indeed hold valuable lessons for us. Next week newspapers will announce an end to collective farming and that farmers will be given their own land – yes?'

Karl-Jürgen nodded.

'This is something most, if not all, Ukrainian farmers want and they will welcome the announcement and think highly of the German administration.' Misha paused briefly before continuing. 'As I understand the plan, this is the main purpose: to make the farmers feel content so that they will plant and harvest, rather than destroy and fight. Yes?'

The German indicated his agreement.

'But there's no true intention to privatise the land.'

'That is also correct.'

'And so, the aim must be to prolong for as long as possible their conviction that privatisation is just around the corner. To achieve this, we need to do two things. First, we must convince the farmers, and especially their leaders, that we know what we are doing – that is where our trip comes in – and second, we must set up State registries.'

'Tell me about your trip.'

With half his mind on Fedir's misadventure with the Reichsführer-SS, Misha related their agreed-upon-version of the tour of collective farms they'd made in the autumn of 1938 for First Secretary Khrushchev. He described the farmers' working conditions, state-imposed planning schedules and impossible grain quotas, out-dated equipment and rogue officials. He told Karl-Jürgen about the dacha where they'd met the First Secretary at the end of the trip, their notebooks overflowing with information and evidence about the farmers' overwhelming desire for an end to collectivization. He explained that, despite his and Fedir's excellent report and Khrushchev's recommendations, Stalin had judged most of what they suggested to be arrant nonsense and threatened to throw all three of them in prison if their scheme – to let farmers decide what they would plant and when – went awry and no one planted wheat or beets or rye. In the end, Misha said, it was only in a small part of Ukraine and for only a few selected crops that Stalin allowed collective farms to do their own planting. For the rest, Moscow continued to know best.

'What I am saying, then, is that next week's announcement must refer to the *faults* of collectivization, as revealed by our Report, in such a way that the farmers understand we're not acting on a whim, that we know precisely what we're doing and why. If they believe this, they will be more patient when privatization is unfortunately delayed, as I assume it will be.'

'Yes, of course it will. But you also say we should set up a registry and register every stick of farm equipment and every animal in the country. What is the use of that?' Karl-Jürgen did not trouble to hide his scepticism.

Misha knew that his suggestion sounded ridiculous, because it was ridiculous. He tried nonetheless to make it convincing: 'Not a *single* registry, but one in every district. Think of it this way: Ukrainian farmers are inured to bureaucracy. If we establish district registries and require all collective farms to register their equipment and livestock, as a condition of privatisation, it will take months for them to do so; during which time, they'll continue to plant and harvest, while waiting patiently to take back their land.'

Misha stopped there and attempted to gauge Karl-Jürgen's reception of his proposal. In truth, he knew that the great majority of farmers would distrust the motives behind the establishment of registries and while appearing to comply, would double their efforts to grow and hide food for their own private use. History told them that state inventories led to more, not less, state interference and could not be trusted; which was precisely the message Misha was trying to send to the farmers; but not to his boss.

'Okay, I understand. I will think about it. But now it is almost four o'clock. We shall finish there for today.'

Misha got to his feet, suspecting his proposal had yet to convince, hoping he hadn't damaged his credibility too badly. Much to his surprise, Karl-Jürgen also stood and smiled broadly.

'Today, Michael, I am fifty years old. I am hoping you will do me the honour of accompanying me to the Oselya for a glass of champagne – yes?'

Startled by this apparent act of friendship, Misha nonetheless managed a smile: 'Yes, of course, Karl-Jürgen, thank you, I would be happy to do so. May I also wish you a very happy birthday?'

Minutes later, Misha and his German boss were heading down a narrow, nameless lane, from where they turned right into a second unremarkable passageway leading directly to Hotel Oselya. Misha knew about the Oselya – most of Kiev did – but had never been inside. He wasn't surprised that Kiev's occupiers had taken it over. Easily passed by, its

376

nondescript brick exterior was widely thought to conceal diverse and myriad wonders. Many believed, Misha among them, that it had once been the hideaway of the last Tsar's adulterous brother, Mikhail. Despite himself, he was looking forward to his glass of champagne in the realm of Russian royalty.

Moments later, Misha's anticipation was abundantly rewarded. White marble pillars set upon red and white marble tiles guarded the entranceway and bordered immense red and blue and yellow bird of paradise wallpaper flocking the walls. A handsome young man dressed entirely in white welcomed them, addressed Karl-Jürgen by name, and invited them to follow him across the lobby to an open door half a football field away, by Misha's calculation.

However grand, the magnificence of the reception had done nothing to prepare him for the splendour that lay beyond the open door. He gasped in awe as he walked through. Over his head, a curved clear glass roof hung with three immense golden chandeliers. Beneath his feet, a carpet magic with gold and red and blue, larger than any carpet his imagination could conjure. Surrounding him, a dozen or more glass-topped tables of the finest Rosewood, encircled by plush chairs of blue and grey velvet. In each corner, two-foot candelabra stood on four-foot plinths, each topped by a congregation of blazing candles and dancing shadows.

Misha was stunned by the opulence. He marvelled that such a place could have survived Revolution, Civil War, and German bombs. He wondered if, each time, enemies had conspired to let it live. Karl-Jürgen's tap on his arm brought him back down to earth.

'We are in for a treat this day, my young friend. Andreas here' – Karl-Jürgen indicated the young man who had escorted them to their table – 'says that only last week, they found a dozen bottles of proper Russian champagne in the cellar and that he has saved one for me. We shall have caviar also. It is my birthday.'

With his mind reeling from the riches of his surrounding and the incongruity of his boss as host, all Misha could summon was a nod and a smile. He was relieved when Karl-Jürgen kept talking.

'I see you have noticed the faded shapes on the wallpaper. It's such a pity,' the German sighed.

Misha had not and quickly glanced around the room.

'Yes, a great pity, and a crime, too. It was your Comrade Stalin. He is quite a stupid man, you know. Not content, after murdering the Tsar and his family, with simply confiscating and keeping their countless works of art and that of the fleeing aristocracy – engravings, paintings, porcelain, *objets d'art* – he sold the lot. I'm told he ruined the international art market for many years. This room was filled with paintings: Impressionists, Dutch Masters and one small Dürer. Now all we have are their shadows. Quite a stupid man.'

The arrival of champagne and caviar saved Misha from thinking of something to say. While Karl-Jürgen spoke to the waiter, he admired the platter of blinis covered with delicate black mounds, each one topped with a slight covering of sour cream and a sprinkle of dill. He had tasted the red before but never the black, never the real thing.

'I have asked Andreas to bring us some of Stalin's champagne as well, Michael, so that we may compare. Perhaps you have drunk some already? No? Well, do not get excited. It is another example of Comrade Stalin's stupidity. Here – taste this first.'

Misha took up the slender glass and sipped slowly. It was his first taste of champagne. He smiled broadly. 'I think I could get used to this. It's delicious.'

'Yes, you are right. It's superb, and that is because it was made in the classical French way. The way champagne should be made. The way it *was* made before Comrade Stalin decided that champagne should symbolise the Soviet good life and ordered twelve million bottles to be produced in one year. It was rubbish, of course.' He sipped slowly, savouring its excellence. 'It is said that the dowager Empress, the last Tsar's mother, commandeered all of the remaining bottles of the good champagne and had sent them here, to this house, when she fled the company of her German daughter-in-law.' He laughed and took another sip. 'Well, the Germans have it now. *Prost!*'

The two men drank and ate in silence, seemingly content, until Karl-Jürgen held aloft a blini covered in caviar and said: 'It's not much like famine, is it, my friend?'

Misha was astounded. What does he know? What could he know? He was grappling with his thoughts when Karl-Jürgen spoke again.

'Theodor has told me of your time in the village, Michael, about your family – wait, do not speak – do not be angry. I also have lost family to starvation, when I was about the same age you are now. You are too young to know about the hunger of the Great War, when British ships stopped supplies reaching Germany. Or to know that turnips – cattle feed – took the place of bread and potatoes.' The German shuddered, as if still disgusted by the thought of his countrymen eating the food of cows. 'Thousands starved to death, my mother among them. I was a young soldier. We were humiliated, because without food our army could no longer fight.

'That is why Ukraine's fertile black soil – *chernozem* – is so important to us, to Hitler's plan to feed German people and German soldiers, and to victory. The Führer has told us such starvation – such humiliation – must never happen again and that the solution is here in the Ukraine. *Lebensraum* – living space. Germany needs more land, good land, to enable our farmers to grow food for our people. The Führer has told us it will be a short war: *a battle for food, a battle for the basis of life. In lightning strikes we will destroy our country's deadliest enemy, bolshevism, and secure its future...*'

Misha took a sip of champagne and tried to smile. He was shocked, not by the recitation of German history and German plans for Ukraine – both of which he knew – but by the revelation that Fedir had shared his family history with Karl-Jürgen. He wondered when and why, and if there were other confidences his so-called friend had shared.

Time passed. Stalin's champagne was sampled and disdained, the platter of blinis was emptied, and conversation faded. Karl-Jürgen suggested it was time to leave, for tomorrow they must work as usual. Before he stood up, Misha decided to take advantage of their surroundings and ask about Himmler.

'With all due respect, sir, I would like to ask what Reichsführer Himmler wants with our department, if you are able to tell me.'

'Ah, the Reichsführer, yes, I wondered if you would ask me that. Did you know he studied agronomy?' Misha shook his head. 'I thought not. We were students together in Munich. Indeed, he was a chicken farmer before he became SS Commissar.'

Misha thought he saw the hint of a smile flit across Karl-Jürgen's face.

'Yes, a chicken farmer. Now he wishes to establish a new colony of chicken farmers for Germany.' The German laughed. 'No, no, you must excuse me. It just my little joke.'

Misha was amazed: a joke about an SS Commissar? Tut, tut, he chuckled to himself, probably prohibited by regulation.

Karl-Jürgen was still speaking, his voice now filled with the importance of Himmler's mission. 'It is part of the responsibilities of the Reichsführer-SS, acting on behalf of the Führer, to strengthen German nationhood, both at home and in the occupied lands. He has determined to establish a colony around his headquarters near Zhitomir, at Hegewald. There will be a trek of ten thousand ethnic Germans from across Ukraine to populate the settlement and each Volksdeutsche family will be given thirty hectares of land to farm. Hegewald will be governed by the SS. It will be the first of many German colonies across the east. Bulwarks against Slavic contamination.'

Finished, Karl-Jürgen leaned back in his chair, hands folded across his chest, obviously pleased with his recitation.

'Thank you for telling me, Karl-Jürgen. It sounds very interesting and I am sure the plan will be very successful.' Misha paused for a moment. 'What will happen to the people presently living there?'

'They will be sent elsewhere.' Karl-Jürgen waved his hand, as if to signify the question was of little importance. 'To Russia, I suppose.'

'I wonder if you would tell me one more thing. What did Herr Himmler say about Theodor?'

Karl-Jürgen looked closely at Misha before answering. 'He said Theodor seems to be a clever young man and that he could use clever young men like him.' He paused briefly. 'Michael, you are a very nice person, although I think perhaps not all of your suggestions are helpful.'

Again, Misha detected a glint of humour in Karl-Jürgen's eyes.

'It might be wise if you were to warn – no perhaps *warn* is too strong a word – to suggest to Theodor that not all that glitters is gold. That it is always wise to tread lightly. Yes?'

'Yes. Thank you, sir. I will. *Guten Abend.*'

When Misha arrived home soon afterwards, he was surprised to find neither Fedir nor Ivan in the apartment. The streets were dangerous and he'd been sure the boy would stay inside. The food alone should have kept him there.

'Hello, Misha, are you here?' Fedir banged the door behind him.

'In the kitchen.' Misha leaned against the counter, waiting. 'That was a long lunch.'

'It was indeed. I think I may have had a bit too much wine.' Fedir grinned and sat down at the table. 'Those Nazi bosses certainly know how to live.'

'Do they?' Misha remained standing, keeping to himself the details of his own outing with Karl-Jürgen. 'I suppose you talked about his plan for a colony at Hegewald?'

'Ah, Bäcker told you, did he? Yes, rather a lot, through the interpreter of course. It's quite a project. It could revolutionise farming in Ukraine, don't you think?'

'It sounds to me more like 'blood and soil' manoeuvring to purge the area of Ukrainians and Russians. Does he want you to be part of it?'

'*Blut und Boden* – yes,' Fedir mumbled, not quite to himself. 'Yes, I think so, although he didn't say so precisely.'

'Would you be part of it?'

'I don't know. Maybe. Hey, where's that guttersnipe of yours? Your so-called Ivan.'

'I don't know. He wasn't here when I got back. I was surprised. He seemed pretty happy to be here when we left this morning.'

'Oh, well, can't be helped,' Fedir said, reaching into the bag sitting at his feet. 'Much more important: look at this.' He handed Misha a small parcel wrapped in waxed paper.

'*Salo*? My God, Fedir, where did you get salo?' Misha was thunderstruck. 'Where did you get the *money* to get salo? It costs bloody near three hundred and fifty roubles just for a pound – that's more than we earn in a week.'

'I know.' Fedir grinned again. 'And it's worth every kopeck. Gorgeous salted pig fat, riddled with garlic: the dream food of every true Ukrainian. Get the vodka out,' he commanded, 'and we'll have some *now*!'

Misha didn't move. He looked at Fedir, flushed with drink, grinning. His mind raced. His body tensed. *Salo. Champagne. Caviar. What have we become? What have I become?*

'Come on, man,' Fedir drawled, interrupting Misha's stuttering thoughts. 'Get the vodka. Let's drink and eat. Better than worrying about some little Jew-boy.'

Misha never saw Ivan again. He went to the Botanic Garden more than once, looked inside the yew tree bower and each time found it empty. Even now, more than a month later, he still scrutinised groups of orphans skittering around corners, as they tried to escape the posse of soldiers sent out daily to round them up. He fought to keep at bay his suspicion that Fedir had been behind the child's disappearance. Fedir would deny it. Misha's accusation would not bring the child back.

He'd seen little of Fedir since his lunch with the *Reichsführer-SS*. He was rarely at the apartment and if asked what he was up to or where he'd been, he would equivocate, talk at length about various projects, some for Karl-Jürgen, some for other people, projects that involved extensive travelling, without giving any details.

Misha was glad Fedir wasn't around much. If he had been, Misha might have had to ask him him to leave. He couldn't stomach his involvement with Himmler. He'd passed on Karl-Jürgen's warning, but Fedir had simply waved it away. Misha now never mentioned Himmler or Hegewald; it wasn't worth the candle. He knew Fedir was working for him and that he would lie about it.

The hardest thing to admit was what he knew about himself. That he wanted Fedir to leave but couldn't tell him to go, because he was afraid of the consequences of doing so. He was afraid of Fedir.

A few weeks back, he'd caught him examining Kola's papers. When challenged, Fedir laughed and dropped them back into the drawer where Kola had left them. You'd better take good care of these, he said, and remember, *bez bumazhki, ty bulkashka* – without the right papers, you're an insect – or at least, Kola is. Since then, Misha had checked the drawer again and again, unable to get Kola's papers out of his mind; afraid they'd disappear; afraid Fedir would take them.

He was on his way out to find somewhere for lunch. It was Saturday midday, sweltering outside and too damn hot inside. As he headed to the door, he spotted an envelope lying on the floor. Hope surged through him: *Kola!* He picked it up: MYKHAILO – STONE STEPS was printed on the envelope. He ripped it open and a small piece of cardboard fell to the floor. Retrieving it, he was at the same time dumbfounded and delighted: a ticket for the next day's football game, the revenge rematch between the occupiers and the occupied: Flakelf v FC Start. He had no idea where the ticket came from or who his mysterious benefactor might be. If truth be told, at that moment, he didn't much care.

The German authorities had decided football games were the way to pacify the people of Kiev and declared the season open in early June. Six weeks later, the Ukrainian team – FC Start – had won every match they played and become folk heroes; a rallying point for Ukrainian pride and a symbol of strength in adversity.

The constant success and growing popularity of FC Start didn't suit the Germans. They decided that both team and city needed a lesson in Aryan supremacy, to be delivered by the strongest German team available: Flakelf, the Luftwaffe team. But as strong as Flakelf were, they turned out to be not quite good enough the first time round and lost the match 5-1. Misha sniggered: so much for German superiority. He looked again at his name on the envelope and reread the accompanying words: STONE STEPS. He knew exactly where they would be found.

'Will I find you there, too?' he asked the empty apartment and for a moment let Kola's name slip back into his mind. He doubted he was that lucky. He grinned at the ticket once again. *I'll know soon enough, I guess.*

The next day he left home in the early afternoon, heading for the stadium long before time. Another searingly hot day, the sun hung uncovered in a deep blue sky. He didn't envy the players and hoped the heat wore itself out before the game began.

Zenit stadium sat beside a small public park, in the middle of a housing estate not far from the city centre. Once past the main gate, spectators followed a long, tree-lined path to the pitch; a path which culminated in a flight of six wide stone steps leading up to the terraces. It was there Misha expected to find his mystery friend and as he walked towards them, he tried unsuccessfully to see over the heads of the fans filling the path in front. Coming early turned out not to have been an original idea.

The soldiers are new, though, and the Alsatians, he mused as he passed one after another lining the path, all holding rifles.

The crowd in front thinned. He got a clear view of the stone steps ahead but recognised no one waiting. He carried on until he was perched on the top step, drew to one side, and waited. Perhaps ten minutes later, just as he was deciding it was all someone's elaborate joke, a voice from behind whispered near his ear, 'Hello, Cousin, still like football, do you?'

Misha swung around in disbelief. It was Kola. He flung his arms around him 'God, it's good to see you. I can't believe it. Why didn't you just come to the apartment? Why the 'stone steps'?'

Kola shook his head slightly. 'Later, not now,' he said softly. Then smiling broadly, he clapped Misha on the back and spoke up in the hearty manner used by men world-wide when they meet a friend at a game. 'Good, you're here now. About time, too. Let's go find somewhere to stand.'

With almost an hour to go before game time, the terraces, pokey grandstand and every available bit of grass were nonetheless filling rapidly. Ukrainian police, armed German soldiers and dog handlers paced the oval running track that enclosed the pitch, pushing back into the crowd anyone who threatened to spill onto the playing field. Misha and Kola headed to a standing area behind the grass verge of the running track and elbowed their way to the front. There was no pre-match chanting, no banners proclaiming support for one side or the other. Even so, the atmosphere was combustible. Everyone knew more was at stake than the simple score of a football game.

Finally, it began. Shepherded by Ukrainian police, FC Start came onto the pitch dressed in red jerseys and white shorts: the colours of the Soviet Union. From the front of the grandstand, they watched their rivals, Flakelf, dressed entirely in white, march across the field. And watched again, as the

German players stood tall, clicked their heels, extended their right arms and shouted 'Heil Hitler' to the roaring approval of German soldiers and German spectators.

'What's our side going to do? Kola whispered to Misha, a pleasurable shiver of anticipation in his eyes.

The stadium fell silent as the same question passed from seat to seat and up the rows. FC Start stood perfectly still, heads lowered, let the seconds tick by and the tension rise. Finally, as if a single being, they slowly extended their right arms in salute, held them immobile for a lingering moment, then snapped them back to their chests and hollered *FizcultHura!* – Long live Sport! – the traditional greeting of participants at Soviet sporting events; the mantra that meant sport for sport's sake, not the glorification of nations. The home fans – Misha and Kola among them – went wild with cheers and shouts, braying at their country's occupiers across the pitch, keeping it up for many long moments before the whistle blew for the game to begin.

Years later, Misha remembered the match as the roughest he'd ever seen, plagued by German foul play, unchecked by the SS referee. Flakelf soon took on board the importance of the Ukrainian star goalie Trusevich and knocked him to the ground each time he came out of gaol. Finally, kicked in the head by a German attacker, he briefly lost consciousness nonetheless, obviously groggy, he played on and let in a goal to wild German cheering.

The violence against their goalie galvanised the Ukrainian team. Playing like a Fury, Kuzmenko – a PoW alongside Trusevich – scored from thirty yards out. The audacity of his kick pushed Flakelf into confusion. FC Start's winger, Goncharenko, took quick advantage and scored a second goal, and a third only minutes before half-time. Suddenly, it was 3-1 in the Ukrainians' favour.

Pandemonium broke out as the whistle blew to end the half. Start's supporters cheered and sang and danced. A dozen or more hotheads raced across the pitch to taunt the German officers and dignitaries in the grandstand.

Kola nudged Misha and pointed to the dog handlers and Alsatians heading towards them. 'Let's go,' he said. 'I can't be caught here.'

The cousins slipped unnoticed through the crowd; all eyes were focused on the riotous behaviour in front of the grandstand. As they reached the exit, Misha looked back: hundreds of soldiers armed with rifles ringed the field, standing shoulder to shoulder, facing the terraces. Sport for sport's sake had never had a chance.

Leaving the stadium behind, the cousins headed towards the cast iron Kissing Bridge high above the end of Petrivska Alley. Their destination was the parkland below the bridge, where they would wander and catch up the ten months since Kola left Kiev. With almost every German soldier and Ukrainian policeman – and probably most of the Gestapo as well – at the football match, Misha had little fear they would be disturbed.

'I've always liked that bridge,' he said. 'Even though I've never been kissed on it.'

'I'm surprised you've been kissed anywhere,' Kola retorted, smirking.

'Thanks. I think you're terrific, too. But tell me, why the mystery with the ticket? Why didn't you just come to the apartment?'

'They shoot the relatives of partisans. I thought, why risk it? Someone else, a friend, got it and delivered it. I thought you'd guess it was me.'

Misha shook his head. 'I thought at first it might be a letter from you. Mind you, when I saw the football ticket, I wasn't too disappointed.

Kola laughed. 'Remember the Christmas you turned ten? When I told you I'd been to a game with my Pioneer group? You were so jealous. But then I told you they'd lost –'

Misha finished his cousin's sentence: 'And that it had rained the whole game.'

'It was so long ago.'

'Another lifetime.'

'Well, I figured you'd think: football – Kola. Who did you think you were meeting?'

'Does it matter?'

'Not a bit.' Kola stopped walking, looking upwards. 'Look, a red kite, hunting for its supper.'

They watched the bird soar overhead. Its immense wings flashed flame-like as they caught, lost, and caught again the lingering rays of the early evening sun.

'You don't see them very often'

They walked on and after a few moments, Kola told Misha he was heading to Stalingrad but had not wanted to go without seeing him first – just in case.

'Why Stalingrad? The army's there. What happened to the partisans?'

'I got sick of being with anti-Semitic bastards doing more harm than good to the local villages, that's what.' Kola's voice was harsh. 'After Babi Yar, I expected Germans to be bestial and they are. Their troops live off the peasantry: take their grain, slaughter their livestock, rape or shoot the women and children. But I didn't expect the partisans to be almost as bad. Christ, you wouldn't believe the amount of food and animals they take off the farms, not caring whether the villagers starve or not, just so long as they don't. Not *all* the partisans, of course, and not all the time. And it was different at first. We did some good things in the beginning, like blowing up bridges.' He laughed, 'I even flew with a Night Witch.'

'The ones who fly planes that sound like tractors?'

'The very same.'

Kola walked on for a minute or two without speaking. 'Those days were good, but then winter set in. Our leader, Ruslan, started planning excursions closer and closer to the marsh villages, which made German retaliation against local peasants ever more likely. Nothing we said convinced him to change tactics, and when spring came, me and one of the others left to join a group near Zhitomir, led by a man named Verestyuk. He was good, not quite so dedicated to killing people on our side. Then Moscow got involved and rolled up all the different partisan groups into one. I couldn't see the point of staying after that.'

'I'm surprised you didn't run into Fedir in Zhitomir. He spends most of his time there.' Misha smiled wryly. 'I guess you didn't go anywhere near Hegewald.'

'Good God, what's Fedir got to do with that place?'

Misha told him about the lunch with Himmler and how Fedir was almost always somewhere else now, away from the apartment and away from the office. 'To be honest, I don't *know* he's working for the *Reichsführer-SS*, just like I don't know for certain he's involved with Hegewald. I think so, but I've given up asking.' He shrugged. 'There doesn't seem much point, he'd never admit it. Even us collaborators have standards.'

Kola looked sideways at Misha but let his last words pass without comment. 'Well, they've picked a funny place to build their utopia. The area around Zhitomir is crawling with partisans. The Germans only control about a fifth of the forests there and not much more of the farms. They're not going to have an easy time clearing the land for their supposed Volksdeutsche trek, if it ever happens. Why do you put up with him?'

401

Misha told him about the Red Army bombs in Kiev and how Fedir had saved his life. He walked on, lost in thought, knowing he hadn't told his cousin the whole story; knowing he'd left out his fear. After a time, he asked again why Kola was going to Stalingrad.

'I don't know how much you hear in Kiev about the war,' his cousin said, 'but it's going very badly for our side. After the Germans turned back from Moscow last December they dug in about sixty miles away. Hitler fired all his generals and named himself commander of everything. He exhorted his troops to greater and greater acts of bravery and resistance whatever the odds. Eventually they wore down the Soviet counter-offensive and the Eastern Front was saved for the Führer. Since then it's been one Soviet defeat after another: Kharkiv, Kerch, Rostov. If the German 6th Army hadn't run out of petrol, they'd probably have captured Stalingrad by now. It's certainly their target.'

Kola paused for a moment. 'I heard Stalin on the radio last week, after he'd issued a new directive. His conclusion about all the defeats we've suffered: it's time to stop the retreat. *Not a single step back! This should be our slogan from now on!* which I suppose sounds brilliant if you're sitting in a warm office in the Kremlin.'

'So where do you fit in?'

'I'm going to Stalingrad to fight. If the Germans take Stalingrad, that's it: game over. And with Moscow taking over the partisans, I'd be fighting with the Russians if I stayed in Zhitomir, so I might as well fight with them in Stalingrad. I don't know if I'll join up officially. My buddy Viktor is coming too and knows some people. We'll talk to them first.' He said nothing for a moment. 'You could come with us,' he added, his voice gentle.

From the time Kola whispered hello in his ear, Misha had been waiting for this moment. Would he go? Would he fight? He was still not sure. He looked at his cousin, his family, the man who could be his twin, waiting, his eyes willing him to say yes. He looked at the magnificent trees surrounding them, oak and pine and elm; listened to some birds chattering in the branches of a nearby linden.

'Last winter in Kiev was very hard,' he said at last. 'There was typhus and freezing temperatures but no food. Thousands starved to death. Men with carts went around collecting bodies off the streets. It was like Hovkova when I was a boy.' He gestured ahead. 'Let's walk on.'

After a short time, he began again. 'Fedir and I, working for the Germans, have been able to do things to keep food in the villages – food that was supposed to be sent to Germany or the Wehrmacht. We have a number of tricks, fake records, double-bookkeeping, that sort of thing. It's not been hard. The Germans have set up this vast bureaucracy, layer upon layer, all the way down to the *starosty* – village elders – all to get food out of Ukraine and into German mouths. However, the Germans themselves rarely ever visit the farms and their paid overseers only go about once every week or two, sometimes less often. So, we went instead, which gave us ample opportunities to work with district leaders and village elders to manipulate the harvest results.' He snorted. 'They were doing it themselves: the Germans, here in Kiev, to hide grain from the army so they could send it to Germany instead and get career kudos. The problem is, we've only been able to help the villages, while people in Kiev have carried on starving.'

'I knew you wanted to do things like that, but I didn't know you'd succeeded.'

Misha smiled wanly. 'How could you? But I haven't finished. There's a rumour I keep hearing, of a plan so evil, so heinous it would make Stalin blench. It's part of the so-called General Plan and summarised in something called the Yellow Folder. They're going to empty the cities by starvation rather than force. It's why they're blockading Leningrad, what they're trying to do here, what they're planning to do in every major Soviet city. *Thirty million people* live in the cities, and they intend to starve as many as possible.'

Misha paused for a moment to catch his breath.

'But they've got a problem: people aren't dying as quickly as the Germans calculated they would, even though last winter was terrible. The food shortages in Germany are getting worse and they've got an extra million forced labourers to feed. So the plan is to speed everything up by eliminating all unnecessary people. They call them *useless eaters*: Jews and gypsies, old people and sick people, Bolsheviks, anyone who can't or won't work for *das Vaterland*. They're going to launch a new campaign against them. Goering apparently says that if anyone goes hungry, it won't be Germans.

'The thing is, I'm pretty sure there's a copy of their plans, this so-called Yellow Folder, in Karl-Jürgen's office, the man I work for, something he said when he'd had too much to drink –'

Kola's surprise registered in his voice: 'You drink with him?'

'He's not a bad man, Kola, just very loyal. Part of me likes him – he reminds me of Zvi's father in some ways.'

'Okay,' Kola said, sceptically. 'So, you plan to pop into this not-bad-just-loyal Nazi's office one day when he's off somewhere else and see if you can find this folder – is that the idea?'

'Yes, it is. Don't mock me, Kola. I know I'm not like you, fighting with the partisans, blowing up bridges. But I think there's a chance – a good chance – that knowing their plans wouldn't just help me figure out ways to get food to people here in Kiev. I'd try to get a copy to the underground. I don't know if it'd help the Soviets to know in precise detail what the Germans' plans are – maybe they do already – but it might.' Misha looked at his cousin, with a smile half-defiant, half-entreating: 'You think I'm crazy.'

'No, I don't, not a bit. I think you're brave.'

'I'm a collaborator, Kola. They aren't brave. They aren't even good.'

'I won't pretend I wasn't bloody angry when you wouldn't come with me last autumn. But I guess I understood. I guess I wouldn't be here today if I didn't. Listening to you today, though, hearing what you've been trying to do, what you have done, I think you're brave and good. You're a good man, Misha, you should know that.'

'I'm a collaborator and you're a partisan. That makes you the good one, Cousin, not me.'

Kola laughed and flung his arm across Misha's shoulders. 'I'll tell you what, *Cousin*, if I get back from Stalingrad –'

'*When* you get back.'

'Okay, when I get back from Stalingrad, and when the Krauts have been kicked out of Kiev, you and me will share a bottle of the best vodka money can buy and argue about your essential goodness or not. Is that a deal?'

Misha smiled. 'It's a deal.'

A few days after meeting Kola, Misha decided to hunt for the infamous Yellow Folder. He saw Karl-Jürgen leave and waited for his secretary to go as well. Fedir wasn't around to help – he rarely was – but Misha reckoned that with both of them gone for the day, he'd be safe without a lookout. The filing cabinet was open and his hands full of folders when Karl-Jürgen came through the door. They stared at one another until, without uttering a word, his boss stepped back through the door and closed it behind him. The next day and every day afterwards, Karl-Jürgen had remained unchanged toward him, and Misha knew that he owed his life to the enemy.

Misha's failure to help the people of Kiev plunged him into misery. He dwelt unceasingly upon the contradictions surrounding him, overwhelming him. Kiev was filled with deprivation and starvation. He saw young men and women snatched by soldiers, to be shipped westwards in closed cattle cars – fodder for German industry. He was importuned by beggars of all ages, wanting not money, just food – however old or stale or foul. He watched people die: some hanged, some shot, most simply starved to death. His private world had food and warmth. He worked every day in a dry, heated office; slept every night in a dry, sometimes heated, sometimes lighted apartment. He ate in canteens and cafés and his own kitchen. He owned warm clothes and leather boots.

As the weeks passed, he was pulled deeper into helping his enemy starve his country, as the incessant pressure to find food for Germany grew relentless. Recognition of his powerlessness, and of the extent to which he had been fooling himself that he could do good while supping with the devil, finally pushed him from self-deception to self-disgust, and ultimately to an all-pervasive despair. Maybe if he'd had gone with Kola, things would have been different. His mind would go down that road many times a week. But then, with a shrug, he'd remind himself that it was all too late now. Far too late.

Winter – the second winter of occupation, the second of food blockades – began inhumanly hard. While the days stayed warm, jubilation at FC Start's football triumph had permeated the city, infecting Kievans with an almost mocking defiance. People had looked nearly happy, as if they still found pleasure in sunshine, leaves turning red and yellow and orange, birds high overhead practicing for migration. Even the arrest of the football players one by one did not fully destroy the sense that somehow things were getting better.

But the short, cold days of winter had cut through the lingering warmth of autumn. Defiance crumbled. In its place, a terrifying awareness of the climate's capacity to destroy bodies weakened by age or hunger or disease. The streets Misha walked in winter were shrouded in darkness, broken only by the lights of German offices and German homes; by the glow of German restaurants filled with German soldiers feeding cakes and wine to pretty young girls; girls selling themselves to survive. Like me, he'd think, and the darkness of the streets would come home with him.

An icy February wind was barrelling down on Kiev from the north, carrying swirling, biting snow that clogged eyes, froze skin, took breath away. Misha almost wept with relief when he saw the dirty grey building where he worked looming ahead. At least he'd be warm. Inside, away from the bitter north wind, Misha climbed the stairs to his office. He was surprised to find Karl-Jürgen there, looking out of the window as if he'd been watching for him. He wasn't late; if anything, a little earlier than usual. He hurried out of his coat and hat. '*Guten Morgen*, Herr Bäcker. I'm sorry to be late. Did we have a meeting?'

'No, no – no meeting. You are not late. Do you wish some coffee?'

Misha said coffee would be very welcome. He was puzzled. Although he and Karl-Jürgen had continued to meet from time to time for drinks and an occasional meal, the

German had never before come to Misha's office. He looked unwell, aged. Misha waited, trying not to let his anxiety show.

'Sit, sit.' Karl-Jürgen waved Misha to a chair.

Misha moved to his desk. Sitting down, he saw for the first time a gun and holster lying on the desktop. The skin on his scalp crawled. *Why a gun? What is happening?* Karl-Jürgen was still speaking.

'Michael, it is all over. Finished. *Kaput*. The announcement will be today. We have lost Stalingrad. One hundred and twenty-seven days fighting, all for nothing. From the stifling heat of August 1942 until this bitter cold February of 1943. Field Marshall von Paulus surrendered two days ago.'

Misha was stunned. He couldn't speak. He prayed that his face didn't reflect the wild confusion in his mind: hope for Kola, fear for himself.

'The odds were terrible, Michael. They had nothing: no reinforcements, no food, no warm clothes. They should have called a halt in November, turned and run away. They were encircled by five new armies.' He dropped his head into

413

his hands, despair soaking his voice. 'Five new armies. Five. It took only one hundred hours after that... almost one million of our troops dead or worse, taken prisoner by savages.'

Karl-Jürgen stood. 'The gun is for you, Michael. Carry it with you. You may need to defend yourself.' The German turned away to leave the room. 'I do not think we will do any work today, Michael. Perhaps tomorrow.'

Misha still had not spoken, but the German appeared not to notice.

Misha left the building soon afterwards, intent on walking home. Germany losing. He needed to think. Defeat. What would it mean for him? For others like him? A sudden heavy snowfall drove him inside Bessarabka Market. He usually avoided public places like the market, but thought he'd chance waiting out the storm with a coffee.

'Sorry, friend – we're not taking those anymore.'

The coffee vendor tossed back the *karbovanetsi* Misha had given him. 'Haven't you heard?' The man looked around quickly before continuing. 'The Krauts lost at

Stalingrad. They're on their way out now.' He grinned. 'So, it's roubles for the coffee, thank you.'

Misha handed over some loose roubles he found in his coat pocket and took his drink to a nearby table. A Soviet victory. He didn't reckon his chances at the hands of the Red Army very highly.

'You're crazy!'

Angry shouts from a nearby bread shop brought Misha back to the cold February day and the café where he was sitting with Karl-Jürgen's gun in his pocket.

'You're a bloody thief.'

A burly, middle-aged man pushed his way out of the bakery and harangued the queue of people waiting to enter. 'He wants ten times the money he wanted yesterday, and in roubles, for some lousy bread. Ten times! Because of Stalingrad. Thinks the bloody war's over. Bloodsucker.' The man started back toward the shop entrance. 'I'll show him what I think of his ten-bloody-times bread.'

No one in the queue spoke or moved. Misha spotted two Ukrainian policemen converging on the angry man, clubs in hand. Within moments, he lay stunned and bleeding on the filthy market floor and was quickly dragged out of the sight of the silent onlookers. An elderly woman sitting at the next table turned to Misha, shaking her head reprovingly.

'Foolish man. The price of milk has gone up five-fold. Everything will cost more now. They think the Germans will be leaving, that Stalingrad is the beginning of the end.'

Misha placed a few small coins on the table. He nodded a farewell to the old woman: 'Perhaps they're right, perhaps the end is near. *Do pobachenya.*' Goodbye.

Not long afterwards Misha let himself into his empty apartment. He took the gun from his pocket, held it in both hands as if preparing to shoot, wondered if he ever would, and almost smiled. After several long moments, he crossed to the small table under the mirror, opened the drawer and carefully placed the gun on top of Kola's identity papers.

Chapter 35

Winter at last thawed into April. Thick cracks skated across the icy surface of the Dnieper, soon to resolve into odds and ends of icebergs. Bits of green disturbed grey-brown branches reluctant to begin again. People on the street hurried a little less. In his apartment, Misha searched the kitchen, hoping to fashion a meal good enough to stay home for. Without warning, his scavenging was interrupted by the sound of the front door opening and closing. A look of hope flashed in his eyes: Kola?

A voice called from the hall. 'Misha, are you here?'

'In the kitchen,' he replied tonelessly, disappointed.

'So, it's you back, is it?' he said as Fedir came into the room. 'What happened to Hegewald? To the great ethnic German Volksdeutsche trek?'

'Hello Misha, it's good to see you again. It's been a long time.'

'Yes, it has.'

'Is there any vodka?'

Misha pointed towards the cupboard and repeated his question. 'What about Hegewald? Why are you here and not there?'

'Hegewald is over. The word they're using at the moment is *postponed*, but in fact it's *kaput*. Too many problems and too many recriminations. The Volksdeutsche claimed they were forced there against their will, that they didn't have enough food or enough equipment. Then the partisans started attacking.' Fedir smiled wryly. 'Europe's California isn't going to happen, Misha. There'll be no white slaves growing wheat for the Fatherland.'

'Was that really Himmler's plan?'

'Oh, yes. We were going to be Germany's India or America's South. Lots of *Untermenschen* – Slavic sub-humans – toiling for the imperial rulers, flags raised and lowered every day, that kind of thing.' Fedir swallowed the last of his vodka and poured more into his glass.

'And you worked for him, for Himmler, to help create a colony of Ukrainian slaves? Is there no one you wouldn't work for? Hitler? Beria? The devil?'

'I don't believe in the devil.'

Misha didn't bother to hide his disdain. 'You know what I mean.'

'It's all about survival, my friend. To survive, to live through it. Look at you: you're morose. Guilt oozes out of you. But why? What have you done? What have you *actually* done? You've survived, that's what. Do you think your mother put that silver spider around your neck just so you could be buried with it? No, she wanted you to live, to live for her and for your sister. You've done what you had to do – that's all. You've survived.' He raised his vodka glass in a mock toast.

Misha sat perfectly still, staring into nothingness. He shuddered He didn't want to face the truth of Fedir's words. A minute passed, then another. 'Fifty thousand didn't survive winter,' he said at last, covering his face with his hands.

Fedir waited a short time, placed his empty glass on a nearby table, and went to the door. 'I'm hungry. Let's go find some food.' He held Misha's jacket in his outstretched hand. 'Coming?'

Misha looked at Fedir, his fellow survivor – collaborator – standing by the open door. After a moment, silent, his mind carefully empty, he too stood, accepted his jacket, and followed his friend into the mild evening air.

A few short weeks later Misha was torn from a troubled dream by the roar of planes overhead, followed rapidly by the dull *crump* of an exploding bomb. He rushed to the window, shouting for Fedir. Outside, bright lamps descending from the sky turned night into day, casting unnatural shadows across the city German rule had decreed should sleep in darkness.

'Bloody hell,' said Fedir, joining Misha at the window. 'It's the Soviets.'

'I know, although I'm not sure I believe it. And look at the lamps: they're tied to parachutes. It's amazing.'

'It's bloody incredible. The whole of Kiev is lit up.'

They watched in astonishment as Soviet planes swooped across the skyline, bombing makeshift bridges crossing the Dnieper, factories repairing German tanks, and hospitals healing German soldiers. Fires on city streets and in the harbour soon replaced the dropping lamps, lighting the flyers to their targets as the Red Army Air Force attacked again and again. A few minutes more and the raid ended. Too excited for sleep, the pair sat talking over coffee.

'Well, that's a poke in the eye for the Krauts. I wonder how much longer before the Reds get here.' Fedir said. 'I didn't see too many Luftwaffe out there.'

'Me neither. I wonder what our German masters will do. Did you know they shot three of the football players who beat the Luftwaffe team? Partisans blew up a factory here in Kiev which was fixing German sleighs, motorised ones the Krauts really need. In retaliation they lined up all the men in Siretz' prison camp and shot every third one. The whole team was sent there last year and three of them had the bad luck to be in the wrong places in the line.'

Misha drank what was left of his coffee.

'That was for just one factory. What the hell will they do when it's half the city?'

Chapter 36

'Michael, you must think about leaving Kiev. It has been too dangerous for us here since August, since *Zitadelle*, and now it is September already. We will leave very soon and you must come with us. Fedir thinks this also.'

Since the resurgence of the Red Army at Stalingrad, Karl-Jürgen had made it his habit once or twice a week to wait in Misha's office for him to arrive, after which they would share coffee and the progress of Germany's downfall. The German was well informed and for the first time, Misha fully appreciated the magnitude of the Soviet effort to rid the country of the invaders. He said little in these discussions. He thought Karl-Jürgen simply wanted someone to listen as his world crumbled.

'Operation *Zitadelle* on the Kursk salient was our last chance for final victory in the east. The Führer said it would *shine like a beacon around the world.* But for every single one of the fifty days, we were outmanned, outgunned, and outmanoeuvred. The front line was three hundred miles long and one hundred and ten miles deep – did you know this, Michael? They had one million troops, 5,000 tanks, and 20,000 artillery pieces, and they simply sat there and waited for us to attack. Which we did – and lost the largest tank battle in history, with thousands dead.'

'Perhaps that's why there wasn't any retaliation for the bombing of Kiev?'

'Perhaps, I do not know. Now they are gone. The Führer has taken the panzers to Italy to fight the Americans. We must go as well and you must come with us. No, Michael' – Misha was shaking his head – 'it would be both foolish and dangerous to stay. You are amiable and clever and far too young to wish to die. You will come with us. But first, there

423

is a great deal left to be done.' Karl-Jürgen stood and left Misha's office, their talk obviously over for the day.

Karl-Jürgen was right about the amount of work to be done before Kiev was abandoned, and the closer the Red Army got, the more the Germans panicked.

The corpses of Babi Yar were dug up and burned. For twelve hours a day, for thirty days and more, three thousand bodies at a time were dragged from the earth by PoWs, stacked between layers of firewood on a plinth of marble headstones from the old Jewish cemetery, soaked in kerosene and set alight; their ashes sifted for gold and silver and jewels; their smell drifting across Kiev.

Paintings, antiques, rare books, and ancient snuff boxes – plundered from the empty homes of the dead – were piled into cars and trucks and driven away, on the run for Germany.

Thousands of documents were destroyed. Young men like Misha stood in offices like his, hour after hour, reading and ripping, reading and ripping; consigning the most damning to the maw of hand-cranked shredders brought from Germany with the invaders.

After a time, Misha stopped reading and ripped and shredded arbitrarily. What does it matter? The Soviets will come. They'll bomb and burn. They won't read reports and if they do, they won't care how much wheat went to Germany, how much to the Wehrmacht. They'll have won: that's what will matter. He dropped the batch of papers he was holding and crossed to the window. Wishing he could see through buildings, he wondered how long it would be before Red Army soldiers reached the far side of the Dnieper. He wondered if Kola would be with them. He turned back to the empty room and scattered the fallen papers with a kick.

'Fuck it. I've had enough of this rubbish for one day,' he told no one at all. 'I'm off.'

Evacuation of the city began in the last week of September. The Soviets were expected to recapture Kiev in weeks, if not days. As the Germans left, people on the streets grew violent. They grabbed what they could and killed whom they wanted.

Returning home late one afternoon, Misha saw a gang of young men gathered around the bodies of two women hanging from adjoining lamp posts. He'd grown used to the sight of death on the city streets but the size of the crowd made him draw near. An icy fear coursed through him as he read the placards strung around the dead women's necks: *Collaborator – Whore*. He turned away quickly and hastened towards the safety of his apartment. As he reached the building, a voice rang out from the pavement opposite.

'There's one – him – he works for the Germans.'

A group of six or seven men and boys rushed across the street and trapped him inside an angry circle.

The man spoke again. 'I used to see him in the building on Bankova Street, calls himself Michael. He's one of them.' The man shoved Misha hard and he tumbled to the ground. 'Fucking collaborator. We'll hang you like the others.'

Misha was terrified. He told himself he wasn't afraid to die, but not now, not like this. He thought of the gun

426

upstairs in his apartment. 'I'm not Michael. It's not my name,' he said, still on his knees. 'I'm not a collaborator.'

One of the younger men kicked viciously at his back, sending him sprawling. 'That's what they all say, scum.'

The pain in Misha's back was agonizing. His hands were pitted with gravel. He pulled himself to his knees. 'Please, I can prove it. I've been in the north, with the partisans, with Verestyuk. I can prove it. I'll show you my papers.'

Misha slowly got to his feet, expecting another kick at any moment.

One of the men surrounding him recognised the partisan leader's name: 'If he was with Verestyuk, he's okay – maybe even a hero.'

'I tell you, I've seen him. Lots of times.' Misha's accuser pushed him backwards, stabbing him in the chest with his index finger. 'You're Michael, alright.'

'No, you're wrong. I swear it. You're wrong.' Misha heard fear in his voice and tried to banish it. 'Michael's my cousin. My cousin Mykhailo Salenko. He was working for the

Germans, on Bankova Street, like you said, but he's gone now. He left with them three days ago. I'm Mykola – Mykola Salenko. People always say we look like twins.'

The man who'd spoken up for Misha intervened again. 'We can't hang him if he's a partisan. We're not murderers.' He turned to Misha: 'You say you've got papers?'

'In my apartment, there,' Misha said, pointing upwards.

'Show us.'

Misha was still shaken a few days later by the encounter with his accusers. He had told Fedir about the incident and how he'd felt like Judas denying Christ when he claimed to be Kola, the partisan. Fedir had said he'd done precisely the right thing: hanging was not a pleasant way to die. They argued about leaving with the departing Germans and Misha hadn't seen him since. He couldn't leave Kiev. He promised Kola he'd be there when his cousin got back. All he had to do was to figure out how to stay alive until then.

'Misha, where are you?' Fedir barged through the front door, shouting. 'Time's up. There's a contingent of Soviet troops on the other side of the river. Karl-Jürgen's giving us room in his car. You come now or you end up dead.'

'You go. I'll be okay here.'

'You're a jackass. You're waiting for Kola, aren't you?' Fedir shook him. 'I've seen the gun, Misha. What are you going to do with it, shoot yourself if Kola doesn't come back? That'd make your mother proud, wouldn't it? Kola's dead. He's been dead for a long time. The average life expectancy of a Soviet fighter in Stalingrad was one day, unless you were an officer and then it was three. He's dead. Take his papers and come with us now or it'll be too late.'

'You don't know he's dead. He could be with the Soviets on the river.'

'When's the last time you saw him?'

'August ninth, 1942.'

'More than a year ago, and you haven't had a single word since then, have you?'

Misha was silent. He had nothing to say.

'I know he's your only family, Misha, but he's dead.' Fedir's voice softened. 'He would've been here or got a message to you after Stalingrad if he was still alive. You have to accept it. You've got to think of yourself. You can survive. You need to get his papers and come with me now. They'll hang you otherwise.'

Since the day Misha learned the Germans had been defeated at Stalingrad, he'd known this moment would come. Now it was here. Did he wait for his cousin and risk being hanged or shot as a collaborator? Did he leave with Fedir and go where … Germany? He wanted to believe Kola was alive. But one by one, they all had died: Mama, Papa, Baba, his beautiful sister Nataliya, Uncle Orest. Why should the only person he had left in the world be allowed to live? And if Kola was dead, he didn't need identity papers and he would want Misha to live. But if he wasn't dead? If he wasn't dead – without papers … *I don't want to stay – I don't want to go… I don't want to die… I don't want to die.*

'Karl-Jürgen's waiting, Misha. We need to go.'

430

'A few minutes – I need a few minutes.'

He was wearing the small silver spider that had been his mother's last gift. He picked up the copy of *War and Peace* which Zvi had given him, that he'd yet to finish. He collected the few pictures of his family he possessed and put them into a small case with some clothes. He found his coat and hat. Then, from the drawer of the table by the window, he took Kola's identity papers and put them in his pocket, leaving his own in their place. After a long moment, he picked up the gun he'd yet to use. He didn't look in the little mirror above the table. He didn't need to. He knew precisely what he would see: the face of a collaborator. He remembered what his grandmother used to tell him. *You have a choice. You always have a choice.* He shut the drawer, looked around the apartment he knew he'd never see again, and once more followed his friend out into the mild evening air, closing the door behind him.

Chapter 37

The end came quickly. The order to liberate Kiev was given in October. On November third, 1943, two Soviet armies, supported by the newly-named First Ukrainian Front, poured across the Dnieper and the rout began. Seventy-two hours later, it was over. At four o'clock in the morning on November sixth, the Soviet 38th Army swept up the Khreschatyk to the sound of German martial music blaring from street loudspeakers. Marshal Georgy Zhukov was at its head in an American jeep; following behind in a second jeep, Lieutenant-General Nikita Khrushchev, a filmmaker at his side. Seven hundred and seventy-eight days of occupation were over.

Kola Salenko stood among the watchers lining the Khreschatyk that morning, thinner and older, but with the same thick dark hair and striking blue eyes. His clothes seen better days and he looked tired. A dog lay at his feet, waiting patiently for whatever came next. He had fought alongside Red Army infantrymen in Stalingrad, street by street and house by house, until a bullet shattered his right thigh. Lucky to have comrades nearby, he was bundled off to a field hospital, where he'd been adopted by the dog who had pulled travois evacuating wounded Red Army soldiers until it was itself wounded. Kola called him 'Dog', which seemed to please the creature as much as any other name. After recovering, he'd gone west with one of twenty partisan groups sent to escalate the attacks on German lines of communication. Now, at last, he was home.

'Come on, Dog,' he said 'let's go find Misha.'

A few days later, Kola stood at the window of the empty apartment, watching withered dead chestnut leaves fall to the ground, one by one, tumbling like small brown birds diving to earth. Not for the first time, he was thinking about Misha: where he was, why he'd left, who he'd left with. He knew his cousin was still alive or at least had been when he'd left Kiev; otherwise, his – Kola's – papers would be there and they weren't, only Misha's. A loud knock at the door rescued him from the cruel answers he couldn't avoid.

'Mykhailo Salenko, also known as Michael?'

Two men stood on the threshold, clearly officials, in coats too heavy for the mild weather, one bare-headed, the other wearing a dark grey trilby. Kola caught sight of a third man standing behind them, slightly apart, poorly dressed in a patched brown jacket and old trousers, cap in hand.

'No, that's my cousin. He's not here.' He held the door half-open.

The third man began to jabber. 'Don't believe him. He's Michael alright. I used to see him in the building. I was a janitor. He worked for them. It's him, I tell you.'

The two officials pushed past Kola into the apartment, shutting the door on the informer.

The bare-headed one spoke first. 'Your name is Mykhailo Oleksandrovich Salenko. You worked for the German agricultural ministry. You helped starve Kiev and feed the enemy.'

'I did no such thing. My name is Mykola Orestovich Salenko. I've been fighting Germans for two years, not working for them. The man is mistaken. He used to see my cousin, not me.'

The second official edged closer to Kola, forcing him backward, deeper into the apartment. 'Show me your papers.'

'I can't.'

'You can't?' The man slapped Kola hard across the face. 'Or you won't?'

Kola staggered but remained on his feet. 'I can't. I don't have them. They're lost. I lost them at Stalingrad.'

'Of course you did.' The bare-headed man gripped Kola's arm and pulled him roughly toward the door. 'Let's go.'

Kola's denouncer was waiting on the pavement outside. 'You got away from me once, but I got you this time.' He spat in Kola's face. 'Dirty collaborator.'

38

The Reckoning

London, 1993

I'm standing at the window, looking out, lost in thought. It's July, a grand English summer day: not too hot, a welcome breeze. I've been watching a chap outside taking down an awkward tree, cleansing the garden before the party. There are only two branches left now, like crossbars up high. The trunk like a gibbet; a gibbet under a gibbous moon, cadavers swinging in the wind. What's done, I tell myself, can't be undone. 'What's done can't be undone –'

'What's that, Nicholas? What can't be undone?'

I start like a guilty cat, unaware I'd spoken aloud. So caught in the past I didn't hear my wife come into the room. 'The tree –' I point out the window. 'Once gone, it can't be put back. I was watching them take it down. Did you say something?'

'I said Natalie is insisting she can't come next week. She's too busy – has to be somewhere else – has something she must do. I don't understand her ...'

I hear the irritation in my wife's voice. She thinks it's all my fault. No doubt she's right. She thinks I'm an old man, too, that she needs to speak a bit slower, a bit louder. Well, she's not wrong there: I am an old man, but I'm not dead yet and I'm certainly not deaf.

'Do you think it would help if I spoke to her?' I say, interrupting.

'Yes, I do.' Her tone is unequivocal. 'She met some man in Bosnia, it seems. Tell her she can bring him along, that might convince her. Bosnia, of all places. I really don't know where she gets her appetite for war zones – some ancient ancestor of yours, presumably. Certainly not one of mine.' She turns away, saying over her shoulder that lunch is in half-an-hour.

I watch her go, sighing deeply. How I wish, sometimes, I was … not. My wife would be shocked, if she knew. She has no idea how wearisome a life of lies can be; what it's like, always pushing the past down, always pretending, night and day, day after day.

By July, I've had enough. I decide to tell her.

But then, every year, August comes and goes and nothing has changed. I'm still Nicholas Salenko. My birthday is still celebrated in July. I'm still silent. I'm not all bad, I tell myself. Others did the same. I had no choice.

I shiver despite the warmth of the room and return to the window to watch the woodcutter. My thoughts go to Natalie, my beautiful, absent daughter. I know full well where she gets her love of danger: from my long dead cousin. I've never told her about him or how much she's like my sister, her namesake; or that when I look at her I remember my long-ago life. If I told her that much, I'd have to tell her everything. I'd have to tell her I'm not Nicholas – Mykola – Kola. I am Michael – Mykhailo – Misha.

A week later, I'm sitting at the end of a weathered teak table, shaded by a wisteria-laden pergola, surrounded by my family, listening to our first-born son, John, regale the gathering with stories of my war-time exploits. The weather couldn't be better. Lunch is finished and was excellent; a birthday treat for me, and a family *command-performance*. There are two newcomers among us: our second son Michael's new girlfriend and the young man my daughter Natalie met first in Crimea and again in Bosnia. I'm happy she's here. The invitation to her new chap appears to have done the trick.

I'm listening to son John with half an ear. For the newcomers' benefit, he's gone back to the beginning or thereabouts. I wish they'd give *Father's Birthday Party* a rest. I don't need a party to see my family and don't want one. My reasons would be hard to explain, though, in large measure because I'd have to begin with the revelation that today is not my birthday, since I was born in January, not July. I almost owned up three years ago when I turned seventy. Almost. But I wasn't quite ready to tell the rest of the sorry tale.

Some people are lucky: the past is a refuge, somewhere to hide if the present goes awry. I would have to hide in a lie. Indeed, I could probably teach Pinocchio a trick or two. After all, my lies have been believed for years without any discernible impact on my appearance; although not believed by me – never by me. I've often wondered how many times a lie must be told before the teller believes it. Ten? Two dozen? A thousand? Maybe liars never fall for their own tricks. Maybe the Russian was right and truth never goes away, no matter how carefully life is nailed shut, and lies stay lies inside, lies and ghosts, always waiting to remind you of who you are and what you did.

I watch my son while I muse, light-years away. He is very like his great uncle in looks and mannerisms, but without Orest's oddball sense of humour. I can't imagine him making silly toasts to borsch and cabbage or raising a glass to his mother and reciting *He went for a wife and returned with a pumpkin* as my uncle did so many years ago. I chuckle to myself at the memory but am pulled quickly back to the present. John has got to *Dad-as-Partisan-Hero*. I let him get as far as the Night Witches – for the newcomers – and then speak up.

'John, that's enough for one day, don't you think? Let's not spoil the sunshine with too much talk of war.'

Always amiable, my son lifts his glass in tribute and the others join in: 'To Nicholas! To Father! Happy Birthday!'

Grateful they don't go in for singing, I get to my feet to say thank you and give the expected birthday speech:

'I once heard someone say that people only understand world events within the context of their own circumstances. This has certainly been true for me. The first time I – Natalie, where are you going?'

'There's someone at the door. I heard the bell. I'll be right back.'

I sit down and chat easily with the young man my daughter brought to lunch – Alan, I think his name is – but gradually realise that several minutes have passed without her returning. I'm about to go myself when she comes back, looking disconcerted.

'Papa, there's someone to see you.' She beckons to me. 'Please, come.'

I stand, inexplicably frightened. My daughter has not called me Papa for many years.

'There's someone here to see you,' she says again. The confusion in her voice is painful to hear. 'He says… he says he's *you*.'

I feel the blood drain from my face. The sounds of the garden, the people around me, all fade into shadow. All I see is my daughter's face. All I hear is her voice. 'What did you say?' I try to remain calm, but feel panic rising within.

'Papa, come, please.'

Her agitation catches the attention of the others. My wife speaks first: 'Natalie, what is the matter? Nicholas?'

An elderly man is coming down the garden path, leaning on a black cane. He speaks slowly but clearly, in heavily accented English. 'His name is not Nicholas, madam. *I* am Nicholas, or Mykola, as I prefer. His name is Mykhailo, although I used to call him Misha.'

443

I think my heart will stop when I hear the voice of the old man standing beside my daughter. Kola? Is it possible? Words won't come. I stand there, mute, staring at the newcomer.

'*Khiba ti zahbuv meme, Misha*?' Have you forgotten me?

Forgotten you? I think of you every day. I have done for fifty years. I live with you, frozen inside me, day after day. 'I thought you were dead,' I hear myself say, limply.

We stand there, two old men, looking at each other. Someone tugs my arm.

'Come and sit down, Papa, you're very pale.'

It's Natalie, trying to lead me back to a chair. I brush her away. Doesn't she know I simply want to look at him?

'No, leave me, I'm fine,' I say, more harshly than necessary. 'Oh, I'm sorry, Natalie, forgive me. I'm fine, honest.' I smile, hoping to convince myself as well as her. Tears well in my eyes. 'Is it really you, Kola? You're not dead?'

The stranger who isn't a stranger nods and we cling to each other, laughing and crying at the same time. I turn to my puzzled family. 'Anne, Natalie, this is my cousin, Mykola Orestovich Salenko. Kola, my wife and daughter, and my sons, Ivan – except we call him John, of course – and Michael.'

'And this is my friend Alan,' Natalie adds, 'and Nancy, a friend of Michael's, and Fiona, my brother John's wife.'

With no room at the outside table for Kola, we move indoors. I sit beside my cousin on the sofa, elated but fearful, dreading what might come next. Kola alive, and not just alive, but here, in England, in my house. What now? I take his hand. 'How is it possible you are here? How did you find me?'

Kola laughs. 'For getting here, you must thank Mr Gorbachev. Without him, we would still be living behind an iron curtain and travelling to England would be impossible or the next thing to it. As for finding you, you must thank my daughter. She –'

'You have a daughter?'

'I do. Later I will tell you,' Kola says, continuing. 'My daughter, Elena, is a biologist, a very eminent one, and she was asked to speak at a conference in Bonn about one and a half years ago. The conference was organised by the German Ministry for food and agriculture and after her presentation, one of the senior people introduced himself: Herr Doctor Theodor Wendel.' Kola is grinning broadly.

'Fedir!'

'The same.'

'Why am I not surprised?' I'm caught somewhere between admiration and contempt, instantly back in time to our final argument, in Spring 1944. We had reached Warsaw. Fedir's plan was for us to keep travelling into Germany: Berlin, Bonn, Bremen – it didn't matter where – until the war was lost and we were captured by the Americans. I wanted to go to Italy. Perhaps it was the lure of Italian wine and sunshine or the thought of Italian food. I didn't know. I didn't care. I knew only that I wanted to be there. I was heartily sick of myself, of Germans, and of Fedir. I could still hear him shouting at me:

You're a bloody fool, Misha, and always have been. I'm the only reason you're still alive. You'd never had made it through Stalin's purges if it hadn't been for me, much less the bloody occupation.

Maybe not, I had shouted back, *but at least I'd still have had some self-respect left when I died.*

Kola is watching me remember, smiling. I smile back: 'I should have known he'd land on his feet.'

'Oh, yes. He's been very successful and continues to work for the German government, as a consultant: he's not getting any younger either. He wanted to know if Elena was part of the Salenko family he'd known in Kiev and if she was related to the Nicholas Salenko he'd read about in the *Financial Times*, who owns *Jones and Cooper's* supermarkets in England. Elena of course told him she wasn't, her father was Nicholas Salenko alright, but he was a retired pilot. Fedir seemed puzzled by this and the next day he gave her the FT clipping, which he'd hung onto. A few months later, she found you – she found Nicholas Salenko, that is – on the internet, along with a photograph of him. And looking at it, I knew instantly it couldn't be anyone other than my long-lost cousin Mykhailo.'

'Kola, I – ' I stop. My face flushes. I want to apologise, to say *I'm sorry*, but if I did, what would my wife think? Or my children? Sorry for what?

Kola pats his leg. 'Later, Misha, we will talk later.'

I nod, relieved, but then my daughter cuts across Kola's good intentions. 'But Papa,' she says, 'why do you call yourself Nicholas if your name is Mykhailo – Michael?'

Kola jumps in first. 'It's a long story, Nataliya – Natalie. I think later would be better. First, I would like to know how Misha came to be here, in England.'

I say nothing for a long moment, wondering if Kola, or the others, can see the confusion that grips me. What is he asking? He knows what I did. Does he want to know why? Does he want me to say it out loud? Through the fog in my mind I hear him speaking –

'Your journey must have been difficult. It must have taken a long time, many years, perhaps.'

'The journey… yes, you're right, it did, many years, almost ten.' I stop. Kola is smiling. I can't read his eyes. I have to say something. 'I left Kiev in October 1943. There was chaos everywhere: everything and everyone was in turmoil. The Germans were fleeing. Ordinary Ukrainians were fleeing. I cadged a lift with some people I knew – Fedir was one of them – and we drove across Ukraine in the midst of an extraordinary exodus of soldiers and civilians, cars and trucks, horses and carts. All loaded with plunder. I had never imagined Kiev held so many treasures – or that Khrushchev had left so many treasures behind when he'd fled. We drove across the country, staying in Zhitomir, then Rivne, each for a few weeks. I kept thinking the Red Army would catch up with us but they were still far behind.

By Summer 1944 I'd left my friends in Warsaw and was walking across Poland, usually at night to avoid the heat. I had the clothes I was wearing and a small amount of money. My coat was far too heavy for summer but I kept it, in case I was still walking in winter. I had good boots and the book Zvi gave me. Do you remember, Kola? *War and Peace*. I even managed to finish it. There's one passage I still remember: "To be able to walk hundreds of miles a man must believe that something good awaits him at the end. He needs the prospect of a promised land to give him the strength to keep on".

'For me, that land was Italy, and after spending three years or thereabouts in an Austrian Displaced Persons' camp, I was sent there as an agricultural worker. It turned not to be quite the Promised Land but I was lucky. As a former partisan...' I pause, my voice thin and strained. I don't want to say this bit. I can't look at him. But it's the story my family knows. I take a sip of water and go on. 'As a former partisan, I was considered to be a refugee and sent on my way to freedom rather than returned to the Soviet Union as a possible collaborator.'

Kola is still smiling.

'About two years later, British officials arrived looking for strong, healthy workers to go to England. I jumped at the chance and within a year I was getting off a train in London. I can still see the landladies lined up on the platform, waiting for us, all hats and gloves and sensible shoes. I ended up in a street full of Ukrainians in Whitechapel, and worked in nearby Smithfield Market hauling meat for most of a year. One day I borrowed a suit from a mate for a job interview with *Jones and Cooper's*; got the job, then met Anne, who turned out to be the boss's daughter, and the rest, well, the rest just happened.'

I draw an imaginary circle encompassing my wife, children, and the house. Some part has been told. It's a beginning, of sorts. 'But what about you, Kola? You have a daughter? She must have a mother – are you married?' I smile, hoping my cousin will say nothing about my lies. I'm not ready, not yet.

'I was married, but many years ago. I came back to Kiev not long after you left, in the wake of the Red Army. I was free for only a few days. I had lost my identity papers – perhaps in Stalingrad, perhaps somewhere else – in any event,

I could not prove who I was and when the police came knocking on the door, I was taken away, as a collaborator.'

My mind reels. I'm afraid I'll be sick. *I thought you were dead. I swear I thought you were dead. You had to be dead.* I struggle to maintain my outward composure.

'It was my fault… if – if only…' I stumble over the words. 'How long –'

Unexpectedly, Kola laughs. 'Twelve years. But you'll have to get used to the idea that, your fault or not, some good came of my arrest.'

I feel completely wrong-footed. 'What do you mean, good? What are you saying?'

'Two years after you left, by which time I was far, far away, the NKVD started rounding up all the former and current partisans they could find. God knows why; afraid of them probably, after what they'd done to the Germans. I wasn't there and only heard about it afterwards. They jailed them or shot them in about equal numbers. So, Cousin, had I been able to prove who I was, if my papers hadn't gone missing, I'd probably have been shot. But that's not all…'

I'm too flabbergasted to speak. I stare at Kola as he recounts how, after his arrest, he was held for four months in Lukyanivska prison in Kiev before being sent to a camp in the far north of the Soviet Union. His journey took more than a month in a freezing train headed to Vladivostok, with little food or water, followed by a brutal voyage in a battered and rusting ship to Kolyma. Where, in Hell's own prison camp, in a coincidence that rarely happens outside fiction or fairy tales, he found his father, Orest, still alive after five years.

Kola pauses for a moment, before adding so quietly that only I can hear: 'Thanks to you, Misha, thanks to you.'

A tremor of joy surges through me *Dyad'ko* – Uncle Orest. Any attempt at words will only bring tears and I gesture for Kola to continue.

'Papa was only fifty-five when I found him, but he looked much older. He was very frail and the people around him were surprised he'd survived the previous winter. Because I'd only just arrived, I was reasonably strong and healthy and able to share my food with him and exchange his rags for my warm clothes.' Kola stops speaking for a moment. 'We had almost six months together,' he says, softly. 'Before he died.'

My mind fills with images of Uncle Orest. I try to speak but words won't come. My daughter takes pity on an old man's grief and talks of other things.

'Cousin Kola – may I call you that? Would you like another drink or something to eat? A cup of tea, perhaps?'

'My dear Natalie.' Kola breaks off and turns to me. 'She's very like your sister, isn't she? The resemblance is remarkable.' He smiles at her. 'Thank you for asking, my dear, but I am fine as I am. Later perhaps.'

'The place you were talking about, Kolyma, is it part of the *gulag* in that book, the one Solzhenitsyn wrote?'

'It is. Kolyma was an almost perfect prison, with mountains on one side, the Pacific Ocean on the other, and the Arctic Circle across the top. The conditions were worse than abominable and there was no escape. It's the coldest place in the northern hemisphere and grey all day: grey with fog and ice and filthy snow. There were 70,000 prisoners when my

454

father arrived and 200,000 when I left. It's a hard place to survive and even harder to forget.'

'So, we are lucky to have you.'

Kola acknowledges Natalie's kind words with a slight nod. 'After Stalin died, when Khrushchev came to power, they declared the majority of political prisoners to be *rehabilitated*, which was the word they used to describe people they'd decided to return to life. Me finding my father had convinced the prison authorities that I wasn't who they thought I was, and eventually I was given permission to go back to Kiev in 1955.'

He turns to me, patting my hand gently. 'Papa spoke of you often, Misha. He told me many stories about you as a young boy; stories I'd forgotten or never knew. He loved you very much and understood. He quoted Tolstoy, saying life didn't stop and people had to live somehow. And he forgave Mariya. He said she'd been a child when she played her part in his arrest and that children should not be held responsible for the evils of the state.'

Mariya. I haven't heard her name spoken for fifty years and more. I still remember, just about, how much I loved her, how pretty she was, her tiny hands, her pale hazel eyes. I wonder if Bobby ever found her, if he delivered my message. Kola's watching. He knows what I'm thinking – he's waiting for me to say something.

'Did you ever see Bobby again, after you came back to Kiev?'

'No, we didn't. We looked for a long time but never found him. We thought he must have been sent to Germany as forced labour and either died there or after being sent back home as a refugee. The Soviets shot thousands of them.'

'We? Who is *we*?' I don't realise I've spoken aloud until I catch Kola's flustered look. I wait for him to continue.

'Mariya and I... I – I met her one day by chance in Kiev, not long after returning. I was completely alone. We were both completely alone. I married her, Misha, that same year, in December 1955.'

'Married! You and Mariya!' I am utterly astonished and leap to my feet. 'Married! She's not dead. You and

Mariya.' I'm suddenly full of energy and begin again to walk about the room, talking almost to myself. 'Mariya… married… incredible – wonderful!' I come back to the sofa. 'And your daughter?'

'Yes, Elena is Mariya's daughter.' Kola takes my hand and pulls me back down onto the sofa. 'But Mariya is not alive. She was not young when Elena was born, almost forty, and was never the same afterwards. She died when Elena was three.'

'Where's Elena now?'

'Here with me. She's at the hotel, near Paddington, the York.'

Without a moment's hesitation, I speak to my sons: 'John, Michael, take my car and get your cousin. Bring her here and make sure she brings all their things – hers and Kola's. Pay the bill as well. Off you go.' I turn back to Kola. 'There's plenty of room here. You're staying, both of you. No argument.'

After our sons leave, my wife Anne comes to where I'm sitting. She looks puzzled, but not upset. I can see her thinking that whatever the story behind this mysterious cousin, it can wait. She kisses me on the forehead.

'I didn't know you had a cousin, did I? Or a sister. It seems we need to talk. But right now, I want to check the spare rooms and make sure there's dinner enough for two more.' She smiles at Kola and leaves the room.

I glance around. My sons' wife and girlfriend are engaged in close examination of some magazines, while Natalie and Alan seem happy just holding hands. I want a chance to talk to Kola alone and suggest we go for a walk.

Chapter 39

It's late afternoon, but the sun is still hot. I head to the local park, holding my cousin's arm as we walk. I still don't quite believe he's real. I find a bench in the shade of a large oak tree and we sit facing a small pond inhabited by ducks and coots and a single grey heron.

Kola speaks first. 'The story you told about your journey here – it was the varnished version, I think. I'm sure it must have been much worse after you left Fedir. You did finally leave him, didn't you?'

'Oh, yes. I left him, in Warsaw. By that time, I'd had enough of him, of anything and everything German, enough of myself. And yes, the journey was grim. I headed south and spent the winter of 1944 in Czechoslovakia, walking when the weather allowed, which wasn't often, stopping in tiny villages, begging food and shelter to stretch my rapidly-disappearing supply of money. When spring came, the chaos on the roads made the confusion of the previous year seem peaceful in comparison. There were endless streams of people, whose homes had been destroyed, cities bombed, villages burnt. Who'd lost everything. Children who'd lost everyone. There were no authorities, no police, no one in charge anywhere. Just thousands and thousands of people.

'For a long time, I was caught up with a caravan of Cossacks – peasants and their families – who'd been on the road for a year, fleeing the Red Army advance. I travelled with them into Austria, sometimes riding on one of their wooden waggons but mostly walking. We saw young girls raped, grandmothers beaten and robbed, women sell themselves for food. We smelled the dead lying untended in burnt fields or spilling out of half-crumbled houses; rank, hideous corpses.

'There was no food. Fear filled people's bellies instead – fear and hatred. Shame filled mine. The horrors I walked through were ones I'd helped create, perhaps not as a rampaging soldier, but as a well-fed, educated collaborator nonetheless, whose job it had been to find food for Germans. Whatever else I may have done or tried to do to thwart their plans, I had helped them. The devastation and death surrounding me – caused by fleeing German soldiers as they destroyed countryside and city alike so that none who remained might live – was one result of that help. It wasn't only you I betrayed, Kola. I betrayed myself.'

Kola takes my hand. 'Papa used to quote Shakespeare: *what's gone and what's past help should be past grief*. You did what you had to do to survive – what anyone would do – what I would have done. You have suffered enough. You must forgive yourself.'

I sigh; shrug my shoulders. 'How was Uncle when you found him?'

'He was an old man and very weak. But his mind was as sharp as it ever was, right to the very end, and his memory – for the bad as well as the good. He remembered everything that happened to him at the University before he was arrested. He was sorry he hadn't told us there was trouble. His disappearance might not have shocked us so much if he had.'

'Did he say what had happened?'

Kola nods. 'He was called to a meeting in the President's office, with Yelenchuk and some NKVD higher-up named Plushenko who somehow manipulated him into agreeing to become an informer, with Yelenchuk as his handler.'

'Uncle wouldn't have liked that. I guess he didn't co-operate?'

'You guess right. And when Yelenchuk began to demand information, he refused. His exact words: "Fuck off, cretin".'

'Was he tortured?'

Kola pauses before answering. 'Yes, beaten and tortured. They used the *stoika* – made him stand against a wall on tiptoe for hour after hour. When he'd slump, they'd club him across his back. He said he'd been lucky, that there were much, much worse things they could've done to him.'

'Were you –' I can't say the word. I can't breathe.

'Tortured? Yes.'

'I thought you were dead.' I look away, anguished.

'They were all dead – all of them – our grandmother, Mama

and Papa, Nataliya, your father – I told myself you wouldn't be any different, that you would be dead, too.'

I fall quiet. When I speak again, my voice is no more than a whisper. 'I've lived with your absence every day, and with my sin, your betrayal. I wanted you dead, Kola. I could leave Kiev if you were dead, with your papers. I wouldn't get caught. I wouldn't be called a collaborator. I wouldn't hang. I didn't want to die and if you were dead –' I pause, my eyes averted – 'I'm so ashamed … I wanted you dead, Kola. Please forgive me. You must forgive me.' I can't go on. My throat clenched. I simply want to howl.

'Oh Misha – Misha, please don't cry. Papa and I talked about you often and about what most probably had happened. He wasn't surprised you took my papers. He knew you, not as an evil or wicked young man, but as someone like the rest of us, with both strengths and weaknesses. He knew you and he loved you, and he helped me understand why you'd done what you did. He allowed me to forgive you. After all,' he says with a wide smile, 'it was only good luck that I wasn't dead, and if I had been, I wouldn't have needed my identity papers, and clearly you did. There's nothing to forgive.'

My tears are falling freely now and there's little I can do to hide them. I hold my cousin's hand and weep. A young couple passing by look at us, clearly wondering if the two elderly gentlemen sitting side-by-side on the park bench need help. I manage the semblance of a smile and wave them away.

After a time, I find my handkerchief and wipe my eyes. I'm calmer; telling him the truth has helped. 'Your father always said you should do what you fear most. I never did. At least, not after the famine. But until I took your papers and left Kiev, I still thought I would be brave, tell the truth, slay dragons. But then, at that moment, I knew I wouldn't – I couldn't – I was too weak. I've been hiding from myself ever since. Even today, I let you lie for me: you didn't lose your papers, I stole them. Well, I've lied long enough. My family deserves the truth. You deserve it.'

'You don't have to –'

I stand and help Kola to his feet. 'I do.'

I slip my arm through his. 'Let's go home, Cousin. They'll be wondering where we are.'

As we get back to the house, my sons arrive with Kola's daughter Elena in tow. She's small like her mother, and graceful. Her smile touches my heart. Mariya's daughter: the child we might have had. I embrace her warmly and introduce her to new family.

'Well, Papa,' she says as soon as she is settled beside him. 'Have you been doing all the talking or have you let Cousin Mykhailo say a word or two as well?'

I grin at Kola. 'Daughters, eh? Who'd have 'em?'

Kola pretends to grimace. 'Well, I might have talked too much, but it has been a long time since we've seen each other. Even so, I forgot something: In one of life's silly coincidences, I was transferred to the camps at Kolyma from Vladivostok on exactly the same ship, five years apart, as Papa: an old tub called the *Puget Sound*. And this – the real Puget Sound – turned out to be somewhere Papa had always wanted to go. He said he used to dream about getting on a

465

boat in Kiev and finding his way to the Pacific and just keeping on until he got there. He said it was the most beautiful place on the west coast of North America. He'd lie on his bed in the camp and paint pictures for me of the islands and the waterways and the birds and sea animals that he'd never seen…'

'Papa –'

'Yes – yes. The point is, after we leave England, Elena and I are going there, to Puget Sound, to the Pacific Ocean. We'll look at all the islands my father never saw, perhaps even sail up the coast to Alaska.' He turns to his daughter, smiling. 'What do you think, Elena – Natalie? Shall we?'

Without a moment's hesitation Elena, understanding her father fully, says, 'I think yes!' She smiles at her new-found cousin. 'Natalie, perhaps you would like to come with us on our voyage? Get to know me, your cousin who could almost be your sister?'

Natalie is on her feet in an instant, squishing herself between Kola and Elena on the sofa. 'I would love to come,' she says. 'There's nothing I'd like more.' She looks up at me. 'But Papa, you still haven't told us why you call yourself Nicholas, or, for that matter, why Cousin Kola said he was you.'

'Ah, well, I –' I stop before I start. Smile weakly at Natalie. It was never likely my clever daughter would forget the mystery of Kola's arrival. I haven't always been the best father over the years and I'm afraid of her knowing the truth, her and my sons; and not always the best husband, either. I cross the room to sit beside my wife, take her hand. Take a deep breath. It's time.

'I should have told you long ago, Anne, at the beginning, but I was afraid if I did, you wouldn't marry me. And I loved you so much and wanted to marry you so much, and have a family together. Then the children came, the years went by, and I couldn't bring myself to tell you. I didn't want to lose you or them. I hope you'll forgive me when you hear what I have to say.' My heart pounding, I stop to catch my breath. 'Kola told the truth. My name is Mykhailo

Oleksandrovich Salenko. Misha. Michael. And today isn't my birthday' – I manage a weak smile, point at Kola – 'it's his.'

Slowly, quietly, I tell them my story. I keep my eyes averted, occasionally looking at Kola but nowhere else. I can't bear to look at my wife or children, afraid of what I might see: Anger? Pity? Contempt? Finally, I get to the end: 'I thought Kola was dead. I hadn't heard from him for over a year and everyone else – all my family – had died or disappeared. Why would Kola be any different? And so, to protect myself from being found out as a collaborator, I took his identity papers and told people I was him – Mykola Salenko, partisan. It was a terrible thing to do and I've regretted it every day since.' My voice catches. 'I thought he was dead.'

There's silence in the room when I stop talking. The look on my sons' faces suggests they aren't quite sure what the problem is: I survived, Kola survived, nothing wrong there. Anne says nothing, sits a little closer perhaps, gently rubbing the back of my hand.

But if my wife is silent, my daughter is not. 'All those years,' she says, indignation soaking each word. 'All those times, we – I – listened to your war hero stories, your refugee-made-good stories, and believed them. You're a fake. They were lies, all of them lies. How dare you sit there and say *I thought he was dead*, as if that excuses what you did or the lies you told us. Is that why no one can get close to you? You're afraid we'll find out the truth – that you were a *collaborator* – that you abandoned your cousin to God knows what – that you betrayed him?'

She turns to the young man she brought to lunch, standing as she speaks. 'I'm sorry you had to hear all this, Alan. It's not very pretty. Shall we go?'

'Natalie, wait.' Kola puts out a hand to stop her. 'Please, don't go. Your father – your husband, Anne – has given you a shallow, very bleak explanation of the choices he made in dreadful, evil times. Life then was much more complicated than his few words suggest. Almost from childhood, he – we – lived with fear: of starvation or arrest or violent death, and worse perhaps, fear of torture, of ourselves or the people we loved. Living here in England, only ever in peace time, you cannot know what fear can do to a man or a woman. What it can make them do. What it could make you do. The line between right and wrong – between bravery and cowardice – is sometimes very fine. Sometimes, in some circumstances, lies and deceit are all there is.'

'But I was the one who was weak, Kola, the one who was cowardly, not you. I knew what might happen if you were alive and still I went, and left you to face the consequences. For years I've heard our grandmother's words ringing in my ears: you always have a choice. It's what, with the arrogance of youth, I told Mariya. But unlike her, I wasn't a child when I took your papers. I had a choice. I've had to live with that, and with not knowing what happened to you, only imagining the worse, year after year –'

'And if you hadn't done what you did, Misha, I would never have found my father again. I would never have had those last months with him. I might've been shot. Life deals out funny twists sometimes.'

I wait a few moments, eyes downcast. I haven't finished, not quite.

'There's something more I want to say' I stop briefly, not sure how to go on; my daughter's words still smarting. 'I have always felt –' I stop once more, then try again. 'I've known love and contentment with you, Anne, without question, and with our children. But it wasn't *my* life, I wasn't me – Misha, who had once had a sister named Nataliya, who grew up in a village named Hovkova, whose dog disappeared in a famine. I was Nicholas. I stole Kola's life so that I would survive and I did survive. But after such an act, such treachery, it's hard to live with honour, hard to be happy, to make others happy. I cheated myself, but more importantly, I cheated all of you, of happiness; of honesty. And for that I am deeply sorry. I hope you will forgive me.'

I'm silent. No one speaks. Moments pass, each one, to me, an eternity. In time, my wife breaks the silence.

'Nicholas – Michael – we all tell ourselves stories, all of us: about who we are, what we do, what we have done. Sometimes the stories are true or almost true, other times

471

they're simply false. I won't pretend your story doesn't trouble me, because it does. But in most marriages – in *our* marriage – people live together minute by minute, day by day. They live the small things. Having a meal together, meeting friends, caring for children, remembering a birthday. We've been happy as a family in the day-to-day. More than that, I've been happy as your wife.

'You, my love, clearly have had more than your fair share of the big things that sometimes crash into people's lives – the life-shattering events – which led you to a life-story based on pretence and lies. It must not have been easy living that life. Would I have done the same – told the same stories – if I'd had your life? I don't know, maybe, probably. My one rebuke is that you might have trusted me more. Our marriage didn't need the stories, we had each other – we *have* each other.'

She turns to our daughter. 'Natalie, your father loves you very much. He always has. He's not a fake, as you called him. Frightened perhaps, but not a fake. I think you might forgive him for that.'

Natalie stands without speaking, keeping her eyes away from me, looking instead at her mother. After some moments, she goes back to her chair and sits down again, beckoning to Alan to do the same. Relief floods through me; relief, and the hope that one day she will forgive me.

Anne gets to her feet. 'Kola, having you here is wonderful: thank you for coming.' She turns back to me. 'My dear husband, I loved you as Nicholas and I love you still as Michael. We'll talk later. But as Kola reminded us, life doesn't stop, and there's dinner to get. Nancy, Fiona: would you like to help? Natalie, why don't you take Elena upstairs and show her the room?' She smiles gently at me as she leaves and I know all will be well.

I glance around a room suddenly empty of women. My sons are nattering at each other as usual, seemingly untroubled. Natalie's friend Alan is examining the bookshelves. Kola is sitting on the sofa opposite, smiling at me. I must look astonished because I am astonished. I don't know what to say. Whatever else I may have expected from my cousin's miraculous reappearance, it wasn't this. I let my head rest back against the sofa. A knot inside melts. Perhaps there's still time –

'What's that? Did you say something, Kola?'

'I did, Cousin. I said, is there a half-decent football team in this city of yours?'

I stare at him, dumbfounded. Then, as the past slips away, as if by magic, I begin to laugh. It could have been so much worse.

Acknowledgements

My journey from academic to fiction writing was bumpy. At times, I thought I was on the wrong road, a view undoubtedly shared by some who read and some who judged earlier versions of *Surviving Ukraine*. One person seemed never to lose faith that I would get there in the end: Anne Faundez, a friend of many years, who read and commented upon each of my attempts. Her help was invaluable and I will always be grateful to her. My husband, Alan Angell, was also a constant supporter, who listened and commented as I read aloud the latest chapter. I thank him, with love. I wish also to thank three people who read very early drafts: Colin Thomas, Hazel Gower, and Robert Service; and Archie Brown, whose comments on this final version both enlightened and encouraged me. Finally, I thank my wonderful granddaughter, Ulla Angell, whose help publishing this book was invaluable.

The impetus behind *Surviving Ukraine* was wondering what my father's life would have been had *his* father had not emigrated to Canada not long before the Russian Revolution. I knew next to nothing of Ukraine's history at that time and read widely to achieve at least some understanding of people's lives. The following were key sources among many.

Applebaum, Anne, *Red Famine: Stalin's War on Ukraine*, Allan Lane, London 2017.

Berkoff, Karl, *Harvest of Despair: Life and Death in Ukraine under Nazi Rule*, Belknap Press, Harvard 2004.

Collingwood, Lizzie, *The Taste of War: World War Two and the Battle for Food*, Allan Lane, London 2011.

Conquest, Robert, *The Great Terror: A Reassessment*, Pimlico, London 2008.

Conquest, Robert, The Harvest of Sorrow: Soviet Collectivisation and the Terror-Famine, Pimlico, London 2002.

Dolot, Miron, *Execution by Hunger: The Hidden Holocaust,* Norton, New York 1987.

Melnyk, Eugenie, *My Darling Elia*, St Martin's Press, New York, 1999.

Smith, Tim, Perks, Rob and Smith, Graham, *Ukraine's Forbidden History,* Dewi Lane Publishing, Stockport 1998.

Fortunately, there is always more to life than sorrow and war, for which the following were highly useful:

Dougan, Andy, *Dynamo: Defending the Honour of Kiev*, Fourth Estate, London 2001.

Gronow, Jukka, *Caviar with Champagne: Common Luxury and the Ideals of the Good Life in Stalin's Russia*, Berg, Oxford 2003.

Turkewicz-Sanko, Helene (ed), *Treasury of Ukrainian Love Poems, Quotations and Proverbs*, Hippcrene Books, New York 1997.

Ukrainian Women's Association of Canada, *The Art of Cooking Ukrainian Style*, Vancouver 1965.

Printed in Great Britain
by Amazon

38697867R00268